10/1℃

THE ROW

J. R. JOHANSSON

THE ROW

FARRAR STRAUS GIROUX
NEW YORK

Farrar Straus Giroux Books for Young Readers
An imprint of Macmillan Publishing Group, LLC
175 Fifth Avenue, New York 10010

Printed in the United States of America
Designed by Andrew Arnold
First edition, 2016
1   3   5   7   9   10   8   6   4   2

fiercereads.com

Library of Congress Cataloging-in-Publication Data

Names: Johansson, J. R., 1978– author.
Title: The row / J. R. Johansson.
Description: First edition. | New York : Farrar Straus Giroux, 2016. | Summary: After
    visiting her father on death row for twelve years, seventeen-year-old Riley is determined to
    find out if he is guilty or not before he is either executed or retried and, perhaps, released.
Identifiers: LCCN 2016001907 (print) | LCCN 2016024166 (ebook) |
    ISBN 9780374300258 (hardback) | ISBN 9780374300265 (ebook)
Subjects: | CYAC: Fathers and daughters—Fiction. | Prisoners—Fiction. | Serial
    murderers—Fiction. | Dating (Social customs)—Fiction. | Family life—Texas—
    Fiction. | Houston (Tex.)—Fiction. | Mystery and detective stories. | BISAC: JUVENILE
    FICTION / Law & Crime. | JUVENILE FICTION / Family / Parents. | JUVENILE
    FICTION / Mysteries & Detective Stories.
Classification: LCC PZ7.J62142 Row 2016 (print) | LCC PZ7.J62142 (ebook) | DDC [Fic]—dc23
LC record available at https://lccn.loc.gov/2016001907

Our books may be purchased in bulk for promotional, educational, or business use.
Please contact your local bookseller or the Macmillan Corporate and Premium Sales
Department at (800) 221-7945 ext. 5442 or by e-mail at
MacmillanSpecialMarkets@macmillan.com.

For Bill Chipp—
Thank you for always considering us your own.
We love you.

THE ROW

1

I STEP INTO THE REGISTRATION BUILDING and marvel at how it smells the same every time. The strong aroma of bleach cleanser that somehow never manages to get rid of the lingering undertone of mildew and rot is a hard one to forget.

For over ten years, I've spent every Friday afternoon from three to five p.m. at the Polunsky Unit except for the two weeks in December it took to get my "hardship privileges" approved by the warden. It still seems crazy to me that I had to get the approval from Warden Zonnberg—the director of death row himself—just to visit my own daddy without Mama present. It was a whole lot of hassle to go through when you consider that I was only ten months shy of being legal at the time. But like Mama says: *Seventeen is still seventeen no matter what color you paint it.* So once Mama's work made it harder for her to attend visits with me, the warden literally declared me a case of hardship in order to approve my visits. I have paperwork and everything. Nothing like putting a label on a girl to make her feel good about herself.

And the stupid teens on reality TV shows think *they* have daddy issues.

Mama sent me with a letter for Daddy—as she always does. I wonder what it says but don't look. It's enough that the guards thoroughly examine every piece of communication our family shares. Me snooping through their messages too would be as welcome as a skunk at a lawn party.

Almost instinctively, I walk toward the desk and begin prepping to pass through the security checkpoint. By the time I step up and sign my name, my shoes and belt are off and my pockets are emptied. As always, I left my purse in the car and only brought my ziplock bag with a paper chess set, my ID, change for the vending machines, my car keys, and Mama's letter—nothing that will raise any trouble. I may not be an honor student, but I am nothing if not a model death row visitor.

Mama should seriously find a bumper sticker that says *that* about her daughter.

Nancy, the correctional officer behind the desk, smiles when she looks up and sees me signing in. "You're prepped already. You've got to be the speediest girl at the airport, Riley."

I incline my head. "I'm sure I will be should I ever decide I want to go anywhere. You've prepared me well."

"You've never been on a plane?"

"I've never been outside of Texas."

She seems shocked. "Good Lordy, why not?"

I place one hand across my heart and give her a wide grin. "Because I love it so. I just couldn't bear to leave."

"Everybody loves Texas," Nancy says, nodding with a smile, obviously not catching my sarcasm.

I provide the expected response. "Absolutely."

Nancy opens Mama's letter and scans through it. When she's finished she puts it back with my plastic bag and moves them both through the X-ray machine.

I put the pen down on her book, handing over my driver's license for her to inspect like she's done so many times before.

"Still not eighteen yet, huh?" She reaches for the red notebook behind her desk where I know my hardship form is kept. The mound of paperwork I had to fill out to get that form is filed away safely somewhere in the warden's office. I swear the prison system seems to have taken on the sole responsibility for keeping the paper industry in business.

"Nope. I decided to delay becoming legal for as long as humanly possible."

"Mm-hmm." Nancy makes a note in the folder. "Are you guys ready for the hearing?"

"Yep," I say with false bravado before swallowing against the fear that clamps down on my throat any time I think about Daddy's final appeal next week.

"What day is it?" She takes me through the metal detector and does my pat-down.

"It's on Thursday." I've grown used to having conversations with people while they're frisking me, but that doesn't make it any less awkward. The trick is to avoid direct eye contact until they've finished. I stare straight ahead as she runs her hands over my legs.

"Well, good luck then. See you next week, Riley," Nancy says, and I wave as I head to the front desk to get my visitor badge and let the receptionist inspect Mama's letter further.

My body follows the usual routine as if disconnected from my brain. I cross the yard and go through the gate to the administration building. I don't even realize that I've passed the green outer door and both steel security doors before I'm sitting in the visiting area designated for contact visits and waiting for Daddy to come in.

It's quiet in the barely-bigger-than-a-broom-closet room and my mind goes over the few details Daddy had told me about the current appeal. His legal team had uncovered evidence that at least one jury member from his original trial might have been tampered with. This may be our first chance to be granted a retrial in the nearly twelve years my father has been in prison. This appeal actually seems promising, and for the first time in years, I struggle to keep my hope in check.

It's what we've been waiting for all this time—a new chance to prove that Daddy didn't do it.

I keep running the envelope containing Mama's letter through my fingers. I pass it from one hand to the other. I wince as the edge slices a small paper cut into my palm, but the pain helps me keep my focus here in this visitation room. My mind should not be behind bars. It should not be distracted by thoughts of what could be happening right now in a jail cell or by what may happen on Thursday in a judge's courtroom.

Today is just one more visit with my father . . . and that alone makes it special.

"Hi, Ri," Daddy says when the officer brings him in. I study my father as I do every week. When I decide he doesn't look any worse this visit than the last, I release a shaky breath. Everyone in Polunsky is in solitary confinement, which is enough to drive a person mad if they weren't already when they came in. That much time alone isn't good for anyone's well-being. He's lost a lot of weight over the years, developing a leaner and harder look. And sometimes he still manages to get bruises he refuses to explain. I've seen enough to suspect they came from a chance altercation with another inmate while being moved around the prison . . . or from the guards.

Once his cuffs are released, he hugs me tight and I hug him back—the same way I do every visit. I guess when you're only allowed two hugs from your father per week, you're never too grown up for it.

The officer clears his throat, and Daddy pulls away from me. We walk over to sit down at the table. Once we're seated, the guard closes the door and stands outside. This is what we're allowed. This is what our face-to-face relationship is defined by: a hug at the beginning and the end of each visit. When I leave, the guard will give me the letters Daddy has written to me this week to take home. While I'm here, we must sit on opposite sides of the table. We can hold hands if we want, but we rarely do anymore. Not since I was little. When Mama used to come more frequently, she and Daddy used to hold hands sometimes. It symbolizes their marriage—their romance—to me now. I couldn't take that away from them.

Mama has had to miss visits and hearings too often in the last year and I know they miss seeing each other, but Mama's new job is demanding. She's been the executive assistant to a vice president at an investment firm since last summer. Her boss pays her well and gives her job security as long as she works whenever and wherever it's convenient for him.

After being fired in the past for reasons like *your presence is creating an uncomfortable work environment for others* or *not disclosing pertinent background information*, Mama *really* cares about her job security.

"How is your mother?" Daddy asks first thing, and I smile. Polunsky has aged him, but the sparkle in Daddy's eyes when he sees me never changes.

"She's fine. She said to tell you that she's excited to see you on Thursday."

His smile falters. "Are you *both* coming to the hearing?"

"Yes." I prepare myself for the argument I know is coming.

"I wish you wouldn't, but you already know that." Daddy sits back in his chair and pushes his hand through his thick salt-and-pepper hair. "Ben can let you know how it goes after—"

"We want to be there. Having your family there to support you is important during your appeals—both to you and to the judge. Mr. Masters even told us that." I shake my head, refusing to budge on this one. Benjamin Masters is Daddy's lawyer, and a longtime family friend. When I was little, I used to think he was my uncle. It wasn't until I was ten that I finally understood that we weren't actually related. He and Daddy were partners in their law firm before Daddy ended up here.

"That's lawyer logic. I know that and so do you." He frowns so deep it seems to create new lines on his face. "I'm not thinking like a lawyer right now. I'm thinking like a father, and I'm just trying to protect my family. I hate seeing the media circle you and your mother like a pack of coyotes around fresh meat. You did nothing to bring this on yourself."

"Neither did you, Daddy." I reach out and give his hand a firm

8

squeeze. "We're in this with you by choice. Besides, I'd hate it if I wasn't there to hear the good news."

He returns a weak version of my smile and I decide to change the subject. Opening my plastic bag, I pass Daddy the letter from Mama before pulling out the paper chess set and putting the pieces in place.

"Now, on to the really important stuff," I say. "I learned a new strategy on YouTube this week that's going to blow your mind."

Daddy chuckles before cracking his knuckles and leaning forward with a grin. "As the things you tell me you find on the Internet usually do."

2

BY TUESDAY, I'VE CLEANED my room five times in an effort to keep my mind off Daddy's upcoming hearing. For the first time I can remember, I almost wish I had school in the summer just so I would have something to distract myself. It's a momentary and fleeting wish, since most of the time I would give my left kidney to not have to go to that hellish place where everyone—students and faculty alike—watches me like I might morph into a killer at any moment.

Still, saying that I'm in serious need of a diversion is a definite understatement.

I slump down on the couch with my somewhat maimed copy of *The Count of Monte Cristo* to read for the billionth time. The whole house is dim and I wish I knew when Mama would be home. Rubbing my fingertips against my eyelids, I let the tension from the week seep down into my legs and out through my feet.

I flip open the book, and end up dropping it after only a few pages. I love the story, that isn't the problem. The house is too quiet around me. It's peaceful, but sometimes it feels more like our home is wrapped up in a blanket of apprehension. It's waiting, just like

I am. Waiting for the next visitation day, waiting for the next trial date, waiting to read the next letter—or, like right now, waiting for the next appeal hearing in two days.

That's all we do in my family. Wait.

My nerves get the better of me in the silence. They're like red ants swarming, creeping in droves under my skin. I can almost feel their tiny feet crawling, but I can't stop them. I cringe, knowing I'm helpless to prevent the stings from coming at any moment.

I rub my hands along my arms, trying to force away the thoughts, the sensation. Wishing I had something—anything—to do. Then I stop and head toward the stairs.

Right now, I can think of one thing I don't have to wait for.

The moment I get to my room, I grab the three remaining unread letters from this week's stack, slip out the one marked May 31, and flop on my bed as I lift the flap. Daddy never bothers to seal these. We learned a long time ago that the guards would open and read every letter he sends home with us anyway, so he doesn't try to prevent it. Pulling the paper out, I hold it carefully as I read.

> Riley,
>
> Happy Tuesday, sweetheart! Hope you're having a good day. I can't believe how fast time seems to move these days. It's always so good to see you. I can't believe you'll be eighteen soon. It feels wrong that my own daughter is growing up so much without me. Every time I see you, it seems you look older. Don't grow up too fast, Ri. I'm still holding out hope that I might somehow find a way to be back at home

*with you before you move out and on with your own
life.*

*All my love,
Daddy*

I read it again, smiling to myself as I remember my last visit. Our chess match this week had been very close. I'd nearly won—something I hadn't done since I turned nine and realized he was letting me win. I had demanded that he start playing for real, and he'd dominated me ever since.

But I'm learning. I'm getting better with every match and he knows it.

I walk over to my closet. The bottom is filled with neatly stacked shoeboxes. The older letters are packed up and moved into the attic on a regular basis to make room for new ones. I've never tried to count how many boxes I've piled up over the years, but there are twenty-two in my closet right now. The one on top is the only one not held closed with a large rubber band. I slip the newest letter into it and caress the tops of a few envelopes before putting the lid back on and replacing the box. Mama helped me set up this system way back when Daddy was still on trial. He'd started sending home letters every time we visited him—one letter for every day of the week except visitation day.

Mama and I both expected him to stop or slow down at some point, but he never did. The shoebox stacks are reaching the point where they're starting to interfere with my hanging clothes again. Knowing I'll have to move some boxes up to the attic soon forms a ball of sadness in the bottom of my stomach.

I always dread doing that. The boxes hold pieces of Daddy—and

Polunsky has already stolen so much of him away. I like keeping the letters close. I wish I could fill my whole room with them, but Mama won't let me.

I used to think Mama might be jealous that he doesn't send her a letter for every day of the week, but I don't dare ask in case it might hurt her to talk about that. I know she misses him as much as I do, and we've all had enough pain.

A bang shatters my thoughts as I hear the door downstairs close and then Mama's voice. "Riley, are you home?"

"Yep!" I respond as I close my closet.

"Can you come help with groceries, please?"

"Yes, ma'am," I murmur as I head for the stairs. I leave my thoughts where I wish I could stay, locked up tight in the closet full of Daddy's letters.

Mama nudges my hands with a bowl of spaghetti until I blink and take it. When I look up at her, it's clear she's been speaking and I haven't been paying attention.

"Sorry," I say, as I carry the bowl to the table and grab the glasses to fill with milk.

"Your mind sure is busy." She waits until I meet her worried eyes before continuing. "Was your day okay?"

"Yeah, it was fine."

"Are you bored? Are you sure quitting your job was the best plan?" Her voice holds a tone that clearly says she thinks I should've stayed, but we've been over that already.

I level my gaze at her. "I'm sure that working in a place like that wasn't worth the money."

She watches me. I turn and pour the second glass of milk before she speaks again. "I know it was hard—"

"It wasn't *hard*, Mama." I put the glass down on the table with a loud *clink* and barely notice when a splash of milk sloshes over the top. "The second Carly found out about Daddy, she told *everyone*. They all started avoiding me, and then someone left those threats in my cubby and on my car."

"This isn't the first time we've seen struggle, Riley." Mama wipes up the mess with a napkin and shakes her head.

"They said I should die like the girls in Daddy's case." The words spill out like the milk before I can stop them.

Mama gives me a sharp glance and I shut my mouth, fuming silently and fighting to calm down. It's hard enough to cope with our situation, but the worst part is when she speaks to me like I'm not strong. When she implies that I'm weak after I spend every day fighting to prove to myself and everyone else that I'm tough enough to face my situation, my life. The pain of her doubting me hurts worse than it would from anyone else.

"Did you do anything fun today?" Mama clears her throat and lifts her chin as she puts her bowl on the table and takes her seat. I can see in her eyes that our previous discussion is now over.

"I did some reading," I answer, knowing that she won't be pleased if she feels like I sat around all day, content with my newly unemployed status.

"Oh? What did you read?" Her smile is hard, but the tone in her voice has a softer edge. She won't say out loud that she understands why I quit, but she does. Her job may be stable now, but it hasn't always been. And I know from her stories that she's had to work twice as hard just to get people to look at how competent she is instead of who she's married to.

Like Mama always says: *If you make yourself priceless, people can't throw you away.*

"It was *The Count of Monte Cristo*." I swirl some spaghetti around on my fork, but don't take a bite.

Mama's frown is back. "Again? A book about an innocent man in prison, Riley? Don't you think you should try reading something new?"

"I like it." I shrug, and then decide it's my turn to change the subject. "Are you still coming with me to the appeal hearing on Thursday?"

Mama nods as she pokes at her spaghetti. "Yes. I arranged for someone else to cover for me for a couple of hours. Should I come pick you up on my way to the courthouse?"

"Sure." I'm relieved I won't be alone this time. I look down and realize that I've just been swirling the spaghetti around in my bowl and haven't actually taken a bite. My stomach is rolling into a tight knot now, and it has nothing to do with hunger.

Maybe bringing up the appeal at dinner hadn't been my brightest idea.

Mama's hand closes over my fingers, stopping them from clutching my fork a little too tight.

"Whatever happens at the hearing, we're going to be just fine." Mama holds her head high and I wish I could sap a little of her resilience through her gaze. When I don't say anything, she gives my hand a squeeze. "You believe me, Riley?"

I quickly nod and try to convince myself that I mean it. "Yes, Mama."

3

WEDNESDAY AFTERNOON, my Volkswagen bakes in the Texas sun like one of Mama's pecan pies. Heat rises from it in waves, but I can guarantee it won't smell even half as good. I stop on the front porch when I see a white paper tucked inside one of Mama's planters. No one in our neighborhood has been friendly since they found out who Daddy was about a month after we'd moved in. Since then we've received lovely messages like this occasionally. I consider just throwing it away, knowing from experience that I don't want to see what it contains, but curiosity gets the better of me and I carefully unfold it.

It's exactly the kind of message I was expecting.

> *People who support murderers don't belong here.*
> *Get out of our neighborhood!*

Shoving my sunglasses farther up my nose with a sigh, I toss the note in the trash can before speed-walking down my driveway and unlocking the car door. I take a deep breath and open it, stepping back so the wave of heat escaping from inside doesn't blast me across the face.

Almost as if to spite my efforts, a wind hot as blazes kicks up like it came from the face of the sun itself. God, even the breezes in Texas can be hotter than hell. Instead of cooling me off, it makes sweat drip down the back of my neck.

I see my neighbor Mary walk out of her house three doors down, and I wave. She raises her hand automatically to wave back, but then recognizes me and quickly drops it back to her side when she sees her mother coming out after her. Mrs. Jones ushers her to her car, shaking her head and whispering in low tones the whole way. I can practically hear her clucking from here. Ducking my head, I ignore the sting of it and pretend not to care what they might be saying about me.

I watch them drive down the street as my car airs out a bit. It's always like this. We've moved three times around Houston—new neighborhoods, new schools, new friends. The same three things always happen with the kids at school. First, they eventually find out about Daddy, and that alone weeds out the vast majority. The few who aren't driven away by him being on death row are strangely obsessed with it. All they want to do is ask questions about what it's like to have a father on death row. Which is weird, but at least I have someone to hang out with—until their parents find out and forbid them to see me or come to our house. That cuts out almost everyone.

Only two remained after that, Kali and Rebecca. They were the two who didn't seem to care on any level about my dad—the two who felt like they were my friends just for *me*. That's part of what made it so hard when my mom and I moved to the other side of town, away from Kali in seventh grade. She made new friends and we lost touch. Rebecca's dad was in the army at Joint Base San Antonio, and then they were transferred to a base in South Dakota. I still get letters from her occasionally, but not often.

The neighbors usually went straight from finding out the truth to wanting us gone. Not all of them left nasty notes, but none of them were what I'd call friendly either.

Eventually I think I got tired of being rejected and started rejecting everyone else before they got a chance. Keeping people at a bit of a distance may be lonely sometimes, but it can also save a lot of heartbreak.

I punch the buttons to roll down all the windows simultaneously. I throw the blanket I keep over my seat into the back with a little more force than usual. When I climb in, I flip the visor down with a grunt to block the glare blinding me as it bounces off the hood of the car, forgetting for an instant about the old and warped photo of Daddy that I hide there. I catch it with gently cradled hands.

His face is so soft in the photo, so young. His eyes hold a touch of the recklessness he always says I got from him. His expression is now hardened by everything he's gone through. I love Daddy as he is, but I can't help but wish I'd known him when he looked like this. I shouldn't have the photo outside of our house. Mama says the ones from when he was younger are the ones people are most likely to recognize. But I can't bear to not have it close. I kiss the photo before slipping it back up behind the visor and starting the car.

Daddy's upcoming appeal hearing is the reason I feel so anxious and worried lately. He's also the reason I can't stay shut up in our house for another minute. Ever since I was old enough to drive, I've made a practice of seeing what it's like to be someone else on a regular basis. That's the kind of distraction I need to keep my mind busy for the rest of today . . . and I think I know where to find it.

I drive in the direction of First Liberty Mall. It takes fifteen minutes on the road before the air conditioner is even worth turning on. At least that still leaves me another forty-five to drive in the nice, cool interior before I get to First Liberty.

There are malls much closer where I could go to get out of the house. After all, I live in northeast Houston. Nearly every mall in the city is closer to home than the one I'm heading to. But I prefer a longer drive in exchange for the invaluable perk of anonymity. At First Liberty, I won't see anyone who knows me. I'm not *that Riley* from school, *that Riley* from the law offices, or *that Riley* from the Polunsky prison unit.

While I'm there, I can pretend to be anyone I want. I don't have to be the girl with the dad on death row. I don't even have to tell anyone my real name if I don't want to, and the nearly-an-hour drive in each direction is absolutely worth it to be *anyone else* on a day like today.

When I pull into the mall parking lot, a smile creeps across my face. No one here goes to my school or would recognize me. The diner across from the movie theater is a great spot, so I head in that direction. Often, I just like to people-watch. Other times I give myself a little challenge to interact with strangers. See who I might have decided to be if the Texas court system hadn't already defined that for me.

Of course, talking to people is always more risky. Folks I interact with look at me closer. And it's still possible that someone could recognize me from the newspaper articles about Daddy's trials and hearings, but that would be a risk anywhere in Texas. I usually stick with people my age, and that group spends about as much time reading newspapers as they do churning butter. With three high schools within spitting distance, this mall is always full of teenagers.

So for today at least, I can have a fresh start. And that's exactly what I need before tomorrow has the chance to crush my family's future.

The moment I enter the mall, a cool draft hits me and instantly puts me at ease a bit. In the back of my mind, I thank the gods of air-conditioning for the zillionth time.

I head straight for the Galaxy Café, and the hostess seats me near the window where I can watch the people walking by. The ambience here is fantastic. I would love this place even if it didn't offer me the freedom it does. It's like a diner lifted straight out of the sixties. They play old music like the Beatles and Elvis and it always reminds me of the music Daddy used to play around the house and how Mama would laugh. But that was long before prison bars stood between them. The seats are covered in bright red vinyl, records adorn the walls, and the ceiling is painted deep blue with tiny white pinpricks of light spread across it in constellations that mimic the nighttime sky.

Galaxy is both old and new. It's kitschy and cool, and I love everything about it.

On a Wednesday afternoon, the mall isn't too busy, but there are about ten tables already taken with late lunch customers. I order a thick Oreo milkshake and start studying the people around me. One nearby table is full of teens. I scoot to the edge of my booth and pretend to scroll through my phone as I try to eavesdrop on their conversation. Before I get a chance to hear much, though, I feel an impact against my right sandal.

When I bend over, the first thing I see is a red Matchbox car. I pick it up and squint at it.

"Sorry about that. Driving skills obviously need improvement." A deep voice speaks from the booth behind mine and I spin to face it. My first thought isn't exactly articulate: *Wow, hotness.* His warm eyes are a slightly lighter shade of brown than his dark olive complexion.

Hot Guy extends his hand. I freeze, not sure if I should shake it or stick the car into it. As if he can read my mind, he drops his hand back to his lap and provides me with an alternate option.

"Unless you're interested in joining our competition? Any experience on a pit crew, by chance?" His eyes now have a wicked sparkle to them that draws me in.

"Pit crew?" I ask.

"Girls don't like cars." I hear a small voice from the other side of his booth and slide to the side a bit to see who spoke. A seriously adorable little boy looks up at me. He can only be Hot Guy's little brother. His Angry Birds T-shirt is just a smidge too big for him. He has the same skin and dark, wavy hair, the same athletic build, the same square jawline and Roman nose—he is his brother in miniature. When he beams up at me, I can see that one of his front teeth is missing. "Hi!"

"Hi . . ." I can't help but smile back at him.

"What's your name? You don't like cars, right?" He continues to smile at me while I consider my answer. The kid couldn't be more than six years old. "I'm Matthew."

"I actually do like cars."

"Then you're cool." He lifts his cupped hands up and releases no fewer than eight cars onto the tabletop. His big brother frantically shoots his arms out, trying to prevent them all from careening off onto the floor.

Matthew slides out of his seat and walks to my table. "You didn't tell me your name."

Maybe all of my friends should be six. The questions of children seem to be so much simpler than those of adults. Something deep in me really doesn't want to lie to this kid. "I'm Riley."

His brother jerks his head up with an embarrassed expression. "Matthew, she doesn't have to tell you her name if she doesn't want to."

"But . . . she already did." Matthew looks at his brother like he just said the dumbest thing he's ever heard. He sticks his small hand out to shake mine.

"Nice to meet you," he says, sincerely. The gesture melts me and I place my hand in his. All my worry about Daddy's hearing dissolves as he grips my hand firmly and shakes it like this is the most important meeting each of us will ever have. "Now, tell me what your favorite color is."

After tossing the cars into a green plastic container, Matthew's brother gets up and puts his hands on Matthew's shoulders. "Sorry, he has no filter with strangers."

"It's fine. I like being told that I'm cool." I shrug before lowering my eyes to Matthew. "My favorite color is purple."

Matthew dives for the green bin and starts digging through it without another word.

"I think that was your official invitation to play . . . in case you didn't recognize it." Hot Guy rubs his hand on the back of his neck. His cheeks flush slightly and then he smiles at me. "I'm Jordan, by the way."

"Your brother is really cute." I lower my voice so Matthew can't hear us.

"Yeah, that's what all the girls say." Jordan shakes his head.

"Oh, I see." I lift one eyebrow, deciding these two might be the perfect pair to distract myself with today. "This is part of your game then? Bring your adorable brother to the mall. Hit girls with tiny cars. Have him get them to tell you their names . . . very smooth. Will he ask for my number next?"

Jordan looks horrified for an instant before he picks up on the fact that I'm joking and a grin spreads across his face. "Or maybe we're part of a research project and he's just a very small scientist."

The server comes with my milkshake and I stick my spoon into it. "What would you be researching?"

"The effects of tiny cars on complete strangers." Jordan sticks his hands into his jeans pockets as his face turns mockingly serious.

"Fascinating."

Matthew drops a bright purple convertible onto the table in front of me. I pick it up to look at it and before I know it, Matthew is pushing himself and his green bin of cars into the seat on the other side of my booth.

Jordan blinks at Matthew and then me before shaking his head. "Buddy, we need to stay in our booth. I think we've bothered Riley enough for one afternoon."

Matthew freezes in the middle of organizing his cars on my table and looks at me in shock. "I'm bothering you?"

I shake my head fast and firm. "Not at all."

"He's fine." I look up at Jordan and then gesture to the seat beside Matthew. "Looks like I'm officially part of your experiment—or pit crew—depending on where this afternoon takes us. Care to have a seat?"

Jordan sits down, picks up a yellow race car, and runs it over the back of Matthew's hand. His eyes lift to me and he frowns like something is bothering him.

"There is something kind of familiar about you, Riley. Do you go to school around here?"

4

I SWALLOW AND LIFT MY PURPLE CAR in front of my eyes, pretending to be very focused on the front wheels as my mind spins. I really don't like the idea of lying to Matthew, because lying to a kid who is so blatantly honest feels wrong for some reason, but I don't want to tell Jordan any more than I have to. There is obviously only one solution here.

Tell Matthew the truth. With Jordan, I'll lie through my teeth.

"Nope. I'm homeschooled, actually." I spin the wheels around once before lowering the purple car back to the table. "Maybe I just have one of those faces?"

Jordan nods slowly and then says, "Maybe . . ."

"Do you play sports?" Matthew jumps in before Jordan can say anything else.

"Not really."

"Jordan plays—" Matthew looks up at Jordan, his forehead wrinkling up. "Do you still play or do you used to play?"

Now it's Jordan's turn to look uncomfortable. "I might play again, but for now I don't play."

Matthew gives me a knowing nod. "He don't play."

I look from one brother to the other, waiting for someone to volunteer the missing information.

"Football," Jordan says, and his expression is surprisingly guarded. I wonder for a fleeting moment if I look the same way to him.

"You stopped playing football? On purpose?" I feign shock. "I didn't think that ever happened in Texas."

Jordan's face softens. "I know. You should take note. I'm a rare commodity."

"You'll cave and go back eventually. They all do." I ram my car into Matthew's and he giggles.

"You're some sort of Texan football expert?" Jordan's eyes are on me and he seems to have completely forgotten about the toy car in his hand.

I cast him a sideways glance and try for evasive. "Um . . . don't you have to be to live here? I thought they took your card away if you weren't."

"Your official Texan card?" He starts using a drink menu and the napkin holder to build a ramp for Matthew.

"Yes." This is good. Keep the chatter light and friendly. No probing questions and we'll all get through this just fine.

"I think I might just give mine back." Jordan focuses on fine-tuning his ramp balance by placing salt-and-pepper shakers at the end.

I'm jarred and stop my car in place, suddenly so curious about this guy across from me that I forget about protecting my own secrets. "Really? Why?"

Jordan notices the difference in my tone and looks up at me for a few seconds before saying, "I don't know. Reasons."

I blink. *Reasons?* And I thought *I* was the one being evasive.

He picks up Matthew's car and slides it successfully down the ramp. It only stops when it runs into the side of my milkshake and Matthew picks it up immediately for another run.

I take my purple car, place it on the ramp to go next, and smile, feeling myself start to relax. Something tells me that a guy who is trying to keep his own secrets won't press me too hard if I don't want to reveal any of mine.

Apparently, six-year-olds have very strong opinions about what they want to do and when they want to do it. Matthew is our leader and we spend our time mostly following his commands.

"Let's go to a movie!" he shouts as we walk out of Galaxy thirty minutes later.

Jordan looks over at me nervously. "Want to go to a movie?"

"Depends . . ." I look down at Matthew and lift one eyebrow. "Which movie?"

He suddenly frowns. "Ugh, do you like the kissy movies?"

Jordan slaps his hand over his eyes with a groan.

I answer like I'm thinking hard about it. "Hmm . . . not today, I don't."

"Oh, good!" Matthew looks so relieved I actually giggle. "Maybe one with explosions or cartoons?"

"Maybe cartoons?" I assume with Matthew we probably need to pick something in the G to PG rating range. "What do you think, Jordan?"

We both turn to face him and he looks up from checking something on his phone. He seems genuinely surprised that we're even asking his opinion. Maybe hanging with a kid Matthew's age all the time has its downside. You never get a say in anything.

"Yes. Cartoons it is," Jordan says as he leads the way toward the theater.

Matthew sits between us for the movie. I glance over at Jordan during the previews. I've had a lot of fun with these brothers already and I've only known them a couple of hours. Could Jordan finally be someone who wouldn't push to know too much about me? Maybe this could actually turn into a real friendship? My cheeks flush as I look away, grateful for the dim theater around us.

I scowl in the darkness. I know better than to get caught up in anyone like this. It *never* ends well . . . no matter how it starts.

Still, on a scalding hot Wednesday afternoon with nothing better to do, why can't a girl dream a little?

When I lift my eyes again, I see Jordan watching me. This time he doesn't look away or seem shy. He just smiles at me . . . and I smile back.

After the movie, we race cars down the slide at the mall playground and get pretzels. Matthew and Jordan are an infinitely better distraction than the people-watching I'd been hoping for. By the time we're leaving, I'm starting to wish I had a younger sibling to hang out with.

They walk me to my car because Matthew informs me "that's what the gentlemens do." Cuteness is surprisingly difficult to argue with.

Matthew zooms along in front of us as we make our way toward the mall exit. We watch him run his favorite car, the silver monster truck, over every flat surface he can find—the backs of benches, around flower pots, across the bottoms of store windows—I'm surprised he hasn't started trying to drive it over the people passing by.

"Thanks for hanging out with us today." Jordan sounds a little uncomfortable. "I hope we didn't keep you from anything important."

"I had nothing else to do," I say. "And even if I had, I would've picked doing this. You two are highly entertaining."

"Well, that's good to know." Jordan tousles Matthew's hair as he zips by. "It seems he's the secret weapon I never knew I had."

"Should I expect to see you here with a different girl every week now that you know you've struck gold?" I grin.

"Nah, too easy. Then it won't be a challenge anymore."

"Yeah, too easy is never fun." I chuckle, then look down when I realize Jordan is watching me more closely than before.

"Seriously, Riley, something about you is so familiar." Jordan squints and that sense of dread creeps over me again. My stomach goes shockingly cold after such a fun day. I plead inside my head. *Don't remember me from a newspaper or a picture online somewhere. Not today. Not you.* "Are you sure I don't know you from somewhere?"

"I don't know." I stall before continuing as we approach my car. "Maybe you saw me here before. Do you spend most of your Wednesdays with your brother at the mall?"

"We've never been here before, actually." Jordan adjusts the green bin of cars that he has tucked under his arm. I hear several tiny crashes from inside it.

"Like I said, one of those faces." I shrug and pull my keys out of my pocket.

Matthew runs his monster truck over the hood of my car and then abruptly hugs me. "Thanks, Riley."

"You're welcome, Matthew." I pat his head. When I open the door to climb inside, my car seems oddly emptier than it did this morning.

"You want me to give you two a ride to your car?"

"No, we're just a few rows over." Jordan opens his mouth to speak again, but then looks down at my car and frowns. "Uh . . . does your tire always look like that?"

"I have a flat?" I ask, but it's more of a statement than a question now that I've seen it. The tire is so empty it looks like the only thing holding the car up is the rim.

"Yes, you do." He follows me to the trunk. When I open it, I see an empty spot where the jack is supposed to go and I groan. I'd lent it to Tony—a guy from my old job—a week before my co-workers had found out and started giving me trouble about Daddy and I'd quit.

My perfect distraction day just took a *very* wrong turn.

I close my eyes and rest my head against the open trunk lid. I almost let a storm of curses burst out of me. How could I forget about the jack? Why did my tire go flat *right now*, and out here of all places? Why on the night before Daddy's hearing?

What am I supposed to do now? Who can I call? Mama is working late and even if I can get her on the phone, I know I'll have to wait until she finishes up before she'll be able to come and get me. Why is Mama never around when I need her most?

The last question ricochets through my body like a microscopic bullet. I don't usually let myself think like that. The thought pierces every cell until there is nothing in me that doesn't hurt, that doesn't bleed. This particular question is the one I actively try not to ask . . . because I'm honestly not sure I can handle it if the truth is that the only parent who really cares about me is on death row awaiting execution.

"Hey, are you okay?"

I turn around and sit on the edge of my open trunk. The still-hot metal heats my legs uncomfortably even through my khaki shorts, but I don't care anymore. I look up at Jordan.

"It appears that I am seriously lacking in the jack department."

Jordan grins suddenly. "I believe I can help with that. Stay here, we'll be right back."

Before I even get a chance to answer, he picks Matthew up and carries him like a sack over his shoulder. Matthew giggles and then makes an *uhh* sound as Jordan jogs across the parking lot. With every foot landing, Matthew's voice gets louder.

"Uhhh UHhhh UHhhh UHhhh UHhhh."

I watch them, a laugh bursting free from my chest. They climb into a blue Honda and drive over to park next to my car.

When Jordan hops out, Matthew follows him like a little shadow.

Jordan hesitates, but then looks down at him. "You can play right around these two cars or inside my car. Nowhere else, okay?"

Matthew nods and starts running his silver monster truck across Jordan's bumper.

Jordan walks up to me and extends a hand to pull me up from my spot on the trunk.

"Thank you," I say quietly, wishing I could've ended our meeting as the cool person they just met and not the helpless girl who isn't even able to take care of her own flat tire.

His hand squeezes mine as soon as I'm up, then he drops it and pops open his trunk. He grabs his own jack and I start freeing the replacement tire from my trunk. Jordan helps me lift it out.

"I'm sure I can do this myself if you need to go." I try to let Jordan off the hook as I reach out for the jack, but the truth is I have no clue how to change a tire. It isn't like I have my dad around to teach me, plus then Jordan would be the one without a jack when he someday needs it.

Thankfully, Jordan is already shaking his head. "Let me help. I'd rather not disappoint my folks' dream of turning Matthew and me into good Southern *gentlemens*."

"Lofty goals."

He shrugs as he pushes the jack into place. "It's good to have dreams."

"I suppose." I can't find a witty comeback this time. I sit down close to the car, watching Jordan so I'll be able to take care of this on my own if it ever happens again.

Jordan frowns at my now hopelessly dirty shorts. "You can just sit in your car or go inside the mall while I do this."

"No way. I've never been confused for a good Southern lady, but even I know better than to leave the guy helping me outside on a hot summer evening while I wait in the air-conditioned building." I look through my bag. "I just wish I had some sweet tea or anything flat I could use to fashion a large fan."

Jordan chuckles as he finishes cranking the jack up high enough to lift the weight of the car off the flat. "I thought girls only did that in old movies like *Gone with the Wind*."

"Maybe the girls you know are *actually* helpful instead of just pretending to be."

He squints over at me. "Maybe they're less creative."

"That's hard to imagine." It surprises me how comfortable it feels to just sit and chat with him. "So, if I can't fan you, I'll have to entertain you with witty conversation."

"Somehow I'm certain you'll be good at that." He glances up at me.

A wave of pleasure goes through me before I continue. "Let's see, I now know that you're an expert in miniature cars and scientific experimentation, you at least appear to know how to change a tire, and you temporarily pride yourself on being a gentleman."

Jordan doesn't even hesitate as he removes another lug nut. "Sounds about right."

Matthew comes over, his hair all matted with sweat. "Can we go home now?"

Jordan pauses and looks up at him. "Remember those things the *gentlemens* do?"

Matthew's eyes go from me to Jordan, and finally to the tire. He sighs. "This is one of those things, isn't it?"

"Yep."

Matthew shuffles away, looking hopelessly bored.

"I'm sorry. I can try to do this—"

"Sorry, can't hear you, this socket wrench squeaks too loud." He holds his free hand out like he's helpless against such a problem.

The wrench is almost completely silent.

I roll my eyes. "Fine."

"Good answer. It's really pointless to argue anyway. I'm a scientific mastermind, remember?"

"I don't remember ever saying mastermind." I frown in mock confusion.

"Weird." Jordan looks up at me with wide eyes. "Pretty sure I heard you say that."

"So anyway, back to my witty conversation. What else should I know about you?" I lean my head back against the car. "Anything else your mom wants her dear son to be? The first mechanic slash babysitter slash tiny-car scientist perhaps?"

Jordan's movements stop abruptly. When I tilt my face toward him, he keeps going, but he doesn't answer, and there is a distinctly pained look on his face now. Perfect. Of course I would somehow manage to hurt one of the only prospective new friends I've made all year.

"I . . . I'm sorry—" I begin.

"No." He shakes his head and his smile is back to almost the strength from before. Jordan removes the final lug nut and stands up straight. "You have no reason to be sorry, Riley."

I climb to my feet and help him lift the tire off in awkward silence. I'm not at all sure what I said that hurt him, but I'm determined not to repeat the mistake.

Jordan and I put the replacement tire in place before he turns to face me.

"Now you aren't speaking, and I don't want that." He pushes his wavy black hair back from his face and glances over his shoulder to make sure Matthew is out of earshot. "Our mom died in a car accident a few months ago. Thinking about her hurts, that's all."

My stomach drops and I feel terrible. "Oh, Jordan, I'm so sorry."

"Thank you." Jordan nods. "Now to make sure I didn't scare you away, promise me that you will talk to me constantly from right now until I finish putting this tire back on."

I raise my eyebrows. "That's quite a request. I'm actually not a big talker."

"Learn to adjust." He grins and then squats down to start securing the lug nuts back into place.

"Okay then." I retake my seat on the ground, trying to think of anything to keep this conversation going. It suddenly feels like a lot of pressure.

Jordan stops and gives me a pointed stare so I blurt out the first thing that comes to mind.

"It sucks having only one parent." I blink at him, and from his expression I can see he seems as surprised by my comment as I am. *That? That* is what I decide to say? What happened to being evasive?

Then he turns his eyes back to the tire. "Yes . . . it does. Your parents divorced?"

"Yes." This lie is too easy and common not to take advantage of, but somehow lying to Jordan after what he just told me feels wrong. I try to leave in some of the truth. "My father hasn't lived with us for years . . . since I was six."

"That's a long time." Jordan's tone is level and measured, but his eyes are filled with such a deep and aching sadness that my breath catches in my throat when he goes on. "Do you still miss him?"

35

"Yes," I respond quietly. "Every day."

Jordan finishes securing the spare and lowers the jack. Several seconds pass before he asks, "Does it get easier?"

I think about that question for a moment. Truthfully, I don't really remember much about the time when Daddy lived with us, so that part would be hard to compare with. But I do remember early visits at Polunsky, back when I would hope that maybe next week, next month, next year, that at some point it wouldn't make me as sad when I said goodbye.

That day had never come. It still feels like I'm leaving a piece of me behind when I exit Polunsky. It's like a part of me has been imprisoned with him for most of my life.

Finally, I reply with the only answer that feels true. "Not yet."

Jordan climbs to his feet and picks up his jack. "All done. We both survived, but I think at some point you owe me that sweet tea you mentioned."

His tone is light, but his eyes study me intently. The idea that he actually wants to see me again makes my stomach wobbly.

"That sounds more than fair." I give him a shy smile as I close my trunk. Jordan pulls a paper out of his pocket and I see him writing on it before he walks to stand beside me.

"Drive safe. You have a full-size spare, so you're set, but you may want to get that flat fixed or replaced soon." He reaches down and presses the paper against my palm. "Just in case you decide to make a habit of getting flat tires."

I feel warm inside as I see a phone number scrawled in heavy black numbers on the tiny paper. "Thank you, Jordan."

"Why is this picture so old?" Matthew's voice comes from

behind me and I spin to see him sitting in the passenger seat of my car. The door hangs open and I gasp when I see my picture of Daddy clutched in the boy's small hand.

I rush over to him, jerking the picture away and sticking it in the glove box before Jordan can see it. When I stand back up, both of them are watching me with wide eyes.

"Sorry, I—"

"No." Jordan cuts me off before I say any more. "I'm sorry he was snooping around in your car."

"I wasn't snooping!" Matthew yells, and when I glance down at him, he's rubbing his eyes and looks very tired.

"I know you weren't." I crouch down in front of him. "It's okay. Thanks to both of you for all your help." I lift my eyes back to Jordan, hoping he doesn't think I'm a total freak after that display. "I had a really fun day."

Matthew nods seriously, then turns his face up to Jordan, a whine creeping into his voice. "Are we done being gentlemens yet?"

"I guess so." He points toward their car. "Go buckle yourself in."

Jordan and I stand together alone. I squirm awkwardly, but he seems to have recovered.

"I'm sorry, it was just—"

"Really, Riley, you don't have to explain." He walks closer and rests one hand on my shoulder for just an instant, but even that shoots sparks through me. Then he pulls out his wallet and shows me a picture of a beautiful Hispanic woman who has Matthew's dimples. Her hair falls in soft curls that remind me of Jordan's. "Of all the people in the world who should understand why you have a picture of your dad hidden in your car, don't you think I'm one of them?"

I can't tell him that my reasoning is different, but I can't lie. Not after he showed me something that is obviously so special to him. But maybe our answers *are* the same. Maybe we both love and miss the parents that we can't be with. Why can't it be as simple as that?

So I just whisper, "Thank you."

"Have a good rest of your week, miss." Jordan tips the brim of a nonexistent hat to me as he backs away, and my soft smile breaks into a full-blown grin.

Matthew waves from the backseat as they drive away. I wave back, amazed at how one afternoon with a guy I barely know could leave such a huge impression on me.

5

THE COURTROOM SMELLS OF SWEAT AND FEAR. People shift awkwardly in their seats. They don't look much at each other, just mostly at us—they don't even try not to stare. I grab Mama's hand and don't look them in the eye, but I can't help but wish we could face today alone instead of with a hundred hostile strangers.

As much as I hate it, I understand them perfectly. They're both fascinated and frightened by my father and his family. We are the circus freaks in this charade. Maybe I should be better equipped to entertain them, but I'm not. I keep my appearance as generic as possible for every court appearance in the hopes that I can bore them into forgetting me. I wear large sunglasses even indoors, no earrings or hair accessories. I keep my dark hair straight and in a low ponytail. If I could find an outfit to blend in with the wooden bench I perch on, I probably would.

I can't even bring myself to look at the people on the opposite side of the aisle. If the strangers in this room have hostile gazes, the glances from the families of the victims are downright hateful. I'm sad for them. I really wish they could find the justice they think they have, but it's not here. I've never seen justice here.

In some ways, we're the same. All bound together by a stranger who committed a few acts of senseless violence. I expected the families of the victims to go away once Daddy was found guilty, but that was naïve of me. They're here for every hearing, every appeal—just like us. None of us, on either side of this situation, have been able to move on.

Mama and I have been told to sit quietly, no matter what the result may be. And we've done our duty every time. We might as well be bound and gagged in this room. We're helpless to do anything here, as we always have been. The fact that we are sure he's innocent doesn't matter, and it never will.

Daddy is here to play their games and guess at their questions. All in the vain hope that the correct answer might convince them of the innocence he has argued for almost twelve years. That he might someday earn his freedom.

I'm starting to believe that kind of freedom doesn't exist—not for us. This holding pattern of a life may be all we ever know.

Mr. Masters and Stacia stop beside us on their way up to the front. Stacia used to be Daddy's assistant. Daddy probably doesn't need legal help as much as the other Polunsky inmates, being an excellent lawyer himself. But they're the only other people in the world who believe Daddy is innocent besides our family, and we'll take any help and positivity we can get.

Daddy says Mr. Masters has watched out for us over the years in ways that he couldn't. All I need to know is that I can trust him, and I don't trust anyone else but my parents. He is the exception, the one person I can go to anytime, anywhere, with anything, and he won't judge or question me. That makes him family in my mind—and God knows I don't have enough of that.

"How are you two holding up?" Mr. Masters crouches down in the aisle at the end of our row and studies us both with concern. Stacia stands beside him, her hands fluttering nervously as she straightens the edges of papers in the stack she's holding.

Mama nods, her face a mask of confidence. "We're just fine. Thank you, Ben."

Masters searches my face and he seems to be checking to verify how much of what she's saying is true. I give him a tiny shrug because I'm really not sure how we are. Maybe he should ask again after we get through this appeal hearing.

"What do you think our chances are?" I ask, keeping my voice soft.

He puts on the same confident expression as Mama and nods. "I think we *have* a chance, which is what matters most right now."

Stacia reaches one hand out to squeeze my shoulder. "We're fighting our hardest for him. We won't give up."

"And we're very grateful for that." Mama swallows hard, and then all of us look to the front as the door they'll bring Daddy through opens.

Mr. Masters reaches over and pats Mama's hand before winking at me. Stacia gives me a nervous half smile before they both head to the front. I know they're here to support Mama and me as much as Daddy, and I'm grateful. Theirs are the only friendly faces that have ever greeted our family in any courtroom.

Daddy is escorted in and joins the rest of his legal team. He's less than ten feet in front of me, but I can't reach him, I can't touch him. I release Mama's hand and clench both of mine tight in my lap. I don't know why seeing him in a courtroom still shakes me in this way. I should be used to it. This is the perfect example of how we've lived almost all my life. He's right here in front of me, but still just out of reach.

He's told me a million times that he would be with us if he could. His wishes can't overcome the steel and bars that have been placed between us by a broken system. My hopes can't erase the words that were spoken in a different courtroom by Judge Reamers when I was only six years old.

Those words crushed my world. They haunt my dreams at night. I've even looked up the recording online to see if I was remembering it wrong—I've watched it more than once. Even so many years later, the words race through my head unbidden every time I sit in any courtroom.

This jury has found you, David Andrew Beckett, guilty of three counts of capital murder. In accordance with the laws of the state of Texas, this court hereby sets as your punishment: death. It is therefore the order of this court for you to be delivered by the sheriff of Harris County, Texas, to the director of the Polunsky Unit, where you shall be confined pending the carrying out of this sentence.

"Riley?" Mama squeezes my hand hard, and I turn my eyes on her immediately.

"Yes?" I study her face, wondering if she feels the same things I do as we sit here. My own mother is so difficult to read.

She gives me a wavering smile. "If you don't feel like you can be here, Daddy would underst—"

"No." I answer louder than I intend and then bite my tongue, actually drawing blood, but I force myself not to wince.

Mama's back stiffens, but I can't back down, not about this. During Daddy's trial, she deliberately kept me out of the courtroom whenever Mr. Masters didn't believe my presence was necessary to help the case. Since then, I'd missed several of the appeals when I couldn't convince Mama that Daddy would want me there. Only when I'd gotten my driver's license had she started to relent and let me choose whether to come to hearings. Even now, though, she still tries to shield me from specific information about Daddy's trial as much as possible. She refuses to understand that I'm not a six-year-old for her to protect anymore, but I will not let her send me away from his final appeal hearing. Not today.

"Please. I need to be here," I say.

She relaxes and takes a deep breath before nodding and patting my knee.

I know Mama is worried about how I'll handle it if this appeal doesn't go well. Daddy says that things look good this time, but he says that every time. At least with this appeal I don't feel like I'm going into the hearing blindfolded. This time, Daddy told me about the juror who was convinced by a family member that she should vote guilty. It's the most promising lead we've had in a while, but all the same, I'm afraid I'm being set up to fall. I can almost feel the ground beneath me starting to shake.

Mama sits so straight, her chin held high, but I wish I could know what is in her mind. Her last visit to Polunsky was over three months ago, and lately I wonder if she's lost hope after all this time. Maybe she's trying to make it less painful for herself if today doesn't turn out the way we want it to. Maybe that's the smart approach, the safe approach.

The bailiff orders us to rise as Judge Howard enters. I remove my sunglasses, sticking them in my purse. I want to be able to see everything that happens clearly. The judge's black robes float about her and make her seem more like an omen of death than the symbol of justice she should be. When we sit, she almost looks bored as she shuffles through the papers in the stack before her. It infuriates me in a way that I know it shouldn't, but she has too much power, and I have none. And I hate her for it.

Finally, she stares over her bench at my father. "Mr. Beckett, I have gone through the evidence you've submitted to this court several times. And while I agree that a juror's family members shouldn't give advice to the juror on rendering a verdict, I do not believe that in this case the advice swayed her decision. That means your evidence isn't sufficient to warrant the retrial you've requested, or even another stay of your sentence."

My breath catches in my chest as though an enormous weight has just crashed down on me. The room fills with the murmurs and rustling of the crowd watching Daddy's show. On the other side of the aisle people are cheering. They smile and hug at the thought of my father being killed. The irony is both maddening and heartbreaking. Being accused of killing is what landed him here in the first place. What kind of system is this? What kind of justice repays the killing of innocent women by then killing an innocent man?

The eye-for-an-eye mentality seems like it will always be alive and well here in Texas.

I feel sick and wish everyone else would just leave. My heart thuds painfully inside me like it wants to escape. My head spins as I try not to let my inner turmoil show on my face. If Daddy turns to look at me, I refuse to let that be what he sees.

Judge Howard pats at her curly gray hair before picking up one of the papers in front of her and frowning. "You've been convicted of the murders of three young women, Mr. Beckett. And they are particularly gruesome murders. Violent beatings followed by strangulation. Is that correct?"

I hear Daddy's voice hesitate. "I . . . I've maintained my innocence—"

The judge frowns down from her bench at him and interrupts. "Just answer the question, please."

Daddy responds immediately, but I can hear the slight edge he's trying to bury deep in his voice. "Yes. The state has convicted me of that crime, Your Honor."

"Those crimes," she corrects him, her gaze growing harder.

"Those crimes," he repeats back.

She glances down at her papers again. "It says here that you've already requested your writ of certiorari?"

My father clears his throat before answering, and my heart aches for him. "Yes, I have, Your Honor."

"And I'm sure that as a former lawyer, you understand how

unlikely it is that the Supreme Court will agree to hear your case?" Judge Howard squints over the bench at Daddy for several seconds until he nods. Then she brings her arm and the paper down onto her bench with a boom that reflects the finality of her dismissal. "Mr. Beckett, you don't have time left for me to mince words here. Assuming you aren't one of the lucky few cases chosen, you've exhausted your final appeal, and your execution will be carried out as scheduled in four weeks. From what I can see here, you've definitely had your due process. I recommend that you and your loved ones prepare yourselves."

Daddy doesn't move or flinch. I'm not even certain he is breathing. My eyes don't seem to be able to blink as I stare at him, trying to absorb the way he looks today, right now, before *everything* changes.

They're going to kill him. They are going to kill my father. And there is nothing I can do to stop it. If this happened on the streets instead of in a courthouse, I could call the police. Here and now, I can do nothing but watch in horror. People around me shuffle to their feet, but my world shifts and spins and I think I might be falling until I realize I'm not the one who is moving.

Mama falls off of our bench and crashes onto the ground in front of us. It takes me a full three seconds before I can react.

"Mama!" In—and out; I remind myself to breathe as I check for her pulse. My entire world locks up, not willing to move forward until it knows that I will at least have one parent left.

Then I feel the light but steady thrum of her heartbeat and a shuddering breath forces its way free from my lungs. Leaning in to hug her close, I hear her exhale quietly against my ear. Mr. Masters has come over to us. He says something I can't make out, and his hands are on my shoulders, pulling me back gently.

All I can hear is my own panicked muttering. "She's still here. She's okay. She's okay."

Stacia is speaking behind me and I realize she's calling for an ambulance.

When I look down, I see blood on my shirt and realize Mama hit her head when she fell. I grab the only thing I have in my purse, a workout T-shirt, and hand it to Mr. Masters, who presses it against her head.

Nothing here makes sense. Mama never shows weakness. She never fails and she never falls. This can't be real. It can't be happening right now. Not after what the judge just told us. If I squeeze my eyes tight enough, I might wake up from this nightmare.

I *have* to wake up.

I'm on the floor with my eyes shut tight. I'm clutching my unconscious mother's hand when I hear Judge Howard dismiss the court. The guards begin taking Daddy away.

"Wait! Wait! My wife fell. Is she okay? Amy!" His voice floats to me from far away and I open my eyes even as tears burn them. Tucking my head low so no one can see, I blink frantically until the traitorous drops fall away and then shove my dark sunglasses back onto my face.

"She'll be okay, Daddy," I yell out, loud enough for him to hear me. "We've got her."

Newspaper reporters crowd around us and start taking pictures. I can't hide myself from them. Stacia goes out to meet the paramedics. Mr. Masters keeps his head down and pretends the cameras aren't there. I do the same, but now that Daddy is gone I've lost my strength. No matter how hard I try, I can't stop the tears that pour down my cheeks.

One of the bailiffs makes his way through the crowd and crouches next to me. He looks from me to Mama and asks, "Do you need medical assistance?"

I shake my head hard and try to wipe the tears beneath my sunglasses away. "We already called for help."

His expression is tainted with disdain as he stands up, and I realize he thinks my mother is faking it. I look at the crowd around me, wishing the bailiff would at least make them go away, but he doesn't, and I'm sure from the look on his face that he won't.

After all the things I've experienced in places of so-called justice in the last eleven years, I would be shocked if he did anything at all. The paramedics come in, and Mr. Masters tugs me back, forcing me to drop Mama's hand as he pulls me into a tight hug, muttering against my head that everything is going to be okay.

Mama is always so tough and strong. All of my worry has been so consumed by Daddy for my entire life that worrying about Mama feels strange. Wrong.

The tears have stopped, or I can't feel the heat from them anymore. For the first time ever, I wish this court was even more of a circus. Because then at least the lights would fade, the crowds would leave, and I could slink away into the darkness.

6

DR. BILLINGS FROWNS AS HE PACES slowly around Mama's hospital bed. Mama sits completely forward with her legs crossed, like the pillow she's supposed to be resting against might burn her. It's a standoff of epic proportions. If we were in the Old West, I'd expect tumbleweeds to come blowing through, and they'd be drawing pistols at any moment.

"I don't think you're hearing me." The doctor speaks slowly. "Your blood pressure is very high, and your blood-test results indicate areas for concern that put you at a significantly increased risk for a heart attack. The medications we've prescribed will help with this, but everything we've seen suggests your stress level is far too high."

"I heard you just fine." Mama crosses her arms to match her legs. "And I don't need to be in the hospital, or resting, or running around picking up medications. I need to be at work."

Dr. Billings drags one hand through his hair and turns his eyes on me. "How many hours does your mom work per week?"

I open my mouth to answer, but Mama shushes me with a single stern glance.

"I work a full-time job just like everybody else, and I'll thank you to address your questions to me instead of my daughter."

"You collapsed. Your body can't take the strain and pressure you're subjecting it to. If you don't change things, it could be much worse next time. You need to, at the very least, be on medication to manage this."

Mama's cheeks flush, and from her reaction he might as well have told her she was weak and utterly useless to humanity. She opens her mouth to respond but I reach out and grab the doctor's elbow before she has the chance.

"I'll take the prescription and pick it up." I speak softly as I urge him toward the door. "Thank you."

The doctor's steps are quicker than mine and it's clear that not only is he relieved I let him off the hook, he's happy to escape this hospital room as fast as humanly possible. I close the door behind me and lean against it.

When I lift my eyes to Mama, I try to imitate the same reproachful look she's given me a million times. "If you want me to take medicine the next time a doctor tells me I need it, you better at least do the same for me here."

For a moment, it looks like she's ready to keep arguing, but then the fight drains out of her and she eases herself back against the pillow. The blood drains from her face, and she suddenly looks extremely frail and small.

I pull a chair over next to her bed.

"I really do need to get back to work," she says softly.

"I know, Mama." Reaching out, I take her hand. Everything that happened in the courtroom seems to settle like invisible rubble around us. "But right now or twenty minutes from now won't make much difference, will it?"

Her eyes settle on mine and the utter despair I see in them squeezes my chest.

"What are we going to do?" We both know what I'm referring to.

She grasps my hand tight before answering. "We'll do what we always do."

"Wait?" I sigh and lower my head onto her bed.

"No, darling." Mama releases my hand and runs her fingers through my dark hair. "We always survive."

Then she moves away. I lift my head to see her pulling her work slacks on under her hospital gown. Something about her getting up and ready for work right now when the doctor just told us she shouldn't feels so wrong. Especially when Daddy just lost his last appeal. When I so desperately need her, and she's leaving me like she always does, leaving me all alone.

Everything about this moment ignites a slow-burning anger in the pit of my stomach.

"What about Daddy?" I watch her as she freezes and then lifts her chin to look at me when I finish. "What if this is something *he* won't survive?"

Her expression flashes both shock and anguish before that ever-present resolute mask falls into place. "Well, Riley, I suppose you and I will survive that, too."

My stomach plummets to my feet at the absolute lack of hope in her words. Then she slips her pumps on, grabs her purse, and gives me a tight hug before she walks out the door. "I'll be home late tonight."

The door closes behind her with the same echoing finality as the judge's gavel.

Thanks to Judge Howard mentioning the gruesome nature of the killings at the hearing, my dreams that night are pelted by the few images and details I still remember from Daddy's first trial.

I stand in front of my house, and when I turn around, I see Mama's body stretched out in the front yard. She looks just like one of the girls from the photos. At first, it looks like she's sleeping. Her long, dark skirt reaches all the way down to her feet and she has black stockings on. Her blouse is done up, her arms folded over her stomach. Everything looks normal except for the angry purple bruise across her neck and her open eyes that stare up at me, vacant. Sobbing, I search frantically for a pulse, but there is none.

Suddenly, we are in a silver morgue with a pendant light swaying over the only table not in shadow. Mama is laid out on the table in front of me, in only her underwear and bra. I can see all the bruises, burns, and cuts that were previously hidden by her clothing. Around us, the walls suddenly light up with X-ray after X-ray, each and every one showing different broken bones. There are more than a dozen, and they feel like they're closing in. I'm surrounded by so many breaks, so much violence. Whoever did this had savagely attacked her, strangled her—and then put her clothes back on so she looked peaceful when placed carefully in our front yard.

I curl in on myself. Unable to look at her anymore like this. So I become nothing more than a small ball in the midst of all this carnage. Backing myself into the corner, I close my eyes. Hoping against hope that it isn't real, and it will all stop. Up until the moment the dream ends and I wake up in a cold sweat.

As I'm getting ready for my visit to Polunsky on Friday afternoon, Mr. Masters calls me. I smile to myself as I answer.

"Hello?"

"Miss Riley." Mr. Masters has a pronounced drawl so thick it'd make molasses look runny.

"Mr. Masters," I reply slowly, mocking his drawl.

When Daddy introduced us a long time ago, Mr. Masters had seemed so tall. I remember thinking that with his fancy and expensive suits, he must be someone important. I'd asked Daddy what I should call him. Mr. Masters had crouched down in front of me and given me a very serious look.

"What do you want to call me?" he'd asked.

I'd hid a little behind Daddy's arm without answering. Mr. Masters told me since I was a young lady I had two options. "You can call me Mr. Benjamin or Mr. Masters."

I'd thought about it for a minute, but Mr. Benjamin just didn't seem fancy enough for this man. "I choose Mr. Masters."

"Excellent choice," he'd said, standing up straight and extending his hand to me. "And I'll call you Miss Riley."

When I'd shyly stuck my hand in his, I felt something beneath my fingers. When I pulled it back, I saw he'd slipped a small pack of Skittles into my palm. They'd always been my favorite candy.

Mr. Masters winked. "I heard you like those."

I'd beamed up at him and I remember thinking that he was like the president, only magical.

So far, he'd never given me a reason to change my mind about him.

"How are you doing on this scorching afternoon?"

"I'm enjoying the pleasures of air-conditioning while I get ready to go visit Daddy. How are things on your end?" The humor disappears on both ends of the phone as soon as I mention my father.

"I'm still working. I haven't given up." His voice is soft now. "How's your mother doing? I've been worried."

"She's still working, too." My laugh comes out with a bitter edge. "What else would she be doing?"

"What did the doctor say?" He sounds gruffer than before. "Stubborn woman isn't taking my calls."

"At least we're in the same camp. She didn't answer when I called earlier either," I mutter. "He said she is carrying too much stress and put her on some blood pressure meds."

His only response is an affirmative grunt on the other end.

"Well, please keep me posted, Miss Riley," Mr. Masters finally says. "Tell me if you think of a way I can help you—either of you. You're the only reasonable one in your family these days."

I laugh in surprise. Masters speaks to me freely. He always has. He doesn't treat me like a child the way my parents do. "Maybe someday you can tell my parents that."

"Perhaps." He chuckles before saying, "Good afternoon, Miss Riley."

"Good afternoon, Mr. Masters."

When I hang up, I sigh and rub the circles beneath my eyes in the bathroom mirror. Between my mind spinning about the hearing and the nightmares, I'd barely slept the night before.

After a long stretch of my neck and shoulders, I decide this is as good as it's going to get. I'd considered applying some powder to try to cover up the signs of exhaustion, but I'm a minimalist when it comes to makeup. Besides, it would take something like a miracle to hide the effects of the last twenty-four hours. Instead, I grab a Coke from the fridge and my keys off the counter, and head out the door.

7

THE REGISTRATION BUILDING AT POLUNSKY is squat and gray; it looks like a block of extremely condensed fog. Which is perfect because my brain can't seem to shake its foggy feeling either.

I spent yesterday evening filling Mama's prescriptions and then stayed up late making sure she would agree to take them. She asked again and again if I was still planning to come for my visit and if I was sure I didn't want to wait until we found a time when she could go with me. I was surprised she'd even asked, because we both knew that would never happen. By the fifth time I assured her that I'd be fine on my own, she seemed convinced. It took all my self-restraint not to slam the door when she asked me to tell him that she was fine.

I don't expect the usual part of our conversation to take long because I'm not going to lie to him.

We're not great, Daddy. Not great.

By the time I say hi to Nancy and make it through the checkpoint, it's clear that she and the others in the registration office know what happened at the appeal. They all give me consoling looks, and no one attempts to laugh or joke with me like usual.

I grab my stuff back from Nancy when she finishes her pat-down, eager to get out of this office that suddenly feels like a funeral wake.

"See you next week, Riley," Nancy says, and as I turn to head to the front desk for my visitor badge, I hear her add, "I'm sorry."

I nod in thanks. My mind drifts back and forth between panic and numb resignation, just like it's been doing since the appeal yesterday. My body goes through the motions, following the normal routine as I try desperately to pretend everything hasn't changed.

It's quiet in the tiny visitation room, and the last thing I want today is to be left alone with my thoughts. The clock on the wall ticks away seconds, and I try not to listen to it. I keep thinking of how many hours are in four weeks, twenty-eight days—twenty-seven now.

When my mind spits out the correct answer to the math problem, my heart sinks. Twenty-seven days is six hundred and forty-eight hours.

I shake my head. No, it's actually less than that. It won't be twenty-seven full days anymore. Every hour that passes is one less. Two hours per visit, with only four more visits, including this one. Two hours each—*eight hours total?*

I have eight hours with Daddy until the state of Texas executes him for crimes he didn't commit. Eight hours before they steal him from me just like they did when I was six . . . except this time I lose all of him forever.

Screw Texas. I hate Texas.

So I refuse to think about the time remaining anymore. It helps no one. I will think about the only options we have left: the writ of certiorari and clemency. No matter what the judge said, we still have a chance the Supreme Court will decide to delay the execution and review his case. And *if* the Supreme Court refuses to hear the case, then our only hope is the governor granting clemency. And a governor granting a stay of execution like that in Texas is almost unheard of. We really need a plan now . . . and a good one.

I stand in the room, pacing back and forth next to the table. By the time Daddy arrives, I'm chewing away at my nails like I have no other alternatives for food despite the fully stocked vending machine I keep walking past.

"Hi, Ri," Daddy says when the officer brings him in. I hug him tight and then study him once we're seated at the table, wondering where we should start.

"How is your mama?" He starts the visit the way we always do, but I feel more like I'm talking to a ghost of my father rather than the real thing. The light in his eyes is gone and he looks completely worn through. It seems like he's lost even more weight since yesterday.

"She's fine. She said to tell you that you don't need to worry about her." I put on the brave smile I have permanently welded to my face for every visit.

"No lies, remember, Riley?" Daddy reaches out and pulls gently on one of the brunette tendrils that fall out of my ponytail. "Not now. Not to me."

Reaching up, I tuck the stray piece back into place. "Let's just talk about our plan, then," I say, changing the subject.

Daddy releases a sigh that sounds so deep it may have started in his feet. He starts to respond, but there's a swift knock on the door, and it opens immediately. On death row, there is no right to privacy.

An older guard I don't recognize steps aside, and I see Stacia behind him. As Daddy's former paralegal, Stacia comes at least once a week to discuss appeals and options on behalf of the rest of the legal team. She usually comes earlier in the week, though, so it's been a while since I've seen her here. Her face is starkly paler than it's ever been next to her dishwater-blond hair. It seems frizzier than normal, and her cheeks have taken on a slightly gaunt look over the last year. Fighting for someone in Polunsky really seems to leave its stamp on people.

She falters a step when she sees me, but the hesitation only lasts a moment. "I'm sorry, David, I forgot today was your visitation day with Riley."

Stacia is awkwardly shy and a little backward, but she's very loyal, and that's what matters. Her feet shift side to side as she keeps her eyes on the floor. She seems even more uncomfortable than usual, and for Stacia, that's saying something.

"It's okay. I'm sure I don't have much time left to worry about whether or not I should spread my visitors out better." He smiles at her, but the sadness and fear behind it take my breath away.

I've never heard Daddy talk like this. He's always been so full of hope. He never talks about the end or how much time he has left. Seeing him like this is more terrifying than anything the judge said in the courtroom yesterday. A cold sweat starts on the back of my neck and my heart speeds up in my chest.

"I-I'm so sorry to have to interrupt with this . . ." Stacia lifts her hand to him and I see she clutches a white envelope. It's pressed so tight between her fingers that each one has left a deep crease. Her eyes flit to me. "To both of you."

Daddy reaches for it. I see the return address on the envelope with the words *Supreme Court of the United States* and everything slows down as he opens it.

We weren't expecting to hear back on the certiorari today. It is our true Hail Mary pass. And now that I know all the answers are in that envelope, I suddenly hope for something drastic to stop us from seeing what it holds. I hope for a fire drill, or a meteor, or the end of the world—whatever it takes to prevent us from reading the answer.

Anything to keep our last scrap of hope alive right now, because I am *not ready* to lose it.

The paper he removes isn't thick, and even from the opposite side of the table I can read the word *DENIED* in bold, panic-inducing letters.

That single word removes one of our two remaining options, and I can't help but feel like someone just ripped off my right leg. It's painful. I feel shockingly off balance.

Daddy reads the entire thing slowly. Then he folds it, puts it back in the envelope, and hands it to Stacia. "Thank you . . . for everything."

She grips the paper with both hands and her eyes are damp, but she can't seem to find any words to say.

Daddy saves her from that task. "I'd like to get back to my visit with Riley now, but thank you very much for coming." His words are kind, but his tone is exhausted and lightly dismissive.

"Of course." Stacia looks down, backs toward the door, and knocks on it. She looks like she failed him, and I feel a sick hope rising up that maybe she did. She's been helping with his case. Maybe she messed something up? We might have another chance at appeal if that were true, and I would do almost anything for that chance right now.

I close my eyes, disgusted with my thoughts. Stacia cares about my father. I truly wouldn't want her to have made a mistake. She would never forgive herself for that.

"I'll come back on Monday," she murmurs as the guard opens the door for her. Then Stacia ducks out through the doorway without waiting for a response.

Daddy stares down at the table in silence as the door clicks closed again, and I wonder if he's forgotten that I'm here.

I swallow back all the fear and dread that threaten to clog up my throat, forcing my voice to come out steady. "Well, I guess the plan I wanted to put together just got even more important."

"Let's not plan, Riley." Daddy closes his eyes and his head hangs forward to rest on his chest for a moment. He looks drained. He's always been a handsome guy, but lately, everything seems to be catching up with him. When he opens his eyes again, they've gone from dull to almost vacant. My stomach clenches just seeing them. What small amount of hope he may have retained after the hearing yesterday just left him—right here in front of me.

That thought terrifies me, so I push forward, my words spilling out over one another in their rush to escape. "I think maybe we should plan out some kind of campaign, you know? See if we can get other people involved, maybe from other states. Have people write to the governor with us and ask him for a stay. I think that outside of Texas people are more likely to—"

"Riley—" Daddy tries to interrupt, but I don't let him.

"Because in Texas, executions are just too common and people are used to it. Plus, I was wondering, is there any chance that anyone on your legal team messed something up?"

"You have to listen—" Daddy frowns, tilting in toward me, and so I lean back. For the first time ever, I'm fine with pissing him off. Let him get frustrated. *That* I can handle. What scares me right now is hearing the utter defeat in his voice.

"And you already have so many people from other countries who write to you here. I know they're all strangers, and probably more than a few are totally nuts, but they're fascinated with your story and say they're on your side. Warden Zonnberg told me." I lurch forward and wonder if I'm blinking at all because my eyes are starting to burn. "We can get them to write, too, and I think with that many—"

"Enough, Riley!" Daddy barks, and the guard in the hall hammers his fist on the door and looks in the small window to make sure I'm okay.

When I wave him off, the guard relaxes, and I watch my father closely. He has never once raised his voice to me—not once. I don't know how to respond or even what to say to that, so I cross my arms and wait.

"I don't think this is good for you anymore . . . and it's definitely not healthy for your mother," he starts.

I can't stop a scoffing laugh from escaping. "Daddy, this has never been *good* for us."

"And I hope someday you can forgive me for that." His face hardens and I fill with immediate regret.

"I'm sorry, Da—" But he doesn't give me the chance to take it back.

"I need to say this while I still have the courage to do it, so please let me!" He doesn't raise his voice again, but instead scoots forward, grips my hand tightly in his, and captures my eyes with a gaze so intense I don't dare look away. "Your mama is struggling but won't admit it. And whether we like it or not, I am rapidly running out of time here. You're stronger, better, and brighter than I ever could've hoped for, and as much as I hate it, I am forced to rely on you instead of your mother. For that I'm forever sorry."

He takes one long, trembling breath without looking away. And then continues in a low enough whisper that I'm the only one who can possibly hear. "Riley, I've been lying. It's time you know the truth. There is no point in fighting this battle anymore. I'm guilty and I'm going to be punished for what I've done."

Time freezes for moments, seconds, maybe minutes. I wait for the punch line of this terrible joke, but it never comes. I can't make sense of anything he's saying. I keep shaking my head, hoping something will fall into place, or that I might suddenly understand why he would say something like this. My heart has stopped, and ice replaces the blood in my veins.

Daddy keeps going, like he doesn't know damn well that my world is crumbling apart. "I'm telling you now so that you can finally let go of this fight and move on with your life. You need to *let me go*. And you need to decide at what point your mama is ready to know this, too. I'm sorry, Riley, but you may have to be the one to tell her."

I blink, and blink again. Then the horrific sound of a howling, moaning wind fills my mind, and even though he is still speaking, I can't hear his words anymore. I'm trying to pull my hand from his, but he won't release it. I can't process what he's saying. It isn't true. It can't be true. It can't.

My heart rips into a dozen partially beating chunks and it shouldn't surprise me that I can't seem to catch my breath. The only thing that could make sense here is that he wants me to stop pushing him. Maybe he's given up, and he is trying to give me permission to give up, too.

But I can't give up on him. And he can go to hell for even asking me to.

I finally wrench my hand away and get to my feet. My ears are working again, but all I can hear is my own voice shouting the word *No!* over and over again—no to being here anymore, no to what he's saying. And no to everything else he is trying to turn into a lie.

The officer opens the door, but he stops in surprise when he sees that it's me and not Daddy who is causing problems.

"Riley?" Daddy stands up, eyeing me warily like I'm some caged animal—like I'm a monster.

Like the monster he just tried to tell me that *he* is . . .

The irony makes me feel nauseous. I take another step backward. The guard looks from my father to me before holding out the stack of letters that my father has written me for the week.

Turning my back on Daddy without a word, I stalk past the officer, deliberately not touching the letters. I don't know what to think or feel. I just know that I can't hear any more from him right now. I walk through the doors and out into the yard. My feet carry me all the way to my car in a stunned daze, and then I stand there. I stare at the car door as my mind spins through everything he's ever said to me, trying desperately to find something *real*—something true to cling to.

I am not a murderer, Riley. Now, how can I know for sure?

I'm guilty and I'm going to be punished for what I've done. I don't even know how to begin to believe that either.

Every attempt to understand only leads to more questions. I thought he could never lie to me, and now I know for certain he has at least once. How am I supposed to tell his truth from his lies? He's always been my favorite person in the world. Who is he now?

I would never do anything to hurt you or your mama. I don't know.

Trust me. I don't know.

I love you, Riley . . .

I kick my car tire hard and pain shoots through my foot, but I'm too big of a wreck to even care. Tears stream down my face as the Texas sun beats down on my back, but I feel so cold inside that I don't know if I will ever stop trembling.

8

THE SWING I'M SITTING IN HOLDS perfectly still, but somehow the sand between my toes feels like it's moving. I decide I don't care and take another swig from the bottle of rum before fumbling the top and almost dropping it in the sand. Then, with a little difficulty, I finally manage to cap it and tuck the bottle back securely under my jacket. Not that I think anyone will come walking through this park at almost midnight on a Friday, but this is the first time I've ever tasted alcohol and everything about it feels rebellious.

I'd been such a mess during the hour drive home from Polunsky. I had to pull over three times because I felt so sick over my conversation with Daddy. By the time I got back to town, I was only sure of two things. First, I needed some time to try to understand what he was thinking when he confessed to me before I talked to Mama about it. Not a problem, of course, because she's working late as usual anyway. Second, I knew that I really, really didn't want to *think* anymore.

I heard in one of our health classes at school that alcohol slows down your brain function. That's kind of what I was after. I parked in front of the house, checked to make sure Mama wasn't home, stole the first bottle I could reach for out of the liquor cabinet, and came straight to this park.

It turns out, that health class info was dead on.

My head hangs to one side against the chains and it feels heavier to hold up than I remember it being. My phone is on my lap for some reason and it slides off, landing in the sand beside me. I think about picking it up, but it feels like it would be a lot of work, so I don't.

I watch the lights of cars passing by on the nearest street. It's well over two hundred feet away, on the far side of the park. Traffic keeps up a steady hum that is only interrupted by the occasional blaring honk of a car horn. Everything around me feels so fuzzy it makes me laugh. I sing softly to myself in the darkness, choosing a heavy metal song to fit my dark mood. It doesn't sound nearly as tough and angry when it's just my voice and no pounding drums or wailing vocals . . . but it's nice.

Tomorrow will be the first day, other than visitation days, that I won't have a letter from Daddy to open in as long as I can remember. I feel empty, my heart aches, and I'm lonely. It's only been a few hours, but I'm already regretting the way I left Polunsky. Daddy had still been trying to talk to me. Maybe I could've begged him to explain. Maybe I could've gotten some better understanding of whether he'd been telling the awful truth . . . or the worst kind of lie—one designed to push his family away.

And now it's too late for any answers. Now I won't even be able to open one of his letters or speak to him for a week, and I don't know how to deal with that.

I've been alone for much of my life, but I've never felt *this* alone.

I wish again that I had someone to call, that I knew anyone who would come meet me in the park at night and talk to me. Friends should do that, but I don't have that kind of friends—not anymore. The only way I can keep any friends is by lying to them, and I know from experience, the truth always comes out in the end. People keep you at a distance if they think killing runs in your blood.

And if I believe what Daddy confessed to me, then maybe they were right—right about me being wrong about him for so long.

Pulling the bottle out, I take another drink. The burning sensation from the first couple of swallows is long gone. It has been replaced by warmth that momentarily makes me feel not so alone.

But then it passes and I'm cold again . . . and lonelier than ever.

I slosh the bottle around in front of my face. Holding it up, I watch the amber liquid surge from one side to the other in the moonlight. My fingers are numb and I lose my grip, dropping the bottle into the sand.

"Aw, hell." I lurch out of my swing and reach for it even though it's mostly empty anyway. When I lift it up to the moonlight again, the liquid definitely has more grit to it than before. "Damn."

I slump down in the sand and accidentally knock my phone aside when I'm reaching for the bottle. The phone flips over, landing with a soft thud in the sand. The screen lights up and I see a couple of missed calls from a number I don't recognize. Probably a wrong number.

I roll over onto my back and stare up at the twinkling starlight. Each star seems to flicker and wink at me. Nothing in my life feels constant anymore, nothing steady or dependable.

How many times has Daddy declared his innocence over the years? One hundred? One thousand? Were those the lies? Or just this last one? How many times can you lie to someone you love before everything you share becomes the lie?

I grab the bottle of rum, sit up, pull back, and chuck it as hard as I can. I hear a crash of breaking glass on the rocks of the shallow pond. My sudden fury washes away as quickly as it came. My hand feels as empty as I do. What if Daddy didn't mean it? What if someone made Daddy tell me that he was guilty? What if—

A soft whistle comes from the shadows behind me, and I whirl around to face the darkness. My motions are too fast for my current state, though, and I tip to one side, my head spinning. "Who— who is that? Who are you?" I ask once I find the words I'm looking for.

"Relax, Riley." A tall, definitely male form steps out into the moonlight, but I can't quite get my eyes to focus on him. He walks toward me with his hands up. I scoot backward across the ground a bit and he slows down.

Now he's only a few feet away. My vision sharpens and when I recognize him I still can't believe he's real. "Jordan? Wh-what are you doing here?"

"You called and asked me to come. Don't you remember?" His dark eyebrows lift and the corner of his mouth turns up.

The missed calls on my phone . . . could that have been him trying to call me back? I groan, embarrassed, and try to fold my arms across myself, but somehow I end up ramming them into each other and have to try twice to get it right. I look down and see a small white paper under the swing; I know before I pick it up that it's his number. I honestly don't remember calling him, but I do remember thinking again and again that I wished there was someone I could call.

Apparently, I found someone.

I place one hand on my forehead, not sure how to even begin apologizing for this. "I can't believe you came. I'm so *so* s-sorry."

Jordan sits down beside me in the sand, stretching his long legs out in front of him. "Don't be sorry. I'm glad that you called."

I glance over at him, trying to read his face in the moonlight. He stares straight ahead, but he doesn't look annoyed or bothered at all. I relax a bit, lying back on the sand so I can rest my head, which is starting to swim again.

He gives me a wry smile. "I think you almost hit me with a liquor bottle when I was looking for you."

I can't help but laugh. "You have great timing. You're there to help with my flat tire. And now you show up in time to catch my f-first time drinking."

Jordan looks a little concerned as I try to prop myself up on my elbows, wobble, and lie back down. "First time, huh? Did you drink the whole thing?"

"No, officer. Just most of it." I give him a fake salute and he shakes his head.

Drawing a deep breath, I pull myself up to a sitting position next to him.

"And I'm assuming you didn't just pick today randomly to start drinking." He sounds hesitant, like he knows he might be prying, but still needs some answers. "You sounded really upset when you called me. What's going on, Riley? Are you okay?"

I look over at him, wondering how to answer his question. Wondering how quickly he'll make an excuse to get out of here if I tell him the truth. A soft sob escapes my throat at the thought of being alone in the park again, and Jordan puts one of his arms around my shoulders for a quick, comforting squeeze before dropping it again.

"Whatever it is, it's going to be okay." His eyes mean it. And after all this time, I'm so sick of the lies. Daddy was the only one I never lied to, but now I find out he has lied to me at least once . . . and maybe more.

No matter the cost, I can't take any more lying. Especially not to the only person who has been a friend to me lately.

"It's m-my father." I pull my knees into my chest, wrapping my arms around them.

"I see." Jordan nods immediately. "Problems with the divorce situation?"

I blink at him before remembering that I had lied about that, too. "Oh . . . kind of, but I lied to you about that. I'm sorry. I'm really sorry for all of this. I just didn't . . ." I'm rambling and my words slur so much that I'm not even sure what I'm trying to say.

Jordan puts a hand on my arm to stop me, with a small frown of confusion. "It doesn't matter. Just tell me the truth now."

"My parents aren't divorced, but Daddy hasn't lived with us since I was six. He—my f-father is in prison."

"Oh . . ." Jordan gives me a sad look. "You don't have to hide that, Riley. You aren't the first girl I've met with a parent in jail."

"No, he's not just in jail." I bury my head in my arms so I don't have to see his face as I say the rest. "He's on death row for m-murdering three women. He's going to be executed soon—too soon."

Seconds pass, a minute—and Jordan is completely silent. I groan.

"If you need to leave now, I don't want to watch you do it, okay?" I whisper into my arms, but loud enough that I'm sure he hears me. My head and heart throb as I finish. "So just go."

Another minute passes in silence and I finally raise my eyes. Jordan sits beside me, a deep frown on his face. His eyes are closed as he rubs his hand against his temple.

"I said you could go." My voice is small and I hate it.

"I don't want to go," he responds immediately, before opening his eyes and looking straight at me. "What's your last name, Riley?"

It's a weird question, but knowing I already lied to him, maybe he wants to check my story. It looks like my family is full of liars. I can hardly blame him. "It's Beckett."

"Beckett, okay." Jordan takes a slow, deep breath. Then he asks the last thing I expect. "How can I help?"

I shake my head in confusion. "Help?"

"Yes. I hate seeing you like this." He places one hand on mine for a moment. "No matter what your father did, you aren't responsible. How can I help you?"

I sit up straight and jerk back my hand. "Who says he did it?"

A slight shadow crosses Jordan's face. "So he told you he's innocent, then? You believe he is?"

My shoulders slump instantly, because the truth is I have no idea anymore. My head is starting to clear a bit, I feel nauseous, and I'm starting to wish I hadn't thrown that bottle of rum. Then I'm softly crying and murmuring things that I know I shouldn't be telling anyone, but I can't hold the weight of them alone anymore. "He always said he was innocent. For eleven years he's said that, but today he told me he's been lying. He said he wants me and my mom to move on. He wants us to l-let him go."

"Shh. It's okay." Jordan scoots closer and puts his arm around my shoulders, pulling me gently against him. After a few seconds, he asks, "Which do you think is the truth?"

I shake my head and it sets my vision swinging. "I really don't know anymore. I hate that so much. How can I live not knowing who he is?"

He doesn't respond; he just holds me and lets me cry against his shoulder. He doesn't hate me because of my father, he doesn't think I'm weak like my mother does. He just whispers that I'm going to be okay, and that's exactly what I need right now.

After I stop crying, I don't move away even though I know I should. His chest is hard and strong beneath my head, and his fingers are warm over my shoulders as he steadies me. He smells like soap and something musky that makes me want to close my eyes and relax. My thoughts are out of my control and seem to go straight to my mouth without any kind of filter. "You smell so good. Did you just shower?"

He laughs in surprise and his breath is warm against the top of my head. "Yes. My dad made me play in a neighborhood football game tonight. I had to shower right after."

"Are neighborhood games always this late at night?" I try to sit up straight, but can't quite do it and end up leaning my head back against his shoulder because it's feeling even heavier than before.

"No, it ended a few hours ago, but they start around dusk. It's better to start late on really hot days."

"Your dad *made* you play?" I try to scratch my nose, but end up nearly poking myself in the eye. "He's not a fan of you quitting, huh?"

"No. Which is one of many reasons I was so glad to hear from you." Jordan grunts, and his grimace makes him look much older. I sit back and look at him again. "The house is uncomfortable after we have chats like that."

"Many reasons?" I ask. My cheeks feel hot, but then I frown. Jordan is swaying and it's making me dizzy. I almost ask him to stop before I realize that it isn't him that's moving. It's me.

"Maybe it's time for you to go home?" Jordan reaches a hand out to steady me and pulls me up to my feet. Taking my elbow in his hand, he begins guiding me toward the parking lot. "Did you bring anything with you to the park besides your friend in the bottle?"

"No. It was just us." Walking seems to make everything worse, and I'm feeling a little sick. "And I'm not sure he's my friend."

"Probably not." He chuckles.

We're almost to the parking lot when I jerk quickly to my left, ripping my elbow from his hand and stumbling away. I put suitable distance between us just in time to throw up my not-friend all over the grass.

After a couple of minutes, I manage to stop hurling, but my throat burns and my stomach hurts and I'm sure I smell like vomit. When I head back toward where Jordan waits, he begins walking to meet me.

I hold up a hand and weakly blurt out, "As a girl with a very tiny hope of still being able to look you in the eyes after today, please don't come too close."

He stops abruptly and laughs. "Fine, but you can't drive home."

"I know, but I can walk. I don't live too far from here and I can walk over to get my car in the morning." I stumble over my own feet, but somehow manage not to face-plant.

Jordan is already shaking his head. "How about a compromise? I'll drive you home in your car?"

I tilt my head in confusion. "But then you'll be at my house . . . you don't live there."

"I know." Jordan laughs again, louder this time. "It will be fine. I'll just walk back to get my bike."

My eyes widen. "You came here on a bike?"

He grins and the skin around his eyes crinkles. "Different kind of bike. I have a motorcycle."

I shake my head far too fast and then have to stop and breathe. "I don't know how to ride one of those."

"I was afraid of that. And doing it drunk the first time isn't the best plan." He winks at me and I see he's come closer again.

I take a step to the side. "So you can jog back here in the middle of the night and I can't walk home now?"

He lowers his chin and stares at me. "Are you really saying that it is the same to let you walk home, wasted and alone, as it is for me to jog back here sober? You're too cute, and I don't know these neighborhoods very well. Don't fight me on this one."

"Ugh, fine." I tug my keys out of my pocket and hand them to him, then walk slowly toward my car. I throw him a frail smile over my shoulder. "I should've called Matthew. I bet he's less stubborn."

"You've never seen him at bedtime."

I climb unsteadily into the passenger seat. "That bad, huh?"

"Plus, he can't drive. Trust me, I'm the best option for you." He turns the car key and I smile to myself as I lean my heavy head back against the seat. His assessment just might be the most truthful thing I've heard in days.

9

SUNLIGHT HAS NEVER SEEMED SO EVIL BEFORE. I vaguely remember liking it at some point, but right now it seems like it's trying to drill a hole through my eyelids and into my brain. I want someone to make it stop. Groaning, I pull my pillow out from under my head and place it on my face to block out the light. It works, but even the pressure from my pillow feels like it might make me throw up.

I tug the pillow off and moan as I roll toward the edge of my bed. Everything hurts. This is what alcohol does? Why the hell do people even drink? This is *so* not worth it.

A light knocking sounds on the door, and I realize I don't remember getting home last night. Much of the night feels blurry, actually. I blink and sit up quickly, relieved to see that I am, in fact, in my room. Then my head explodes with new pain and I lower it into my hands as I hear the door open.

"This is only the beginning of your punishment, my dear." Behind the anger, I hear notes of sympathy in Mama's voice and I know she isn't as mad at me as she probably should be.

"I'm sorry," I whisper, and my voice sounds like a frog with one foot in the grave. Even more pleasant, my mouth tastes like I ate that frog in my sleep.

Mama steps over to the bed and rests one arm gently around my shoulder. "We're going to have a talk about last night, but first let's see if we can help with the pain you're in. I'll grab you some ibuprofen and coffee. Then you take a shower while I make you something to eat. Okay?"

"Okay, Mama." I lean my head on her arm, but then lift it again when even that increases my pain. "Sorry again, and thank you."

The coffee is bitter. I'm not a big coffee fan, but it helps me open my eyes a bit and feel more ready to face a shower. By the time I'm out of the scalding hot water, the ibuprofen has kicked in and I'm in less physical pain. I've also had the time to fully remember everything that happened with Jordan at the park last night, and so emotionally I'm flip-flopping between embarrassed that he saw me that way and horrified that I had called *him* of all people when I was in that state.

I am never drinking again. Ever.

I told him things I never should have, cried my eyes out on his shoulder, and then puked in front of him. It seems a reasonable conclusion that I'll never see him again, and I honestly can't blame him. Then again, even after he'd seen all that, he'd taken my keys, helped me into my car, and driven me home. But he barely knows me. Why did he do all of that for a complete stranger?

While I'm very grateful that I was able to talk to someone about Daddy and his confession, I'm definitely having morning-after remorse. What if he told someone? Then again, what would that change? Daddy is scheduled to die in twenty-six days, whether he confessed to the crime or not.

Does it really matter who I told? I can't seem to figure out the answer to that with my head still sending dull, aching waves down the base of my neck.

I pull on a pair of jeans with more force than necessary, mad at myself more than anyone else. I pick up my phone and see a text message pop up. I groan when I see the name I apparently saved his number under.

Hot Guy: How are you feeling this morning?

I quickly change the contact name to "Jordan" and bite on my nail for a minute while I try to think of a fitting response. Finally, I send back:

Like I was hit by a truck that then backed over me . . . and ran me over again.

I think for a few seconds before adding:

Thanks for everything. You were great last night, despite how not great I was.

Sticking the phone in my pocket, I sigh. Then I remember to silence it so it won't interrupt Mama and me having our "talk about last night." Clean, dressed, and now feeling like a rather unpleasant vacuum has replaced my stomach, I walk into the kitchen to find my breakfast done—and almost burning on the stove. Mama is nowhere in sight.

With a sigh, I turn off the burner and scoop the only slightly browned omelet onto a plate. I grab a fork and set out to find her. She's in her room with one of Daddy's boxes open beside her, a deeply sad expression on her face. Her hands are clenched at her sides and she has an old family picture from when I was a toddler on her lap.

I cross to her, taking a bite of my food, but her eyes remain on the picture. "What are you doing, Mama?"

She looks up at me, her eyes focusing and blinking a few times. "Oh, Riley . . . nothing, honey. I'm just trying to straighten a few things before I put them in the attic."

The entire box beside her is full of old photos she had suddenly taken down off the walls a few months ago. When I angrily asked her what she was doing, she said she thought it was unhealthy to live surrounded by reminders of something that was over. They would prevent us from moving forward. She said we were trapping ourselves in a life that we couldn't ever have again because even if Daddy came home, everything would still be very different. I didn't speak to her for five entire days—not that she even noticed since she was so busy with work.

Setting my plate on the nightstand, I pick up my favorite photo: the three of us laughing in a park. Daddy has his arms around us both, and Mama is resting her head against his shoulder and looking at him with adoration in her eyes. It had been taken almost one year before Daddy was arrested.

My heart thuds painfully against the wall of my chest. I hadn't realized how much I missed the pictures. But after my visit with Daddy yesterday, they only cause confusion. Did he smile and laugh with us, then become someone else afterward?

If his confession to me was true, then he'd already started killing by the time that photo was taken. I stare at the photo, wondering how I could ever be convinced that this smiling, laughing man had taken a life.

Crimes like that shouldn't be easy to wash off. No one should be able to murder someone and then come home to his family and pretend like nothing happened. He should have that blood staining his hands forever. If he stole even one life, his world should never be the same again . . . let alone three lives.

Of course, Daddy's life did change, whether he deserved it or not. He's been in Polunsky for most of his adult life. He's going to die in twenty-six days, and I still don't know if he did the things he'll be dying for.

"Riley?" Mama grips my shoulder and I snap out of it and turn toward her. She takes the picture I'm still holding and puts the remaining photos back in the box with a shake of her head. "I'm sorry, sweetie."

"For what?"

She points to my slightly burned omelet, forgotten on her nightstand. "Your breakfast."

"Oh." I pick it up and shovel a bite into my mouth with a forced grin. "It's delicious."

Mama laughs and puts the lid back on the box, moving it over against the wall. When she turns back to me, she clasps her hands before her and puts on her best Stern Mothering look. "Now, about last night . . ."

I sigh and plop down on her bed, waiting for the lecture that I not only know is coming, but that I *absolutely* deserve.

Mama tilts her head toward me. "Why would you do that to yourself?"

"I don't know," I mutter, studying the omelet on my plate. "Maybe we can just assume I've learned my lesson and will never do it again?" I give her a pleading look.

"Doubtful." Mama grimaces. "*Have* you learned your lesson?"

"Yes, ma'am," I answer quickly. And from the way she levels her stare at me, I realize, *too* quickly.

"What on earth were you thinking? What made you decide to drink like that?" Mama asks, and then a new and more disturbing thought seems to occur to her. "Please tell me the truth, Riley: Was this the first time?"

"Yes. I promise." I tuck my left foot under my right knee so I'm facing her. Above all else, I hope she doesn't press me further on the one question I haven't decided on how to answer yet: Why?

"Do you have new friends that are a bad influence on you? Did anyone pressure you into this?" Mama watches me closer with each new question.

It takes enormous self-control not to laugh. My worry about her asking *why* is obviously unfounded. She doesn't really know me if she thinks I have any friends or know anyone that I care enough about to allow peer pressure to affect me at all.

Peer pressure lost any power over me when I decided I didn't care what anyone outside our family thought. The kids at school all believe I'm the daughter of a killer and treat me with a mixture of fear and disdain. I think most of them are dumb as rocks and I try to believe they don't matter, pretend they don't exist. Our feelings are somewhat mutual, and I've learned to be okay with that.

"No, Mama, I think I was just feeling a little rebellious after the appeal and all." It's not a complete lie. What happened at the appeal had only been the beginning, but she doesn't need to know that— not yet.

Mama sighs and then reaches out for my hand. "I know you're tough as a boot, girl. But whether you admit it or not, everything with your father has been hard on you, Ri. Harder than it should be for any seventeen-year-old. You promise not to do anything like that again, and I promise it will get better, okay?" Mama leans over until I meet her eyes. "*I* will make sure it does."

"Yes, ma'am." I squeeze her hand and smile until she nods and turns to search for something in her closet; then the smile melts from my face like a piece of ice on the Texas asphalt. It isn't that I'm not happy she wants to make things better. I want her to take care of herself, if nothing else, for her sake as much as mine. It's likely that in twenty-six days, she'll be the only parent I have left. As much as I often try not to, I need her.

I just know that whenever I tell her what Daddy confessed to me, it could destroy her even more than it destroyed me.

10

I SPEND THE WEEKEND rereading old letters from Daddy and sleeping off my hangover. In my mind, I keep replaying my conversation with Daddy at Polunsky. I think that maybe if I'd asked the right questions somehow I could have gotten to the truth.

But I hadn't. I'd freaked out, and now I have to wait a week before I can have another chance to get my answers. The next time I see him, though, I will find a way to make him explain and tell me the truth.

I *have* to know.

It's become an obsession now and I feel like I can't understand anything about my life without knowing what he is. A martyr or a monster? A hero or a demon?

And whatever he is, does it change who I am?

Every time I think about telling Mama about my last visit with Daddy, about asking her to help me find the truth, I chicken out and just end up texting with Jordan instead.

I'm sitting in my room on Sunday rereading a letter from after Daddy's conviction when my phone buzzes beside me.

I see Jordan's name and pick it up, feeling nervous. This is the first time *he's* called *me*.

"Hello?" I know the smile in my voice shines through even over the phone and I don't care. I'm letting my guard down with him and even though I know it might be stupid, I can't help it. Despite my instinctive need to push everyone away, something about him tells me I can trust him.

"Hi. How are you?" I can tell he's smiling, too.

"I'm much better, thanks." I don't know why, but talking instead of texting makes me more nervous. I can't fix my mistakes before pressing Send. "How about you? Been forced to endure any more neighborhood football games?"

He laughs. "No. Thank God."

"I have to admit, I'm intrigued," I say, flopping down on my bed and staring at the ceiling. "What makes a Texas boy who used to like football start hating it?"

I'd been teasing, but the other end of the line feels more silent now and I know I've crossed into territory I shouldn't have.

Before I can apologize, though, or try to let him off the hook, he responds and his voice is soft. "I don't hate football. I still like to watch it. I even miss playing sometimes. I miss my team, but my mom came to every game I've ever played—from flag to tackle to school football teams."

I close my eyes and my heart hurts for him. No wonder he doesn't want to play.

"I just don't want to be out there and look up at the spot where she always sat and not see her. I'm not ready for that." He clears his throat. "I'd be useless to the team anyway."

85

After a few moments of silence, I say the only thing that feels right. "Maybe we have more in common than I thought."

He chuckles softly, but I can hear the pain behind it. "I think you're right."

I decide to change the subject. "I've been thinking and I might have an idea to remedy our situation."

"What situation is that?" The warmth is back in his voice and I feel for the first time all weekend like I've accomplished something.

"The one where I mortally embarrassed myself in front of you and you have yet to do anything embarrassing in front of me."

"Mortally?" He sounds amused by the word.

"Yes, mortally." I tug on a piece of my hair. "It's a chasm. We aren't on equal ground."

His tone has a bit of an edge when he speaks again. "Just stick around. I'm sure to even us out at some point."

I shake my head even though he can't see me. "No. I'm too impatient. We need to fix it now."

"Okay." Jordan seems like he's trying to sound reluctant. He's not pulling it off. "What sort of embarrassment did you have in mind?"

I'm surprised he caved this easy and I don't have an answer yet. "I'm—working on it."

"Well, be sure to give me fair warning once you figure it out." Then there's a huge crash in the background like ten pots and pans being dropped on the floor. I jump and sit straight up at the sound.

"Matthew! Stop getting into the cupboards!" Jordan calls. He curses softly. I hear the thud of footfalls and it sounds like Jordan is running across the house. Finally, he sighs. "I'm sorry. I think I need to go. Talk tomorrow?"

"Sure."

We say goodbye and hang up. I'm left on my bed, staring at my phone and already missing the distraction. When it's your family, your life, and everything you've ever known that you don't want to deal with, it's so much harder to run away. With a groan, I pick up Daddy's letter and start reading again.

By Monday, Mama has gone back to work and I'm going crazy just sitting around and accomplishing nothing. I keep thinking that maybe a visit with Daddy isn't the only way to find answers. Actually, now that I know I can't trust Daddy not to lie, it's probably better to find some other way to verify whatever he tells me. As difficult a task as it may be, I have to find some way to *know* for sure that he's telling the truth.

If only I could figure out how to do that.

I move to my laptop with an open can of Coke and a few pieces of red licorice. Closing my eyes, I try to gather the little strength I have left. I've done a handful of online searches about Daddy's case in the past. I usually can't get through more than the first article before I feel sick and end up closing the browser. It isn't easy, seeing people say such awful things about my father. Back then I did it because of morbid curiosity. Now it's out of necessity.

If he's innocent, then we must still fight.

If he's guilty, then I'd rather know now. And with only twenty-four days left until his execution, I can't afford to waste any more time without at least trying to find out for myself.

My phone *ding*s next to me and I pick it up. I'd honestly expected Jordan to run when he found out way too much about me in just one night. Instead, he's done the opposite. It's like my secret connected us in some way that I don't understand. It makes me both nervous and hopeful. My biggest secrets are all out with him, so I've been able to talk about my whole family freely. He's told me about his mom's car accident and how hard it's been on them. I'm not sure what it says about him that he hasn't run from me.

I just know that I really like having him only a text away.

> Jordan: You have any plans tonight?

My smile widens as I respond:

> Since I decided to ditch my alcohol friend from Friday night . . . No.

> Jordan: Good choice. Want to hang out with me instead? I can't promise to dull the pain from all the crap you're going through in the same way, but I can try very hard not to make you sick by the end of the night.

> Me: Ha ha, don't remind me. What do you want to do?

> Jordan: Let's meet at the Galaxy Café again, but this time the one in the Valley Vista mall by your house. Does 7 work?

> Me: Yep! See you there!

I put down my phone, wondering for a second whether Jordan thinks this is an actual date, before I decide it doesn't matter.

He's funny, really cute, and he wants to spend time with me. That's all I need to know right now.

Time to start my personal research. I take a breath and remind myself that I am doing this for me, for the truth. Popping a piece of licorice in my mouth, I open my laptop and type Daddy's name into the search engine. The first article that pops up makes my stomach clench: "Perfect Gentleman to Vicious Murderer?"

I take a deep breath and scan through that article first. It talks about his happy home life and successful law practice. Then it poses some theories about what could have turned Daddy into a murderer.

> **Is it possible that this monster was always inside David Beckett? Could it have been lying dormant until something or someone woke it? At which point, it could've become too hard for this killer to go back to the gentleman's façade again—or maybe he chose not to.**

I've never heard that one before, but it isn't exactly groundbreaking.

> **Could Mr. Beckett have an undiagnosed adult-onset mental illness? Could he be seeing and hearing things that aren't real? If so, he's an expert in the art of deception.**

I shake my head. These theories could be presented about anyone who'd been accused of murder. Nothing so far is specific to my father's situation. No clues. This isn't helping me.

Perhaps the happy home life Mr. Beckett appears to have isn't everything he would have us believe. Could this be the reason the victims in this case have similar features to the defendant's wife, Amy Beckett? Could this supposed happy home be more like a nightmare? We already know he had at least one affair. Could he have been that unhappy? Did David Beckett kill these women to fulfill some deep-rooted desire to kill his wife?

Taking a deep swig of my Coke, I sit back in my chair. The affair information was nonsense. I'd known this since the trial. The prosecution had accused Daddy of having an affair with one of the victims, but Daddy had denied it. And when I'd been old enough to understand a little about what it meant and ask, Mama and Mr. Masters backed up Daddy's story. It was simply a lie meant to tarnish his reputation in the eyes of the jury, nothing more.

The theory about killing the women because he actually wanted to kill Mama is also one I've heard before, but that didn't make it seem any less absurd. The victims were blond and similar in age. Other than that, they weren't very much like Mama. If Daddy *really* had wanted to kill Mama, why not just do that instead of killing these other women? It made no sense. I would know if I was living in the nightmare they'd described. And our home life only became messed up *after* they threw my daddy in prison.

I go back to the original search and read through article after article, but most of it is the same old stuff I already knew. I find a few details I didn't know about Daddy's childhood on a site called—of all things—Murderpedia.

It mentions that Daddy's father, Joseph Beckett, was in and out of prison for the sale and use of recreational drugs. My parents had said Grandpa Beckett was dead and we had never talked about him. This article says he's alive and living in Florida. I frown, rereading the lines about Grandpa. Why would Mama and Daddy lie about that? And who updates this site anyway? Maybe this information isn't even correct.

Below this is a single line about Daddy being in a few foster homes when he was young, before his mother cleaned up her drug habit.

I put another licorice in my mouth, sucking on it instead of chewing. Daddy's father was in and out of jail, and his mother was a drug addict?

I read through the whole page again, wondering if this information is reliable or not. If this article is true, how many other things don't I know about Daddy's past?

I glance at the clock in the corner of the laptop screen and am amazed to see it's already almost six. Maybe I can check out one or two more articles before I have to head out to meet Jordan.

I go back to the search page, scrolling past the other similar articles and looking for something new. My eyes stop on a page that makes my mouth dry out: "Captain Vega Rides Arrest of East End Killer Straight to the Chief's Office."

It's an old article—this happened almost ten years ago. Still, my body trembles with anger as I click the link. I skim through the article and a few sentences stick out, making my blood boil.

It was standing room only as Mayor Yardley introduced the newly appointed chief. As Vega approached the podium, the crowd broke into applause . . .

Despite a slow start to his career, Nicolas Vega has been a hero in the Houston area ever since the arrest and conviction of David Beckett for the East End Murders two years ago.

The mayor finished the conference with a simple statement: "I feel we can all sleep better knowing that Chief Vega is now guiding our men and women in uniform to protect this city. They will grow by having such a solid representative of justice to lead them."

I growl to myself. The idea that one man benefited so much from putting my father in prison makes my stomach roll. I scroll through the rest of the article and stop when I see a picture. It's easy to recognize Chief Vega. He's the one who came to our house, handcuffed my father, and took him away while my mother cried and held me tight against her. It had been the most terrifying moment of my life.

It still fills my nightmares. I can't forget something like that.

The mayor stands with an arm around him, and on the other side of Chief Vega stands a tall, beautiful woman with a bright smile and long black hair. She looks familiar, too. Odd, because I'm pretty sure I've never seen her before. Close by her side stands a little boy, and I squint at the photo, sure I must be seeing it wrong. It looks so much like Jordan's brother, Matthew.

I zoom in on the boy. Frowning before quickly scrolling through the article, I look for the paragraph I skimmed over about Vega's family. When I find it my heart shatters as I read.

Celebrating this day with Chief Vega were his wife, Anna, and his son, Jordan.

11

I STARE AT JORDAN'S NAME ON THE SCREEN, willing it not to be true. I hadn't known him long, but I'd felt like there could be something real with him. Whether intentionally or not, I'd trusted him with things—so many things. I'd believed he really cared about me.

I think back through all our texts and our conversations and don't understand how I'd never asked for his last name. My mind whirls. Had I given him mine? Yes, he'd asked me my last name when I told him Daddy was on death row.

My hands go to my mouth before curling into tight fists at my side. The way he'd responded, taking that deep breath, the way his hand shook . . . he'd known exactly who I was in that instant. More importantly, I'm almost entirely certain he knew his father had been the one to arrest my father.

And he hadn't told me.

I stand up so quickly my chair falls over behind me, but I ignore it. I pace circles around it as red-hot anger bubbles through my veins. Jordan had talked to me, comforted me, taken me home, and then texted me to check in. He'd called, and we'd chatted a few times. He'd had plenty of opportunities to tell me the truth, and he'd chosen not to.

I glance at the clock. I'm supposed to meet him in thirty minutes. Would it be better to just stand him up? Or to go and tell him exactly what I think about him, his secrets, *and* his father?

His father . . .

My feet seem to lock to the floor and I stop pacing.

I told Jordan—the son of the man who put my dad on death row—that my father had finally confessed.

It may not matter. If Daddy is sticking to this story, then he might have told all the guards and the warden by now.

But if he was just doing as I hope and simply wanted to help Mama and me move on . . . if he truly isn't giving up, if he still wants to fight, then . . .

I pick up my car keys from my desk, grab my purse, and run out the door.

By the time I walk into Galaxy Café my body seems to have turned into a roiling mess of anger and sadness. I'd really started to like Jordan. I don't blame him for being Vega's son. He's no more responsible for that than I am for being the daughter of a man in Polunsky. But how could he have not told me when he found out?

For that, I absolutely do blame him.

I'm right on time, but Jordan is here early, already in a booth in the corner. He waves at me and smiles widely.

I stalk past the host trying to ask me how many are in my party.

When I reach the table, the smile and most of the color have drained from Jordan's face. As I sit down across from him, the server walks up.

"Can I get you a drink or an appetizer to start with, miss?"

I don't even glance up. I'm too busy trying to glare a hole into Jordan's forehead. "I won't be staying."

"Oh . . . okay." The server stands there awkwardly for a moment before Jordan looks up at him.

"Could you give us a couple minutes?"

"Sure." The server turns his back, but I hear him let out a low whistle as he walks away.

Now that I'm here, I'm silent. I can't seem to say the words that brought me here. I hold on tight to my anger because I know that if it leaves me, right here, with Jordan watching me with guilt and sorrow in his eyes, I will only be left with the pain of losing another friend.

And I've felt that enough for a lifetime.

"Riley . . . ," Jordan starts, and I look down immediately, staring hard at my firmly clasped hands on the table in front of me. He sighs deeply and continues, "I'm so sorry."

"Did you realize it that night at the park? Or did you know before that?"

"At the park," he answers softly. "I had no idea before that, but I knew who you were the moment you said your dad was at Polunsky. You only confirmed it for me when you told me your last name was Beckett."

I shake my head. "How? Your dad must've put more than just my father in there."

"He has," Jordan says, then hesitates before evading my question. "It's hard to explain."

My anger increases at even the idea that he thinks he still has a right to keep *any* secrets from me after I've exposed all of mine. "Fine. I don't care why."

Jordan flinches, then starts talking. "I deliberately don't pay a lot of attention to my dad's cases and I think that's because of you."

I frown, caught by surprise. "What? Why?"

"When I was much younger, I remember seeing my dad's name on a newspaper. I was excited, and so I picked it up and started reading. It started off talking about a serial killer he had arrested." He pauses and looks down at the table for a moment before finishing. "But at the bottom, there were pictures from the arrest. The first one had a man being walked out of his house with handcuffs. But there was a girl standing in the doorway behind him. She had on big fluffy slippers and pajamas. Her hair was all tangled on one side like she'd been sleeping. She was sobbing and I'd never seen that kind of pain on another kid's face before. It was an awful picture. I decided then that good men didn't make little kids cry like that. I never wanted to know any details about his job after seeing that."

We sit in silence for a while as I fight the urge to feel anything toward him but anger.

"It was your dad he arrested, Riley. I would never forget his name after seeing that picture." He looks up at me, and his eyes are so sad.

"I only have one question for you." I straighten my back and stare him in the eye. "Have you told *anyone* what I told you—about what my father said at my last visit?"

His spine stiffens but he doesn't answer.

"Tell me."

There is something cold in his gaze now. I realize with a touch of malicious satisfaction that I've offended him. "Of course I haven't."

"No one? Not even *the chief*?" I lean forward, trying to sense if he's lying.

"No one." He doesn't blink, and his expression begs me to believe him. Then he continues, "Telling anyone won't help or change anything. He's lost his final appeal anyway, so him confessing doesn't matter much."

"That's all I needed to know." I get to my feet and walk away, forcing myself not to look back at him when he says my name.

12

ON THURSDAY MORNING, I lie awake in bed. The phone on my nightstand vibrates and I grab it immediately. When I see it's just an email from the library about a book due this week, I sigh and drop it back in place. It's not like I've responded to Jordan's texts since I left him at the Galaxy diner on Monday, but it somehow still depresses me that I haven't heard from him since Tuesday, when he'd texted me three times with similar messages.

> I'm sorry.
> I didn't mean to hurt you.
> I'm so sorry, Riley. I only wanted to help you, to be
> there, but somehow I ruined everything instead.

His final message broke my heart into pieces. Because having someone to talk to was everything I've wanted for so long, but it was coming from a guy I couldn't trust anymore to give it to me.

Since then he has left me alone, and I feel so alone.

There is a deep longing in the pit of my stomach from not

having Daddy's letters to read every day. Even after planning what to ask him all week, I can't decide if I want to go visit him tomorrow. I don't want to hear him say those awful words again. I don't know if I can take it.

I curl into a little ball as another wave of sadness hits me. All my favorite memories from visiting my father roll over me. They used to smooth my rough edges like water on the stones in the sea, but now they slice deep canyons of pain in their wake.

Daddy and the times he would tell me a joke and we'd laugh so hard that the guard would check in and tell us to keep it down.

Daddy and the stories he used to tell me of his court cases before he landed at Polunsky. He made even the boring ones sound interesting.

Daddy sharing his love of chess with me and teaching me how to play.

How could this man be a killer? I couldn't make sense of it. My father the wronged innocent or my father the murderer? I don't know which is the lie, I just know that he lied.

I pull my blanket up under my chin as I tremble under the weight of this burden. I don't want it.

Three weeks. Twenty-one days. Five hundred and four hours.

Time is passing too fast. Everything in me tells me to go to Polunsky tomorrow. Everything but my own fear. It will be a Friday. Going to Polunsky is what I do on Fridays, right?

Clenching my blanket tight in my fingers, I close my eyes and fight the tears that burn from the inside out. What if what he said is true and Daddy murdered those women?

If I cry for a monster, do I become one? How can I mourn a murderer?

Deciding that lying in bed isn't helping anything, I sit straight up, staring into my reflection on the mirrored closet doors. My skin is so pale it looks ghostly next to my messy dark hair. Heavy shadows haunt the skin beneath my eyes and only enhance the effect. I smack my cheeks quickly with the palms of my hands, trying to force some color into them. I glance at the clock and see it's only eight, so I flop back onto my pillows.

My phone vibrates again and I grab limply for it. When I see Mr. Masters's name, I click the Answer button.

"Hello?"

"Hello, Miss Riley." His voice sounds rushed and not at all like him. "Listen, something has happened, and your mother didn't answer, so I need you to pass on my message to her as well."

My stomach sinks. We've had one phone call like this before. Daddy had been beaten up in Polunsky and ended up in the infirmary. I say a quick and silent prayer before asking, "What is it?"

"My informant just contacted me. There was a murder last night. A new victim was found. I can't be sure until I get there, but it sounds the same as the others." Masters starts talking very fast, but none of the words he's saying are things I've prepared myself for. It takes me a minute to understand what he's talking about.

He starts rattling off details and my head spins. These are words that I've heard dozens of times before: strangulation, blond woman, mid-thirties, tortured. But they've always been things Daddy was being *accused* of doing. Never something he couldn't possibly have done due to being locked up in Polunsky.

"When? Who? Do they know who did it? Where did it happen?" I start shooting off questions just to signify to him that I'm still here.

"I don't know, but I'll find out. I'm heading there now. I'm almost to the corner of Barlow and Prairie, so it isn't far from here." I hear the ticking sound of a blinker in the background and realize he's in his car. "I'll head your way as soon as I finish talking to the detectives. You just sit tight, Miss Riley, and I'll get back to you with answers as quick as I can."

Then I hear a *click* and he's gone. I stare at the phone without seeing. My brain is a tumbling mass of confusion and excitement.

This news is what we've always wanted. A reason to cast doubt on Daddy's entire case. Finally, it's something to make people start questioning everything they accepted as truth more than ten years ago.

This is *it*. But it comes the week after Daddy tells me he is guilty. Does this mean that what I'd hoped is true, and he only said what he did because he'd given up? I blink and breathe and just keep thinking. What I want to do more than anything is drive to the scene of this new murder right now. I know it doesn't make sense, but I feel it pulling me all the same. Half of this need I'm feeling comes from the hope that I could possibly find answers to the truth there. The other half is something more like morbid curiosity. I've always believed Daddy was innocent, so I've always wondered about the person who had *really* committed these crimes. If they caught him, will he still be there? Handcuffed in the back of some police car? What kind of monster could he be? Does he look like a killer or does he keep all that darkness locked up inside?

The murderer had been tricky in the past, but now he's out of practice. After all, twelve years is a pretty long break. It was more likely someone could catch him now than ever before. But seeing if they'd finally caught the real murderer isn't my only reason. I've seen so many awful things over the years in pictures in a courtroom that the scenarios have felt like a TV show. This is the chance to see what they've been holding over Daddy's head for most of my life—in person—and as sick as it seems, it's also more morbidly tempting than I can even try to explain.

And I could be there in twenty minutes.

While I was considering, I threw on a pair of jeans, a striped T-shirt, and a baseball cap without even thinking about it. My body seems to have decided for me.

So I decide not to argue. I pick up my keys and run out the door.

I drive through the streets like the devil himself is hot on my heels. When I arrive at the intersection Mr. Masters mentioned, the actual crime scene is easy to find. Everything looks exactly as I expected. Yellow police tape blocks off the entire parking lot in front of the pharmacy on the corner, as well as the entrance to the alley behind the building. I park a block away and run toward the crowd gathering at the edge of the yellow tape. The first news van has arrived, and I have to dodge around it to get closer. As I pass, the words of the reporter drift over me. She raises the same questions that have been plaguing me.

"Sources have told us that this murder seems to mimic those of the East End Murders from over a decade ago. This is especially shocking because the convicted perpetrator of those crimes, David

Beckett, is currently on death row. Mr. Beckett lost his final appeal last week, and is scheduled to be executed at the end of this month. The police now have a big question to answer and a limited window in which to do it. Do we have a copycat killer on our hands? Or has the district attorney kept an innocent man in prison for the last eleven years?"

At least I'm not the only one asking these questions anymore.

I slip in and out between people until I'm at the front of the growing crowd, my stomach pressed against the police tape. I try to get a peek, leaning to one side, then another, but I can't see anything from way out here, and there is an officer only five feet in front of me to make sure I don't think about getting any closer.

I give him a tentative smile and he looks surprised, but then smiles back. His badge reads Officer Romero. He's short but has a very muscular build. I'm not sure if he could catch me if I tried to run past him, but he would absolutely squash me if he did. Obviously, I need a different tactic.

"So, what happened?" I ask, playing dumb.

Romero shakes his head, and his black mustache grows much wider when he frowns. "This is a murder scene." He looks down at the way the tape is pressed against my stomach as I try to see past him again. "Which is why you really need to stay back."

I take one step away and smile again. He watches me closer now than before, and his smile doesn't reach his eyes. I walk back a bit and then slide to the area where the police tape attaches to the wall of the building. It's a different officer on this side. He's drinking a coffee and has his back to me. Maybe I can find a way through here . . .

Before I get a chance to try it, there is some motion in the alley. I hold my breath, hoping they bring someone past in handcuffs. Someone I can hate from a distance as the city apologizes and releases Daddy from Polunsky. Instead, a couple of officers roll out a big black bag on a stretcher toward the waiting Houston City Coroner truck only fifteen feet away from me.

My blood turns cold and I feel nauseous. It's a body bag. Nothing about this feels like TV and I can't believe I'd wanted it to feel real. There's a murdered woman in that bag who was probably alive just last night. My knees buckle and only the brick wall next to me keeps me from losing my balance. How could I have been excited about coming here? How could *this* be a thing that had made me feel hopeful?

What kind of freak had my life turned me into?

At the same time, at the back of my mind I keep wondering if somehow that bag holds the answers we need. The officers who brought it out turn and go back into the alley. The only person guarding the body bag is in black scrubs and banging stuff around inside the coroner's truck.

Drawing in one quick breath, I push aside any sick urge to see the body and instead decide to check around back near the alley. An insane curiosity gets the better of me. Maybe the killer dropped something. No officers assigned to the crowd are looking my way, so I grab hold of the tape and duck under it.

Before I even make it all the way to the other side, a strong hand grips my elbow and jerks me back. I grunt in surprise as someone pulls me away. I flip around to see who it is and the only thing I know for sure is that it's definitely a man. He's wearing a tailored gray coat and a hat pulled low around his ears. I open my mouth to scream, but then he pivots to face me and holds one finger up in front of my eyes. "Don't you think you've brought quite enough attention on yourself already today, Miss Riley?"

I jerk back as I recognize the blue eyes looking out at me from the shade of his hat. I'm so shocked I have to blink a few times to make sure it's him. "Mr. Masters? Wha—you—?"

"Yes, eloquently put." He gives me a wry smile before looking over my shoulder. "Now, kindly follow me to my car before anyone else decides to look our way."

He walks two feet, but I don't take another step. When I speak I can hear the slight whine in my voice. "I have my own car. And I'm here because I *need* to know what's happening."

With a sigh, he gestures for me to follow him a few feet to a spot where the TV vans block our view of the police. "And did you learn anything important so far?"

"Well, no . . ."

"And you won't, Miss Riley." He slips an arm around my shoulders and starts guiding my reluctant feet toward his car again. "At least come and let me explain a couple of things to you before you make a mistake that you can't take back."

When I don't move, he whispers low in my ear, "The second you cross that tape, the officers guarding it will push you back. If you happen to make it to anything important, they would catch you and charge you with tampering with evidence."

"I'm not an idiot, Mr. Masters," I say hotly. "I know that's a possibility."

"Are you planning on following in your father's footsteps

early, then? He may not have broken the law, but it seems you plan to. Why even wait until graduation? Let's go on a crime spree." His tone has an edge of disappointment, and it stings to hear it.

I stop responding because he never talks to me this way, and it hurts to have someone who always watches out for me snub me like this . . . especially when I can see now that he has a point.

I look back toward the crime scene one more time and see Chief Vega leaning out from the alley and squinting toward the coroner's truck.

The moment I see his face, I duck down and follow Mr. Masters quickly through the crowd and around the corner.

As soon as we're in his blue BMW, he starts the air conditioner and then turns to me. He tilts back his hat and I can see concern in his eyes, along with that look that tells me he's thinking hard about something.

"I'm sorry for treating you like this, but you need to start thinking straight." His tone is stern; his eyes plead with me to listen.

"Well, that's not the best apology I've ever heard." I drop my chin and glare at him.

"Okay, let's see how badly this scenario could've played out, shall we?" He lifts one eyebrow in a challenge.

"That's really not—"

"Let's say you make it across and actually get to the body. What do you see?"

"I don't know. I don't think that's where I was going." I sigh, then decide to play along. "Maybe I would see the same types of injuries from the first murders—"

"Which would be reported to me anyway *without* you going to jail, but continue. Anything else?" His voice is soft but firm.

"I don't know, maybe I could find something in the alley they didn't see." I'm starting to feel less sure that coming here was a good idea with each answer I give.

"Doubtful because they're trained professionals, but even if you did, then what?"

"I'd tell you."

"Okay, so you would call me from the police station where they're holding you until your mother gets there . . ." His words drift off and he waits.

I stop responding. Leaning forward, I rub my forehead against my hands.

"It gets so much worse, Miss Riley. This is just the beginning." He continues. "Let's say you somehow are the one to find the key to proving your father's innocence. Except you forgot something. Your dad isn't even a suspect in this crime. Being in Polunsky gives him the best alibi known to mankind. So, since they can't look at your dad for this, the first thing they'll look for is a copycat."

I may not show it, but I'm following every word and my whole body starts to feel cold even in the hot sunlight.

"They'll look first for people who might be close to the man they believe is the original East End Killer. Someone not in jail who has an excellent motive to want to cast doubt on the state's case, someone who loves him and visits him all the time." He now looks sympathetic.

"Maybe someone who's terrified that he'll be executed in three weeks?" I mutter under my breath, trying to shake the fear from the tale he's weaving for me.

"Exactly. And then you go and place yourself at the crime scene and start tampering with evidence? You're now in jail. He's still going to be executed because with your tampering they can't even consider the evidence here anymore. Not sure about you, but that's certainly not the happy ending I'm looking for." He squeezes my shoulder and shakes his head. "Riley, do me a favor and just try to make them look a little before volunteering to be the next easy mark they can pin a murder on, will you?"

I reach over and give him a tight hug, knowing he's completely right. Coming here had been stupid. I'd let the need to *do something* override any common sense. "Thanks. I didn't realize how bad it could have been."

"I know you didn't." He leans away, and I see a bit of fear in his eyes now as he shakes his head. "This is no game. You can ask all the questions you want of me, of your parents, but now is the time you need to trust *me* the most. I've been fighting for your father as long as you have with very few weapons at my disposal. This morning, someone handed me a loaded gun and only twenty-one days to use it."

"You think this will finally give us some of the proof we've been looking for?" I clench my hands against my sides.

He winks and pats my shoulder. "The way this looks right now, I'm gonna give them hell or die trying."

13

ON THE DRIVE HOME I bite my nails, thinking how close I'd come to landing myself in a heap of trouble. Everything feels upside down today and it isn't even noon yet. The sick feeling in my stomach is almost as bad as my hangover had been.

Hangover . . .

My world comes crashing down as I remember my own confession to Jordan. I close my eyes and groan as I make a quick right turn. At the next stoplight, I pull my phone out of my pocket and bring up Jordan's info—which is now filed under a very different name. I send him a text just before the light turns green.

Meet me at the park. 20 minutes.

Two minutes tick by without a response. I wait, listening for my text notification as I drive and focusing on breathing slowly. Maybe he'd given up on me. Maybe he didn't want to see me again after I hadn't responded. Maybe—

Then my phone *ding*s and I glance down at the screen.

Massive Jerk: I'll be there.

The sound from the text echoes in my head long after it stops. It sounded more like a death knell.

I wait in the park for Jordan to arrive. The sky above is filled with ominous clouds. Rain in Texas is not something to trifle with. That's fine. I want to keep this short anyway. The idea of seeing him again already fills me with a bittersweet pain. I'd been so wrong to think we have anything in common. Our lives couldn't be more different. *We* couldn't be more different.

People believe Chief Vega is someone to admire and look up to. He works hard to keep us all safe—or at least that's what everyone thinks. When Jordan and Matthew support their father, they're heroes. They're martyrs for sacrificing time with him for the good of the community.

But when I support my father, I'm a monster. The same people call my father a murderer. He is the lowest of the low and we are either sick or foolish for believing him and standing by him when he tells us again and again that he's innocent.

Devotion counts for little once the world has made up its mind about you.

I see a big dark motorcycle pull in and recognize Jordan's wavy black hair from across the park when he tugs off his helmet. He pulls a pair of sunglasses out of his pocket and puts them on his face, despite the lack of sunshine. When he gets to me, I silently watch him from my spot on the swing. I'm not at all sure where to start.

"I'm glad you texted me." His face is hard to read with his eyes hiding behind the sunglasses, and he keeps his head straight ahead instead of looking down toward me. All I see when I search his face is the reflection of the dark sky above.

"We need to talk." I force the words out before we can get sidetracked. "I know you said you haven't told anyone, but this morning it became really important that you don't." I push off my tiptoes, swinging closer to him, and then reach up for his sunglasses. He freezes as I pull them down on his nose until I can see his warm brown eyes. "Please, Jordan. You can't tell anyone what I said—*ever*."

He doesn't respond. I wait for a few seconds, deciding I need to hear him speak the words. To say out loud that he won't tell anyone, but a new thought occurs to me and my breath catches in my throat. "You haven't told your father since we talked last, have you?"

"No." He pulls the glasses the rest of the way off his face and they dangle from his fingers.

"Good." I somehow feel more empty and miss Jordan more than before he came. "I hope you're telling the truth."

Jordan's voice floats to me as I head toward the grass, but his words hold a weight that flattens my heart like a rolling boulder. "We should talk about this morning, Riley."

I stop walking. "Why?"

He crosses to me immediately. Worry, guilt, and sorrow play across his features. I don't know which I trust to be real. "Why won't you just *talk* to me? I've known about your dad's confession almost as long as you have and I haven't told a soul yet—even though we both *know* my dad would want to know. What would prove my loyalty to you more than that?"

"Maybe telling me the truth from the start?" I shake my head. "We've already discussed my father way more than we should have."

He reaches out and rests a hand on my shoulder. It sends an unexpected shiver through me. "I just want to help you, Riley. Besides, Dad insisted on heading up this new case. He'll have to look at the evidence and decide whether this is the same killer, won't he? Does what your dad said even matter anymore?"

"Chief Vega *insisted* on it, did he? Well, that's just super." My defenses immediately rise like walls against the enemy. "Go ahead, assign the one cop to the case who actually benefited from putting my father in prison. Like he's going to be interested in looking for the evidence that says he made a *huge* mistake in the first place."

Jordan inhales sharply. He doesn't speak, but he refuses to look at me, studying the park around us instead. I think over my words, regretting them instantly but not taking them back. I meant what I said, but I hadn't been trying to hurt Jordan.

"Listen . . . ," I finally say, but he doesn't let me get any further than that.

"My father is a good man, and he knows he's capable of making mistakes." Jordan's eyes are on me and I can't look away from their intensity. "I promise that he doesn't want to put the wrong man in jail. He would *never* want that. Besides, from what your dad told you, it seems his so-called *bias* about your dad being guilty may have been right all along."

His words rip the wind from my lungs. When I speak again, my voice comes out smaller than I want. "Fine. I don't know what to think anymore, okay? I need to know the truth. There is still a good chance my dad could be executed in three weeks and I'm running out of time. If you tell your father that he confessed to me—"

"I don't know. It seems like a confession is something he'd want to know now. And how would telling my dad change anything?" Jordan steps in front of me until I have no choice but to look at him. This time there's a hint of remorse in his eyes.

"Come on. Don't be naïve." I can tell the words bite as I say them, but he has to know better than this. "Your father is investigating whether he could've been wrong when he worked on this case initially. He could believe my father has maintained his innocence the entire eleven years, or he could believe that he confessed one time to being guilty. You don't see how that could make an incredibly big difference to the way he considers evidence? You have to admit that you can see what I'm saying."

Jordan looks away. I swallow hard—there's no denying that we both have solid points. I'm only slightly surprised to find that the idea of having someone to talk to about all of this feels more comforting to me than confining.

"Three weeks, Jordan." I look up at him, pleading. "You of all people have to understand this. If you needed me to keep a secret for three weeks that could've saved your mom's life, what would you have done to convince me?"

He sighs and drops his chin to his chest before answering. "You said you need to know the truth. You don't want me to tell anyone. Let me help and I won't. What are you planning to do?"

"Isn't this considered blackmail?" I glare at him as the sky over our heads rumbles.

"I don't want it to be." His expression softens. His hand reaches out to brush the tips of my fingers before falling back to his side. "Please, Riley, let me make my mistake up to you. Let me help."

I look away. Fear of letting him get close enough to hurt me again wars with a betraying sense of hope at the idea of spending more time with him. I tug my fingers through my hair and sigh. "It sounds like I don't really have a choice."

"Then what's the plan?" Jordan's frown doesn't leave his face as he nods. It might not be the response he was looking for, but it's all I can give him right now.

I blow out a puff of air. "To start, I'm going to try to force my parents to tell me the truth about what happened twelve years ago that could have landed us in this situation now. I have to know how their marriage was, what he was like before prison, and most importantly whether anyone who knew him actually believed that Daddy was capable of murder. That begins with talking to my mom as soon as she's home today and going to visit my father tomorrow. From now on, no more keeping me in the dark."

14

WHEN I WALK THROUGH THE FRONT DOOR, Mama jumps up from the couch and my first thought is that someone died. She's at home? In the middle of the day? I literally don't remember that happening—ever. I hesitate to come in because I'm not sure I can handle any more unwelcome revelations without cracking.

She smiles and suddenly I know exactly why she's home right now.

"You heard?" I say, closing the door behind me.

Mama walks across the room to me. "It's what we've been waiting for."

Mama grips my shoulders with her long, thin fingers, and they feel like a vise. She looks happier than I've seen her in as long as I can remember, so I slap a smile on my face. I feel queasy at the idea that we're celebrating something that involved a woman's death, but we've had so little hope for so long that I refuse to take this moment away from her.

"I can't believe we finally have something like this to fight back with," she whispers.

I hug her before guiding her back to the couch and sitting down beside her.

She puts her arm around me and kisses my forehead. "We need to have the biggest celebration ever, if—or perhaps when—your father finally comes home to us."

My stomach clenches in pain at the word *when*. That isn't a word we use. We learned not to use it the first time the jury found Daddy guilty and I don't think either of us has used it in this way since. I feel an intense urge to make her stop, to take that word back and lock it away. I want to protect us both from the false and agonizing hope the word *when* can bring with it.

"Maybe we should be careful . . ." I start slowly, wanting to let a little bit of the air out of her balloons, not massacre them all with a machine gun. "Let's see what Daddy has to say about the news before we make too many plans."

Mama's smile wavers, but not for long. "Who raised you to be so practical, huh?"

I pretend like it's a hard question. "Hmm, I'm going to say you."

"Maybe we've been too practical for too long." She rests her head against mine, and I stiffen because her words are taking her further into the hopeful arena than I'm ready to go.

"Riley?" Mama sits back and stares at me until I meet her eyes. "What's wrong? How do you feel about this?"

In the face of her hope, I lose control of the emotions I've been holding in check. Mama pulls me into a tight hug as tears flow down my face.

"I so hope you're right." I try to force what I'm feeling into words.

"Last week—last week when I visited him, Daddy told me something. I'm sorry I haven't told you, but I've been worried about you since the hospital and I didn't want to make things worse."

Mama scowls, but she keeps her arms around me as she clucks. "Pay no mind to those doctors, Riley. I'm tougher than they know."

"I know you are."

"What did he tell you?" she urges.

"He—he said he did it, Mama. He said he was guilty. That he's getting what he deserves, and we should move on with our lives." Even saying the words out loud feels like a betrayal, especially now that we know someone outside of Polunsky is capable of having committed the murders themselves.

Mama seems to be holding her breath. When she pulls back, her eyes are wide open and all hint of a smile is gone. "He *actually* said that?"

I nod. My tears have stopped and I wipe those that remain off my cheeks.

The color drains from her face and I worry that the doctors and Daddy were right. Maybe she really isn't ready to deal with information like this.

"Mama?" I reach out and place my hand on top of hers. It's cold.

"He told *you* that?" Her eyes go to my hand.

"Yes . . ." I frown. "Why are you shocked he would tell *me*?"

"Did he tell you not to tell me?" Her voice is so soft I have to strain to hear it, but when she looks up the unmistakable anger I see in her eyes makes me draw back instinctively. She grabs my hand before I can get far and squeezes it hard. "Did he?"

"Kind of. He said he wasn't sure you could take it right now

118

with the stress you're under, and he left it up to me." I look down at my hand. It's starting to ache as she grips it tighter and tighter. "Mama, you're hurting me."

She releases me immediately, shaking her head and murmuring low enough that I can't hear her.

"What did you say?"

"He never should have told you that."

"What does that mean?" I'm so confused by her reaction. It only firms up my resolve to get answers and I reach for her hand again. "Mama, I have so many questions."

"Not now." Mama stands up suddenly and walks toward her bedroom. "I think I'm going to lie down and rest for a bit."

I stand up, confused. "Don't you have to work today?"

She stares me straight in the eye and the utter lack of emotion I see in her feels like I'm looking into a void. As she moves through her bedroom door, she says the last words I ever expected my mama to utter: "I'm taking a sick day."

I stop her before she can fully close the door.

"What are you thinking, Mama?" I keep speaking even as she goes to sit on her bed. "Why wouldn't Daddy tell me? What's wrong?"

"Because you're our child! We are supposed to protect you." Her face is full of defeat and I catch a hint of anger in her eyes. "Do you know how many times he could've told *me* this over the years? If he wanted to confess to someone, why not me? True or not, he shouldn't have put this on you."

"I'm *not* a child anymore. You have to start telling me what's going on and stop treating me like I can't handle anything. I'm

119

strong enough to know the truth—whatever it is." I sit down by her and go on without thinking, but I know the words are hurtful before they even leave my mouth. "And of course he told me! You haven't visited him in months."

She jerks back and her eyes narrow, but she doesn't respond to my accusation. "I've been thinking about this for a while now and knowing what happened during your last visit only makes me surer. I don't say this lightly, Riley, but I think maybe you should stop going to Polunsky."

I blink once—twice—certain that I'm missing something. Then I laugh until she frowns deeply in response. Finally, I say, "Stop? What do you mean stop?"

"Just for now. Just for a little while . . . ," she begins, and there is a pleading note buried deep in her tone.

"Stop going *completely*?" I raise my voice and lean away from her in shock. "I don't understand, he only has a few—"

"You don't think I know that?" As she interrupts, her voice matches my pitch before she takes a breath and reaches her hand out for mine. I jerk away before she gets close. "Not forever, Riley. Just until the police get this new murder sorted out."

"You want me to stop visiting Daddy *right now*?" I shake my head because I'm still not sure how she can be saying this. I may have considered not going back, but thinking about it myself and being told not to by Mama are very different things. The wary look on her face tells me she really means it, and I stand up immediately. "You're asking me to stop visiting when he could have less than three weeks until . . . when he has only three weeks—"

I still can't finish the sentence, but she doesn't let me anyway.

"Riley, I know it's hard to understand." She climbs slowly to her feet.

"What's wrong with you? How could you possibly think this is even an option for me?" My voice gets louder and then I just stare at her. She feels like a complete stranger to me. "He's my father!"

Mama's chin sticks out a bit and her words fall with a staccato emphasis. "And I am your *mother*, Riley. You don't speak to me like this."

"You—you're being crazy! This is insane. How am I supposed to talk to you when you're saying things that make no sense at all?" My hands clench so tight at my sides that my short nails feel like they're cutting into my palms. "You know *someone else* killed that girl this morning, right? You know that there is more chance now than ever that he's actually innocent? Why?"

"It's complicated."

"Not more complicated than everything else. Tell—me—why!" The last three words are half plea, half demand.

"Young lady, *you* don't tell *me* what to do." Mama actually quiets her voice instead of raising it. I recognize it as a technique she uses to get me to calm down, which only pisses me off more.

"What went on between you and Daddy back before he went to prison?" If I keep asking, maybe at some point she'll accidentally answer me. "What haven't you told me?"

"Enough!" Mama slams her fist down against her side so hard I wonder if she might have a bruise later. We both pant into the huge divide that's been planted between us. Has it always been there? Did I just never see it before all this?

"I don't even know who you are, Mama. We live in the same

house, but you don't talk to me. You don't trust me. You don't tell me *anything*. Nothing you're saying makes any sense and I'm so tired of being kept in the dark. I will *not* just leave him alone now. I can't do that. I won't!" My hands ball into fists, my eyes burn with held-back tears, and I realize I'm shouting. Mama's brows draw together in warning, but I don't care. All the frustration, sorrow, and fear I've been bottling up inside explodes. I can't control it—and I don't want to. "Do you know why I'll never abandon him, Mama? It's because I am not—like—*YOU!*"

Her cheeks drain of all color and her mouth opens once, then twice before she closes it. Mama points one shaking finger in the direction of my bedroom.

"Go. Now." Her words land hard and I know I have to get out of here. I've crossed dozens of lines that I've never come near before. "And you will do exactly what I say, whether you like it or not."

My eyes and chest burn but I go to my room and slam the door because I don't want to see her this way.

I don't want to see me this way.

And I'm afraid if I stay, we'll both say more things that we can never take back.

15

I KNEW MAMA COULDN'T MISS an entire day of work. Within twenty minutes of me slamming my bedroom door, she was gone. She must've pulled an all-nighter too, because by the time I leave for Polunsky the next afternoon, I still haven't seen a glimpse of her.

The drive out to Polunsky is torture. I spend most of it with my emotions swinging drastically between excitement about this possible new hope and dread about how the upcoming visit may play out. I've never felt this way about visiting before and I hate it.

Of course, I'd never *really* considered the possibility that my loving father could actually be a murderer either. My, how times have changed.

When I'm not torturing myself about how the visit will go, I try to puzzle out what is going on with Mama. Why? Why after all this time, after raising me to take a trip out to Polunsky every week, after teaching me to love and adore my father, after telling me every day that Daddy was/is/will always be wrongly convicted?

Why try to keep me away now?

I, of all people, understand how shocking Daddy's confession was. But what is she thinking now? Could it really have been enough to make Mama entirely change her mind about him, or is she just as confused as I am? One single confession under circumstances like those we've been under . . . should *that* be the one we believe? Or the years and years of maintaining his innocence that came before it? And right now, in the face of the best evidence we've ever had that he could truly be innocent? It's hard to believe that she would suddenly be convinced that he's guilty. But if not, why forbid me from visiting him now?

And how will she react when she finds out that I didn't obey?

My fingers rub across the cracking leather on my door. The car had been Daddy's before he went to prison, and it had been beautiful. Now, eleven years later, we're all significantly more run down than we were then.

I look at the road before me and am overcome by anxiety. Polunsky is coming up fast on my left. Despite my distractions, it would be hard to miss. It's built like a fortress. I'd wanted to come up with a plan for how to handle this visit on my drive over, but I'm still not prepared, and I'm already here. The sight of the prison only reminds me that I have no idea how to get the answers I need from Daddy.

When I pull into the parking lot, I wait there for a minute, breathing heavily. I'm not sure how long I've been sitting there before my phone *ding*s.

Unwelcome Conspirator: I'm worried. Are you sure you're ready for this?

I glance at myself in the rearview mirror. Forcing my gritted teeth into something a little less like a grimace, I whisper the answer into an empty car. "I have to be."

When the guard brings him in, Daddy looks surprised to see me. It's possible that, after last time, he expected I'd never come back again. That thought breaks me a little inside, and when he meets my eyes I look away, memories of the last visit still painful and confusing. How am I supposed to see him now? Who is he? Who does he want me to believe him to be?

When the guard removes Daddy's cuffs, I stand back and study everything in the room except him. I bite one of my nails and then head for the table to take a seat.

"Riley?"

I whip my head up, surprised he's speaking before the guard leaves.

Daddy holds his arms out for the hug we always share at the beginning of my visits. His eyes don't seem to hide anything. They're unguarded and show me nothing but gratitude and an unspoken plea for me to love him like I always have—to imagine him the same way now as ever. It's something I can't fully give. Not yet.

His words are far simpler. "I'm so glad you came."

My gaze holds his and I'm surprised to see him look away first. Then I answer. "Of course." I walk over and put my arms around him like I've done a million times. He kisses the top of my head. I hold on tight, scared to let go. Scared that if I release him, everything will change, even when we both know it already has.

When I try to pull back, he won't let go. His voice is so low I can barely hear it. "Thank you."

Confusion fills me and I push with my hand firm against his chest. I feel anger deep within me and I'm not even sure exactly why I'm mad, just that I am. I want him to grovel and apologize and say he's sorry for what he said, to take it all back, to tell me he was lying when he confessed and explain why he would do such an awful thing until I can't possibly doubt him anymore.

But he doesn't do all of that the instant the guard closes the door—and I hate him a little for it.

"How are you, Riley?" Daddy watches me with pensive stillness.

"I'm not good." I lean back, putting some distance between us. "You heard about the new murder?"

"Yes." Color flushes his cheeks in a way I haven't seen in a long time. He looks more alive, hopeful. "Masters was here for a couple of hours this morning. We can't file any motions until the police finish their preliminary investigation. If they concede that this newest murder opens the door for the possibility that it isn't just a copycat, they'll have to reconsider giving me an extension at the very least."

I frown, momentarily putting aside our many other issues at the prospect of some solid trial information. "How long could the investigation take?"

"Depends. It could be days or months until—"

"Months?" I interrupt in shock. "You only have twenty days left."

"Believe me, I know, but it actually plays to our advantage that Vega is still working in Houston. He's the chief now, so they might not assign him the case. But if they do, I think it would be a good thing. He knows the details better than anyone else. He can make that call faster than a new detective would be able to." Daddy looks nervous now and I find myself analyzing every word he says, every tic. Hearing him speak the name *Vega* sends me into an entirely different train of thought. What would Daddy think if he knew that I've met Jordan, and that we've spent time together, and what I've told him?

I clear my throat and then mutter, "I guess it's lucky that Chief Vega is already assigned to the case."

He lifts his eyes to mine, his gaze abruptly piercing, and I recognize my mistake an instant too late. "Where did you hear that?"

I blink twice before scrambling together a response. "I heard someone mention it on the radio when I was out running errands earlier."

He nods, seeming to accept my answer, but I catch Daddy watching me closer than before. I decide to change the subject away from Vega.

"How will they be able to tell it isn't a copycat?" I ask, gathering my courage to bring up the last visit.

"There are always details from cases like these that are withheld from the media. A copycat would get some of the details right, but not others." Daddy takes a deep breath and closes his eyes for a second before looking down at where his fingers clasp together on the table in front of him. "At this point, we just hope that every detail is the same. That way they can't rule out the possibility that I am innocent. That this new victim was murdered by the same killer as the others they've believed I killed."

I lean back in my chair and cross my arms over my chest. My eyes follow Daddy's movements, his expressions. When he goes over this information, there is a slight smile at the corners of his mouth that turns me cold. Is it because he's hopeful for this new chance at a future or because he hopes he can somehow fool everyone?

My brain hurts from trying to decipher this code. My heart aches because I have to.

On the other hand, am I seeing these things in him because deep down I now fully believe his confession? Or maybe it's because doubting Daddy is easier than fighting with everyone else against the idea of his guilt anymore?

"Just say what you're thinking, Riley." Daddy finally breaks the silence.

"My brain is going to explode. What the hell am I supposed to be thinking?" I push my hands into my hair and then stare at him.

"Watch your language, Riley." Daddy's brow lowers to match his voice.

"My *language*?" My voice tilts with a hint of the crazy I've been trying to keep buried all day. "My language is quite tame, Daddy, considering our location. Or have you forgotten that we're in a *prison*? You're lucky I'm not breaking out my big-girl swear words after what you told me last week."

Daddy flinches like I've struck him. He looks genuinely shocked, and then his shoulders hunch. "Riley, sweetie, you have to know that I was lying."

My mouth falls open an inch before I catch it. I *have* to know? He dares to give me this burden of his confession that he's never even hinted at before and then try to take it back and expect me to see that coming? At the same time, the blossom of hope takes root in my heart. I don't know whether to nurture it or pluck it out like a dandelion from the grass. As if I wasn't confused enough already.

I say nothing, studying his breathing and wishing I could read him the way he's always been able to read me. I want to see the truth through his body language instead of his words. As agonizing as it feels to recognize it, I know that I don't trust his words anymore. I can't. Either he lied last week, or he's been lying my whole life.

Either way, he's a liar now. Something he never was to me before.

After a few seconds he leans toward me, raw anxiety plain on his face. Even through the arrest, the trial, and all the appeals, I have *never* seen him look this desperate. "Riley, you *must* believe me. I am innocent. I've always said that, haven't I?"

My soul feels like it's being ripped just seeing him like this. My heart pounds loud in my ears, my voice chokes with the emotion I'm fighting not to show him. "Until last week."

Reaching out, he grips my hand tight in his. I want more than anything to believe him completely when he says, "*Please*, I only said that to help you and your mama let me go when I'd given up hope. Please don't use my one lie to trap me now that I finally see a light that could free us all."

I pull my hand away. My voice breaks and a couple of tears roll down my cheeks before I can stop them. "And what a horrible lie to tell."

"Don't you see? I need *you* to understand. Your confidence in me matters more to me than what anyone else thinks." His face cracks and I see my own emotion reflected back at me. "I thought it was over. I was trying to do the right thing for the ones I love the most. I hoped that if you thought I deserved what was coming to me then it'd be easier for you and your mama to move on. You've been stuck in one spot your whole life because of me. I couldn't stand the thought of leaving you without making sure you'd be free to *really* live."

His words are the ones I've been hoping for. They're the only reasoning that makes a twisted kind of sense. They dull the edge of my anger, but it doesn't disappear—and neither do my doubts.

Daddy tentatively takes my hand again in his and this time I don't pull away. I quickly wipe the tears from my face with my sleeve.

"You didn't do it?" For some reason, I need to hear him say it again.

"I. Am. Innocent, Riley." He emphasizes each word separately, trying to force them into my brain.

"I'm not done asking questions."

He squeezes my hand. "I'll have the answers."

I don't say anything else, but I feel the weight of everything that's happened in the last week through my neck and shoulders. I hang my head with a deep breath, trying to release some of the tension there.

"You deserve better, Riley. You always have. I know this is all so hard, but please don't give up on me," Daddy whispers, his eyes pleading with me.

"I haven't," I whisper back, and I hate myself because as much as I want to completely believe him, I'm not *convinced*. Being his daughter has taught me not to trust easily and now that I know he himself lied once, I can't trust him again without some kind of proof. At the same time, I don't know how to give up on a man I've loved and fought for my whole life.

How could an innocent man choose to leave this world with those he loves believing he is guilty of something so awful?

Even though I know for certain that going down this rabbit hole will rip me to pieces, I need to find the answers for myself. I need answers from Mama, from Mr. Masters, from Daddy.

From now on, taking anyone's word as truth is not enough.

16

I PARK MY CAR across the street from the address Jordan gave me and wait. Maybe I should've argued with Jordan when he asked me to come to his house tonight. I thought about it, and he must've known it would bother me to come here, because before I could say anything he told me all the reasons he couldn't leave. He was watching Matthew, and it was getting kind of late, so leaving around bedtime wasn't an option, etc., etc.

The truth is, though, I feel a kind of dark curiosity about their house. His dad put my dad in prison. Vega had always been the monster of my nightmares, but Jordan and Matthew have kind of shattered that idea. So what is left? Could the monster who stole my dad away also be a loving father? Do they have a happy home?

Is it how my home would've been if Daddy had never gone to Polunsky?

Plus, I did promise to come and tell him how things had gone during my visit with my dad.

But now that I'm here, I'm terrified. He said his father would be gone for the evening, yet just the idea of him suddenly showing up is keeping me here in my car—where I have been for the last ten minutes.

With a sigh, I fold my arms over the steering wheel and rest my head on them. The idea of simply walking up and knocking on their door is extremely daunting. Maybe I shouldn't have come. Maybe I should've told Jordan he had to wait until we could meet somewhere, anywhere else, but I didn't.

Oh, screw it, I'm going in.

Pushing away my fear, I step out of the car and cross the yard, jogging up onto the porch before I can change my mind. My hand shakes as I raise it to knock on the door, so I get the three raps over with quickly and hide it behind my back.

1 . . . 2 . . . I count in my head just to keep my thoughts from going crazy while I wait. 3 . . . 4 . . . Please let Jordan be the one who answers. Please. 5 . . . 6 . . . Does Jordan have any other siblings besides Matthew? How have I never asked about this before? 7 . . . 8 . . . I take two quick steps down the porch, sure that I should just go home—

The door opens, and Matthew looks up at me with a puzzled frown that clearly says *I know you, but I don't remember from where.* His Avengers pajamas have creases like they just came out of a drawer. The dark, wavy hair that perfectly mimics Jordan's is all messy. He must've figured out where he knew me from because he suddenly grins at me, both front teeth now missing. "I remember you!"

"Hi, Matthew. I remember you, too." The toothless smile is infectious. Resistance is futile. "Is Jordan here?"

"Yes!" He continues to stand there, smiling at me. I imagine he should be in bed by now, but I've never really been around kids this age and certainly don't know what to do with this one. "You're Riley, the girl who likes the purple car!"

It probably would've been better for him not to remember my name—in case he tells his dad about the girl who came by later—but it isn't like I'm the only Riley in Houston.

"Yep, that's me." He sounds so excited, I chuckle and wonder if I should start introducing myself this way all the time. It's definitely better than my other options: *I'm Riley, the girl who visits death row every week!* Or *the girl who got drunk that one time and told her biggest secret to the completely wrong guy!* No, Purple Car Girl is definitely my best option. Shifting my feet forward, I peek around Matthew, hoping to possibly see Jordan lurking somewhere in the background, but no luck.

"Thanks for visiting," Matthew says like an usher who opens the door for people when they're leaving a museum. He sticks his small hand out to shake mine again and my worries about coming here dissolve.

"You know you're not supposed to open the door by yourself." The door suddenly jerks back and Jordan pokes his head around the edge. His expression goes from concerned to apologetic when he sees me, and he puts his hands on Matthew's shoulders. "Sorry, we're still mastering door etiquette. I hope you weren't out here very long."

Matthew holds tight to my fingers and I'm not sure how to pry him off without offending him. So I just keep shaking and say, "He's better company than you anyway."

"I don't doubt that." Jordan grins down at his brother. In one move, he lifts him up onto his shoulder, effectively freeing my hand.

He turns his back on me and walks inside, leaving the door open behind him. In between bouts of Matthew giggling I hear Jordan say, "Come on in, Riley."

I stand still on the porch. Every inch closer to the Vega family feels like some sort of betrayal. What would Daddy think if he knew I was here tonight? What would he say?

I draw my shoulders back and stand up straight as I walk into the brightly lit interior of Vega Central. I don't know if I'm expecting it to look more like a holding cell than a house, but as I close the door behind me and my eyes adjust, I'm surprised by how welcoming it all feels. Everything in the living room I've stepped into is warm and inviting. It's decorated in a southwestern style with brown couches and white pillows with accents in pops of teal and terra-cotta.

Absolutely nothing reminds me of my nightmares about the man who lives here, and I'm grateful for that.

Everywhere I look, it feels like it has a woman's touch and I'm hit by a wave of sadness as I remember Jordan's mother's accident. Daddy has been gone long enough that I don't see constant reminders of him when I look around our house. I can't decide if the memories would make it easier or infinitely harder. Probably both.

One corner of the room is filled with a massive pile of blue plastic rectangles. I don't have a clue what they're for, but when Jordan puts Matthew down, he runs straight over and starts putting them together. I realize they make a track and then I see the familiar green tub of race cars nearby. There is a big section of racetrack that is already put together, tucked back on the other side of the kitchen table.

"Wow, that looks like quite a project." In my head, I try to picture all the pieces of track connected, and it's quickly obvious that the finished track would take up more than the length of the room.

"Want to help? Jordan helps," Matthew shouts at an impressive volume without even looking up.

"Thank you, but no. I have zero track-building experience. I would only slow you down." Matthew considers my response carefully, then goes back to work like he's decided that I'm probably right.

I remind myself again where I am and—now that I've seen it—how badly I would like to be gone from here before Jordan's dad shows up. I have a feeling he wouldn't be nearly as welcoming as his racetrack-building kindergartner.

Jordan has his eyes on me and I tilt my head toward the door. "Can we talk somewhere else?"

"Sure. Just give me a second." He turns to face Matthew. "Sorry Matty-boy. It's time for bed."

"But Dad isn't home yet." Matthew drops his track pieces into the bucket, his pout clear in his voice even before he turns to face us. When he slowly pivots around, I'm surprised to see tears in his eyes.

"I know. He might not be home until very late, but I promise he's safe." Jordan crouches down and pulls his brother in for a hug. The underlying reassurance from his words comes through perfectly. How hard would it be for Matthew to understand his mother being taken away so suddenly when he was so young?

A sudden vivid memory sneaks up on me and steals my breath away. I remember lying alone in bed, afraid to sleep because I was terrified that if I closed my eyes the police would come and take Mama away, too. I'd been in bed asleep when Vega came for Daddy. The commotion woke me up, and I'd watched with tears burning my cheeks as they walked him out in handcuffs. Somehow I felt like if I'd stayed awake I could've stopped them. I was small and powerless. Not sleeping was the only thing I could think to do to make sure it didn't happen to Mama, too. I haven't slept well since that night.

"We can't see him. How can you be sure he's safe?" Matthew's tiny voice asks.

My soul hurts, both from my own memories and for what Jordan and Matthew have been through. When Jordan sits and pulls Matthew onto his lap and against his chest, the raw pain I see in Jordan's eyes wrenches my heart. He takes a shaky breath and then puts on a smile. "Tell you what. You go get your favorite blanket and I'll let you watch cartoons on the couch in the living room while you fall asleep. Okay?"

Matthew sniffles and nods.

As I watch Jordan with his brother, some of the anger I hold toward him starts to melt away. The intense pain of sudden loss is something we share intimately. There are few who can really grasp that. No wonder Jordan seemed to understand me so quickly in a way that others in the past couldn't. We *are* very different, but we're also tied together in strange ways. I glance around the room and am suddenly aware that there are no pictures—anywhere. I see a few conspicuous mounting nails sticking out of a nearby wall. Somehow I doubt they've been empty for long.

A memory of the day that Mama took down all our family

pictures floats back to the surface. The pictures made me feel like a piece of Daddy was still with us, but then he wasn't anymore. It was like he'd been ripped away from me again, but this time by someone I loved and trusted. I've never told Mama that.

I stand quietly in the corner like a fly on the wall. I try not to feel like I'm intruding on this deeply private scene as I watch Jordan help Matthew gather his things and turn on the TV in a nearby room. Within five minutes, his brother is settled and Jordan comes back to me. He's rubbing his shoulder with one hand like there is a knot there that will never quite go away.

I think I have a knot in the exact same place.

"He has nightmares if he goes to bed before our dad is home. I don't usually let him stay up this late, but it isn't a school night, and I can't stand to hear him wake up screaming in his room." He states this simply, like it isn't the most heartbreaking thing I've ever heard.

I hesitate, but something in me wants desperately to reach out to him. "I used to have nightmares like that."

"Really?" Jordan leans back to sit on the edge of the couch. "About what?"

"I was always afraid. I kept thinking that he might come back and take away my mom, too." I meet his eyes and although I see sympathy in them, we both let the conversation drop there.

Neither of us wants to bring up the truth that hangs over us: the fact that the monster from my nightmares is the same man that Matthew is so terrified to lose.

"Well, in five minutes he'll be sleeping peacefully anyway. Do you prefer not to have an audience? We can go outside to talk."

The desire to leave is only getting stronger and stronger with every passing moment. "I'd rather go outside, but are you sure you can leave the house? What if he needs you? I can always meet you somewhere tomorr—"

"No," he responds before I even get the whole word out. "Just wait a sec."

Jordan walks softly to the living room doorway and peeks in. After a moment, he nods. "He's already asleep. I can't go far, but we can go out to the front yard if you want. Is there a reason you don't want to talk here?"

I hesitate before just saying exactly what I'm thinking. "I'd rather be anywhere where there is less of a chance of *someone* coming home unexpectedly and interrupting our chat."

Jordan's face twists into a strangely pained and rueful expression I've never seen on him before. "Not much chance of that, but okay."

I feel like maybe I shouldn't, but concern forces me to ask anyway. "Why not?"

"Dad works a lot anyway, but with this new murder he might not be home again for a day . . . or two." Jordan shrugs it off.

I shake my head, giving him a sad smile. "For being from completely different sides of this, we sure have a lot in common."

"You noticed that too, huh?" He winks at me before holding the front door open for me to walk through.

I consider asking him if his dad has always worked this much—if it was like this before his mother died—but I hold my tongue. Of all the people in the world who should understand not wanting to answer questions about absent parents, I'm definitely one of them.

Hell, I should be their president.

"Long hours are a common occurrence at my house, too," I say instead.

He laughs, but the normal roundness of the notes is soured by a bitter undertone. "Long hours is an understatement around here."

I follow Jordan over to a beautifully carved porch swing that I hadn't noticed on my way in. It hides in an alcove behind a large pecan tree. Jordan plops down and I take the seat beside him.

Once we're alone out here, the silence hangs between us, awkward and smothering. I don't know how to ease it, but I really wish I could.

"I wish you would relax a little." Jordan watches me, half of his face hidden in shadow. "Why can't you believe that I'm sorry? I wasn't trying to hurt you. You can trust me."

"Trust isn't my strong suit." The seat is only wide enough to give us about six inches between my leg and his. Being this close to him makes me nervous even though I'm not sure why. "So what exactly do you need to know about my visit?"

"Wow, right to business." Jordan laughs. "Is someone a lawyer's daughter or what?"

"I prefer the terms *ex-lawyer, reformed lawyer,* or *born-again criminal*," I reply, playing along as I fight to keep my face straight.

"Noted, counselor." Jordan shakes his head. "Fine. Maybe just assume I want to know anything important. How was the visit?"

My toes push off absentmindedly and the swing starts moving. Jordan stretches his long legs out in front of us and he listens as I tell him an abbreviated version of what happened at Polunsky.

When I finish, he clasps his hands together in front of him and taps one finger at a time against the back of the opposite hand. I can tell from his expression that his mind is as busy as his fingers. "So he's denying it now?"

"Yes." I bite the word off and end my statement there. My instinct is to defend Daddy, to say all the reasons why what he told me makes sense and why I believe him . . . except for the fact that I'm not completely sure if I do now.

Jordan's hands stop moving. "Riley, seriously. Take a breath. I'm not attacking him. I'm not even saying I don't believe him."

My arms are crossed so tightly that I can feel the knot of tension at the back of my neck balling up. Forcing myself to relax, I drop my hands to my sides. "Okay, thank you."

Before he can respond, I speak again. "I don't understand. Why can't you just pretend you never heard about him confessing?" I ask him. My voice is small, but my exasperation at my own mistake shows in my tone.

He stops swinging, turning his head toward me. His eyes are such a rich dark brown that in these shadows they seem nearly black, and now he stares hard, like he's looking right through me. "Can *you* pretend you never heard it?"

"That isn't the same." I shake my head.

"Are you saying this confession wouldn't be pretty important to my dad, too?"

"Fair point." I wince from the sting of truth in his reply.

"But it really isn't about that. No matter how mad you are at me, I want to help." He leans closer and his eyes move from the shadows into the light. "Maybe if you tried to think about it that way, you might be able to relax and let me help you?"

I consider what he said for a few minutes. My instincts doubt him now, but eventually I realize that he's right. If I want him to keep Daddy's secret from Chief Vega, then I'm stuck with him. Does it really matter what his reasons are? If he can help, let him help.

I shrug. "I think I just need time to figure this out. I'm going to ask my mom and dad's lawyer first. He's a family friend. Maybe he has information that could help clarify things for me. Before I do that, though, I need to find the right questions."

Jordan closely watches me as I piece together the only plan that has any hope of providing the answers I need right now. "I'm going to do some research. Find out everything I can about the case, refresh my memory. I'll figure out what I should be asking and who I should be talking to. My dad lied, and I never thought he could be a liar. I have to figure out if he's the man I thought—or someone else entirely."

"Riley . . ." Jordan waits a few seconds. He seems reluctant to say whatever is on his mind. "You know—you know that whatever you may find, it probably won't be something that can change the actual case. After all these years of people looking on both sides, it's hard to imagine you finding anything new to prove his innocence in court."

"I know," I answer, so soft that he leans in closer. Then I look straight into his eyes. "I don't need to find answers for *them*. I need to find them for *me*. I need to know what *I* think, not what my parents have told me to think. I need that—before he's gone."

Jordan sits back in the swing, his eyes still on me. He doesn't say anything.

"Does that even make sense?" I ask finally.

"Yes." His response comes with no hesitation. "I think—I think I'd feel the same way."

The pictures of the victims from Daddy's trial play through my head. Mama had tried to cover my eyes during that part, but I'd seen enough to have nightmares for a very long time. I finally got over them after several years, but now, with just the mere thought of digging into his case, my mind immediately fills with the images.

Jordan's fingers close over mine as he stands up and pulls me to my feet. "You *have* to let me help you."

I fight the instinctive urge to be suspicious. The warmth of his hands sinks into my cold fingers, branding me. The idea of sifting through details of my father's case with Jordan sounds like the worst plan ever. It was horrifying just hearing bits and pieces of the case when I completely believed Daddy couldn't have done it. This time with the doubts that linger now, it will be so much worse. I open my mouth to argue, but before I can, he goes on.

"I hope you want me there, but even if you don't, I think you'll need me, Riley." Jordan's face is a confusing mess of confidence and desperation. "This won't be easy for you, no matter what you find. You have to stop trying to do everything on your own, and I can help. I *want* to help you."

My mouth, which had been open, poised to argue, is left hanging. I close it, realizing how near we're standing to each other, and how much I want him to stay here, to stay with me.

But no one ever stays—I know that. Just because he hasn't left me so far doesn't mean he won't.

"I'm not . . . ," I begin softly, but he cuts my argument off again by pulling me into a tight hug.

"Let me help you." His voice pleads against my ear and I lose all will to argue with him anymore.

"Okay," I answer finally. "For now."

"Deal." He releases me with a smile and then leads me toward my car. I walk along in his wake as my mind fights to find firm footing for why this isn't my best option. When we get to my car, he opens the door for me and says, "You won't regret it. Occasionally, I can even be helpful."

Moving around to the inside of my door, I watch him for a few seconds before finally accepting the fact that I want him to be here with me through this as much as he says he wants to be.

But he definitely doesn't need to know that.

"I hope you're right." I eye him warily for a moment and then climb in and start my car.

17

I FIND MAMA'S NOTE on the counter when I wake up Saturday morning.

> *I have to work today, but I'll be home tomorrow. Plan on being around. I know you went to Polunsky yesterday even after I asked you not to. We need to talk.*
> *—Mama*

The metallic taste of blood is on my tongue and I realize I've been biting my lip a bit too hard. It isn't like I expected that Mama wouldn't find out. I just hoped it might take longer. I pick up my phone and text Jordan.

Busy today? I think it's time to do some research.

It takes less than a minute before my phone *dings* with his response.

Jordan: I'm free in an hour. What did you have in mind?

I think for a minute, then decide that since Mama will be gone all day, we might as well take advantage of it.

Meet me at my house. Bring a laptop if you have one.

Jordan: See you then.

A thick fog of anxiety hangs over me as I hop in the shower and get ready. I keep trying to relax my shoulders, but they've tightened again on their own within minutes. I take one deep breath and check my clock. Jordan should be here in about ten minutes. Maybe there *is* something I can do to calm myself before then. I go to my room out of habit and grab Daddy's letter that he's written for today, opening it hastily.

Riley,

Happy Saturday, my dear! I'm so sorry about last week and I hope you can forgive me for lying. Sometimes people do the wrong thing for the right reason. I hope you can understand that. I need you to. I can't imagine finally getting out of here only to have lost you along the way. That would be a harder punishment for me than all these years I've spent in Polunsky.

Now that we have hope again, please keep my mistake with you alone. There's no need to involve your mother in something that only has the potential to hurt her further.

All my love,
Daddy

I sigh. Too little too late. If only I'd read this or talked to Daddy before I told Mama. This wasn't the right choice of letter to ease my stress. Usually Daddy's letters find a way to make me feel better, but apparently not today.

I walk back to my closet in a daze. How can it have already been eight days since Daddy told me the thing I never wanted to hear? Time seems to be flying faster than small-town gossip, and I'm being dragged along behind it no matter how hard I fight.

It feels like my universe collided with another one, imploded, and then formed an entirely new solar system. And here I am left standing in the middle of utter chaos. I keep digging for the truth, making a giant mess in the rubble and just trying like hell to figure out this one crucial detail.

If everything around me changes, am I still the same?

I search through the shoeboxes, looking for one with letters from several months back. The top portions of the stacks wobble as I dig and I hope to God everything in the whole closet doesn't fall out and flatten me. Although, wouldn't that be one fantastic headline?

Death Row Man Finally Released, Only to Mourn Daughter Crushed Just Weeks Before by Avalanche of Shoeboxes

I smile to myself as I turn and lean against my wall. The correct shoebox is finally in my hands. I open the top envelopes and start scanning through them.

By the time the doorbell rings, the dull pain at the base of my skull has eased a bit—all thanks to Daddy and his letters.

I lead Jordan to the kitchen table, where my laptop sits alongside two notebooks and some pens. His eyebrows lift and he throws a questioning glance in my direction.

"Before I can try to get the answers I need"—I release a shuddering sigh—"I need to make sure I understand what *everyone else* thinks happened."

He hesitates before speaking. "Are you sure you want to go down this road, Riley?"

I give him a firm nod. "I'm not saying it's the truth, but I need to know the details of what the state says happened before I can even attempt to figure out what questions I need to ask."

Jordan watches me closely as I take my seat, then he pushes up both sleeves and opens his laptop. After I give him our network password and he's online, he asks, "Where do you want to start?"

"I know most of the details of what happened to the victims—how they were killed. I also know they falsely think my father had an affair with one of them," I say, and he squints so I hurry on before he can get caught up in the wrong details. I'm not ready to consider the idea that this could be just another lie. "I need to know what else I'm missing. I need to understand their arguments better."

Jordan shrugs. "Sounds good to me."

"Good. We'll each look up several articles that go over the evidence and the details of the case. Let's take notes, then we'll compare and see if either of us finds anything new."

Jordan gives me a grim nod, then turns to his screen and starts typing.

"And Jordan?"

He waits for me to finish.

"Thank you . . . for wanting to help."

He appears to hesitate before reaching out and grabbing my hand in his. The gesture is so sudden and unexpected I nearly jerk my hand back. He squeezes my fingers lightly twice and I'm amazed at how warm and strong his hand feels around mine.

"It's going to be okay, Riley." Then he rubs his thumb across my knuckles slowly before releasing my fingers without a word and turning back to his screen.

When I place my hands back on my own keyboard, I can't help but notice how much warmer the hand he'd held still is. It's like he left a bit of his life and warmth with me. I smile softly to myself, but it slides slowly away with each key I press as I type the words *East End Killer* into the search window.

We've each been jotting notes on our pads in silence for over an hour when I finally look up again. My finger goes down my list as I read through some of the words I've written. Seeing details that condemn my father in my own handwriting feels like treason.

I stare at the screen still open before me for the fifteenth time, but nothing here is new information. All I can think about is everything I've read so far and how awful it is. And how Jordan is reading it, too. The silence between us that was just starting to become comfortable again now feels dreadful and humiliating. He's still reading and has a look on his face that is half horrified, half fascinated. It's the same one people wore during Daddy's trial every time they talked about what he did.

I remember that look. I hate that look.

The information in the articles feels so vastly different when looking at it as something that could be true. I'm not ready for these differences. Especially when every description conjures images of my father as a living, breathing nightmare. My hand shakes, and I pull the notebook onto my lap before Jordan can see it.

I'd been so young during the trial. Some of the details are familiar, mostly the ones that mattered because we'd argued for appeals based on them. Mama and Daddy had told me that the things the prosecutors said were lies and I should forget about them, and I'd believed my parents completely. Reading through these documents of evidence now—now when I'm older and understand each and every detail, and now that I know that my parents are liars, too—it's an entirely different experience, and my stomach is a turbulent mess.

I strive to bring my emotions to balance and get a grip. Inhale and exhale. I tune out everything but the air in my lungs and breathe slow and deep. If I can't even read through the evidence of this case with an open mind, how will I be able to face the other things that could be coming my way? The reopening of his case, his possible release, his probable execution.

If I want the truth, I must be strong enough to handle it when it comes.

"Riley?"

I fight for control, forcing myself not to whip my head up or react suddenly.

Instead, I stay exactly as I am and softly murmur, "Hmm?"

Only when his warm fingers slide down my arm do I realize how chilled my skin has become.

"Are you all right?" His words hold none of the judgment I was afraid he was feeling, only concern.

When I finally make myself look up with the intention of brushing him off, I find that I can't. A deep frown creases his brow and makes the shadows around his eyes appear deep, haunting. He seems nervous and worried—and scared. Exactly what I feel. I don't know how to react to that. Jordan should be my opposite. He is the son of the cop who put my father in prison. His life has always represented justice and the right of the law, while my life represented injustice and the mistakes of humanity.

How can we possibly ever be on the same page?

"No," I say, the emotion in my voice catching both of us off guard. I'm suddenly uncomfortable with his gaze on me, so I gesture to the notebook in front of me, hoping to draw his attention away. "Nothing here is all right."

Jordan does as I was hoping and looks back down at his own notebook. He opens his mouth to speak, but then hesitates and meets my eyes. "Are you sure you're ready to deal with this?" His hands spread out over the mess around us and his shoulders actually droop. It's like his question is too heavy for them to carry.

But it isn't a choice. I have to carry that weight, and I have to do it now, before another nineteen days pass without me knowing what I truly believe, and Daddy gets executed for a crime he didn't commit or—equally unthinkable—he gets released from prison and exonerated for a crime he *is* guilty of. How do I live without telling anyone if I decide he *is* guilty, and I'm the only one who heard his confession?

"I'm ready." From the steadiness of my tone, it almost sounds like it could be true.

18

AFTER VERIFYING WE BOTH have all the same general information about the case, we start separating the details into groups. Agreeing with Jordan on where specific points should go is harder than I expect.

"But shouldn't that be listed under the evidence that speaks to his guilt?" Jordan taps his pen against his lip, and I resist the sudden urge to rip it from his hands.

"No, it definitely casts doubt. It needs to be listed there." I clasp my fingers tighter in my lap, trying to hold my anger in check, but the jab still slips through. "Maybe if you weren't so biased against him, you'd be able to see that."

Jordan makes a sound like he's choking on something, his eyes go wide, and he slumps down low in his chair, mumbling, "You're impossible."

"Well, it's true," I mutter, reaching for his notebook to study what he's written. Instead, Jordan sits straight up, grabs his scribbled notes in one hand, and my wrist in the other.

I'm stuck now, and I've leaned so far forward that my arm is actually over his shoulder. I have no choice but to rest it there to catch my balance or fall forward out of my chair.

"Riley," he whispers an inch from my face, his eyes firing sparks at me. "You, my friend, are a hypocrite."

His words make me want to jerk my hand away, but I don't. I stay there, leaning close with my wrist in his fingers and my heart pounding in my throat. My balance is so off-center. With a slight shift of his weight, he could drop me to the floor.

The frustration in his eyes fades as they search mine, and I say, "I am not."

"Not what?" His response is lightning fast and playful, but he helps me regain my balance and releases me. "A hypocrite or my friend?"

A laugh bursts from my chest and it is as unexpected as his words. He grins wide, but I force myself to focus. If we're going to make any progress, we need to stop getting distracted by disagreements . . . and each other.

"Fine, then we're both hypocrites." I lean back, crossing my legs beneath the table as I try to think of the best solution. The one I come up with doesn't sound fun, but it's the only idea I have. "Okay, so maybe we need to flip sides and switch arguments. You are only allowed to think of reasons why something could cast doubt. I'm only allowed to consider ways it could speak to guilt. Deal?"

Jordan gives me a look that can only be described as grimly impressed. "That isn't going to be easy. And it requires trust. Are you *sure* that's the best approach?"

"It's the best way to make sure we're seeing it clearly." I pick up his notebook and look at it again, trying it out. "If I convince us both that he's guilty, no matter how much I don't want him to be . . . then it's obviously true. Right? And vice versa for you."

Jordan doesn't speak until I lower the paper.

"You need to know, Riley, I do *not* hope your father is guilty. If we can prove him innocent, I'll be genuinely happy for you both. It will be anything but disappointing." His tone is stern, almost as if holding a rebuke toward me for misjudging him.

"It doesn't seem like that, though. Every point you make and the things you say . . ." I'm not sure whether to defend my opinion or apologize.

"I've been arguing for that evidence because I believe my own dad is a good cop." He lowers his chin and finishes, "I *think* your father is probably guilty, but with this new murder, I'm really not sure right now. And I definitely don't hope he is."

I force myself not to flinch when Jordan says those words. I'm used to everyone thinking that Daddy killed people, but I've learned not to get close to people who believe that, and this is why—no matter how I prepare myself for it, it hurts to hear them say it. I don't blame Jordan for it, but it still stings.

I push aside the pain by pointing to a different note I have written down. "Okay, so this evidence could speak to his guilt because all of the victims of the East End Killer are blond, attractive women in their thirties." This is a good place to start. It's one piece of evidence for which I remember the reasoning of the prosecution at trial very clearly.

Jordan switches gears, too, having no problem keeping up. He takes the notepad from my hand, frowning as he reads through it. "But it really means nothing, because thousands of men across Houston are attracted to women like this."

"It's common for serial killers to have a person they fixate on and then for them to kill people who look similar. In this case, evidence suggests he has a carefully constructed f-façade." I falter for only an instant and then push forward with the prosecution's words that still haunt my nightmares sometimes. "An intricate smokescreen of a life that he cares greatly about protecting. He feels a great desire to kill his fixation, but it would threaten his lifestyle. So he replaces her and kills these victims to satisfy that urge."

I organize the papers in front of me into a pile and make sure no emotions show on my face. He looks sad, but the expression disappears the moment my eyes meet his and I'm grateful.

"You're talking about his wife," Jordan says, carefully following my wording to leave any mention of my relationships with these people out of our conversation and again I'm filled with a brief rush of gratitude.

"Yes."

"That's ridiculous," Jordan says simply. Hearing him truly defend my dad is so unexpected that my jaw falls slightly open. "The argument could just as easily be made that this victim profile makes him an unlikely suspect. He and his wife have a good relationship, a happy marriage. She hasn't cheated—that anyone knows of. There has been no evidence of any reason he should have that kind of anger toward her."

He shrugs at the end and waits for me to refute him, but I'm too overwhelmed to speak or say anything. I've never, *ever* had anyone, besides Mama or someone who was being paid to do it, defend my father in front of me. It doesn't matter that in the moment I know he doesn't believe it. It doesn't matter that I know he's just meeting his end of our arrangement. All that matters is that he has a choice right here and right now and he is *choosing* to argue for my father's innocence in order to help me.

I scoot forward and quickly put my arms around his neck in a tight hug. Tears I don't expect wet the shoulder of his shirt and I try to wipe them away before he notices. I whisper, "Thank you."

Jordan seems alarmed at first, then he leans forward and wraps both arms around me. I withdraw before I become too comfortable in that position and clear my throat, trying to carry on as though nothing strange has just happened.

"Reason doesn't apply here. Sociopaths don't need reason," I say, daring him to refute the statement that has kept me awake at night.

"Yeah?" Jordan smiles, and doesn't mention my more than slightly awkward and abrupt display of emotion. Instead, he plays right along with me. "Well, then *prove* to me that David Beckett is a sociopath."

I smile back, thinking for the first time that looking at all the facts presented in Daddy's case ourselves might not be the worst idea I've ever had.

19

AFTER THE INITIAL FINDING of—and subsequent arguing over—the details of the case for the last two hours, Jordan and I have come to one conclusion. The relatively small amount of information in the papers isn't of much use without specifics from the new case.

Unfortunately, since that case is still open and active, there are even fewer details about it online than about the other murders.

"The victim is—" I look down at my notes again—"Valynne Kemp. She's blond, same age range as the others, and she was strangled like the first three."

"Does it say if she was beaten first?" Jordan asks.

I shake my head, wishing I had that detail. "Not anywhere I read."

Jordan nods and then chimes in, "I found an article that quoted a source within the police department. He said that the bodies were posed in a similar fashion."

"All things that could've been copied," I answer softly.

"Or done the exact same way because it was the exact same

killer," Jordan says, refuting my argument without even raising his eyes from the paper.

I scan my notebook one more time before dropping it back to the table. "I think that's about everything the Internet will be giving us today."

Jordan sighs and sits back in his chair, stretching. "So what's next?"

I'm quiet for a moment, debating whether to ask the question I have on my mind before diving in. "I don't suppose your dad would be open to answering questions you asked him about the new murder, would he?"

Jordan stiffens and I regret asking almost instantly. "I'm sorry . . ."

"No." He shakes his head and gives me a sad smile. "You couldn't know this. It makes sense for you to ask, but my father and I haven't been speaking much lately."

"Oh." Now I feel worse. I figure we really have no room for secrets anymore, so I don't hesitate this time. "Why?"

"A lot of reasons," he begins, and when I wait in the quiet, he continues. "He doesn't agree with my choices lately, I guess."

I groan. "Join the club."

"Yeah. First I quit football, then I stop hanging out with my friends." He runs his fingertips across the table and looks so deep in thought that I wonder if he remembers he's talking to me. "But I haven't been around constantly to watch Matthew all the time either. So he thinks I'm doing something to rebel, like drugs or drinking—"

"Or hanging out with the daughter of everyone's favorite death row inmate?" I fill in with a rueful chuckle.

He rewards me with a big grin. "Yeah, or that."

"That sucks. I really am sorry."

"Yeah." Jordan shrugs. "I am too."

I try to think of a good backup option for getting information on the newest case, but my brain comes up empty.

Fear churns like a spinning pit in my gut. I know that I want the truth, but until this moment, I never considered the possibility of never *truly* knowing.

Daddy is Daddy. He's loving and warm and stunningly smart. I've always wanted to be more like him. How can *that* man be guilty?

But this isn't just about who he was. It's also about who he *is*. It's part of who I've always been, part of who I am. If he was a murderer—still is a murderer—that would make me the daughter of an honest-to-God serial killer. If that's who he is, then I'm the girl who has spent her life defending a monster. I hate the very idea of being *that* girl.

But if I am, I refuse to be kept in the dark by his lies anymore.

Opening my eyes, I see Jordan studying me, his features tight with worry. His warm earthy eyes meet mine, and I can see him bracing himself for my next move. Still, all I can think is to wonder what he sees when he looks at me.

Does he see the daughter who believes in her father's innocence against the odds?

Or does he see the fool with the DNA of a killer, who believes a liar when everyone around her knows the truth?

Whatever he sees, he's here when he probably shouldn't be. He keeps my secret even from his own father when, in truth, he owes me nothing. He helps me when anyone else would've ditched me after my drunken shenanigans in the park.

I climb slowly to my feet, and Jordan does the same. Without meeting his eyes, I walk forward and reach both arms around his waist for a quick hug. "Thank you."

He wraps both arms around me. "This isn't over yet, Riley. Don't give up."

His words and closeness steal my breath away. I step back instantly because it's clear from that one moment that he is worse than any drug. All my nerves fire off in response to the way he smells, the way he feels, the way he looks at me. When I'm not furious with him, he creates his own brand of potent intoxication.

He's a drug I *can't* become hooked on, because I know he'll leave eventually.

"Okay then." I turn and close my laptop, then my notebook, and stack them up. "We'll just get the information another way."

Jordan watches me, curious. "What do you have in mind?"

"My father used to be a lawyer. I mentioned it before, but his former partner is a close family friend and he's represented Daddy in all his trials. He knows this case better than anyone." I twist my lips to the side, thinking for a minute. "Maybe he can help me."

"When are you going to contact him?"

"I'll go to his office Monday." I stretch my arms up, trying to relax the tight muscles down my back. "I'm in kind of a time crunch here, and he should have all the case details with him if I meet him there."

He jumps in quickly. "I have to watch Matthew, but I should be done early, around eleven."

I freeze in my semi-stretching position. "Uh, I'm not sure if—"

"Let me come." Jordan's eyes plead with me and I drop my arms to my sides, uncertain. "Maybe I can help somehow?"

I consider his words. Bringing Jordan with me could have no effect, or it could knock Mr. Masters off his game a bit. It could also make him angry, and he might not tell me anything, but playing it safe isn't getting me anywhere. It's time to start pushing boundaries. "Fine. You can meet me Monday afternoon, then?"

"Absolutely." He beams down at me, looking a little too pleased with himself as he follows me to the front door, and then out to his black monster of a bike.

I chuckle with a rueful grin. "See you then."

"Text me with where you want to meet up." When I start back toward the house, he continues. "Oh, and Riley?"

I pivot back to face him, waiting.

His eyes flash a challenge at me from across his front yard. "This time, I drive."

When I wake up the next morning, Mama is waiting for me on the couch, sipping a cup of coffee. I sigh, deciding to take the bull by the horns, and walk straight up to her.

"I know we're going to talk, but I have some questions for you, too," I blurt out before she has a chance to speak. "And I'd like to be awake enough to formulate them, so I'm taking a shower first."

I phrase it like a statement, but we both know it's more of a

162

question, so I wait. She watches me for a full thirty seconds before inclining her head without a word.

I grab some clothes, head straight for the bathroom, and proceed with the hottest shower I've ever taken. By the time I'm done and have brushed my teeth and hair and gotten dressed, not only am I fully awake, but I've got a list of questions for Mama that may make her wish she hadn't given me the time to shower.

My hair drips wet and cool on my neck and back as I enter the room. A fresh plate of toast and a cup of juice are in front of the spot on the couch beside her, so I walk over and sit down.

"Thank you," I say, and before she can get started, I keep going. "Daddy says he didn't do it. He says he had finally given up and was just trying to give us a way to a fresh start."

Confusion crinkles her brow, and I can honestly say I know *exactly* how she feels. "He said that?"

"Yes."

"Thank you for telling me."

"You're welcome. I thought you would want to know." And I brace myself.

She nods and takes a single deep breath before starting in. "Why did you go to Polunsky after I asked you not to?" Her voice is stern, but I see hurt behind her eyes.

"You know why I went, and I told you I was still going to go," I respond without emotion.

"You've never blatantly disobeyed me before." Her tone softens.

"You've never told me not to go see Daddy when he's only weeks from execution before," I respond back, matching her tone. She's silent, but when I glance over she's frowning. I decide it's my turn to start asking questions.

"Why did you tell me not to go? Why now?" I watch her face closely, and what I see there surprises me more than anything else could—it's fear, and then it's gone.

"I just think maybe this is a time to keep our distance."

I pounce. "Why? Right now, for the first time in years, we have hope. How could you turn on him so quickly? Why back away now?"

"I haven't turned on him, but he's never told anyone that he's guilty before," Mama hisses before sitting up straight and looking abashed.

"Of course he hasn't. Doesn't it make sense to you that he could've given up? That he was trying to do something unselfish and help us let him go?" I settle back farther into the couch cushions, like I can use them to fortify my defenses.

"Now is quite the time for him to start being unselfish," Mama growls out so soft it's almost like she's talking more to herself than to me.

I gasp and my muscles stiffen.

"What do you mean? You think Daddy is *selfish*?" I frown in confusion. Mama has never spoken about Daddy like this. "He does nothing but worry about us when he's the one stuck in that awful place."

Now the anger grabs hold and I stand up, raising my voice to her. "I have literally never even heard him complain. How can you say these things? It hasn't been long since you started choosing work over him, over *me*, over everything you're supposed to lov—"

Mama is on her feet before I've even finished my sentence. I hear the crack when her slap lands brutally hard against my left cheek before I feel the burning sting of it. I lift my hand gingerly to my face and back away slowly, gaping at her. I'm in shock, and in pain, and I'm even more confused than before. Not only has Mama *never* struck me, but she's never reacted with violence. Ever.

Her mouth hangs open as she watches me put several feet between us, then she looks down at her hand like it's some foreign object she doesn't recognize. She hides it behind her back and shakes her head wordlessly as she stares at me.

My left eye is stinging badly enough now that it starts to water, but I won't let her see that. I turn and stalk toward my room.

She yells after me, "Riley, wait!"

I slam and lock the door. I know Mama has the key, so I slide my chair over to block it, but there's no need. I don't even hear her moving outside for at least twenty minutes. My own fuming movements and the soft sobs I can't quite silence completely are the only things that break the stillness.

Picking up my phone, I consider texting Jordan, but don't because I don't know what to say. He might be handling it okay that my father is a monster, but what if he knew that my mother has this penchant for violence inside of her also?

Who *are* my parents? Are they anything they've always raised me to believe?

I hear a soft knock on my door and I freeze, holding my breath.

"I'm so sorry, Riley." Her voice sounds near tears. "I didn't mean to—I'm sorry."

Something hardens inside me and I don't answer. I just wait and listen.

"I'm leaving an ice pack out here for you. You should put it on your cheek." Her voice breaks with remorse on the last word and my heart aches to get up and open the door. She goes on before I have a chance. "I'm going to the store for a while. I'm sorry. Please know, Riley, that I'm not your enemy."

My head echoes with her words. Each painful throb in my face makes me wonder if they're true. Who are my mom and dad? Do I really know anything about them? They lived entire lives before I came along. How can I really know them when so much of their past has nothing to do with me? Everything I've built my world around cracks inside me and begins to shatter, then I'm crying for an entirely different reason than the pain.

I sit in the quiet and ask myself the one question I've been avoiding for most of my life.

How can we *really* know anyone?

20

BEFORE I EVEN GET IN MY CAR the next day, I've already texted Jordan, asking him to meet me at the park. I arrive first and find some semicool shade to sit in while I hide from the blistering afternoon sun. I probably shouldn't have come early. A hot day can make you feel like a Sunday pot roast in under five minutes.

Thankfully, Jordan pulls in on his motorcycle a few minutes before I'm expecting him. When he takes off his helmet, his black hair shines in the sunlight. I carefully adjust my large, dark sunglasses against my sore cheekbone and wipe some sweat off the back of my neck. Why must Jordan always show up looking *so* good?

He crosses toward me. "You going to tell me how you plan to get answers at the law offices tonight? Or is it some kind of requirement that you keep me in the dark?"

"Not a requirement, but more fun." I climb to my feet, dusting off my faded blue jeans. "Seriously though, it's just one more place where I'm hoping that asking questions might get me somewhere."

"Still cryptic, but fair enough."

Before I can take a breath, he's stepped up beside me. Jordan digs in his pocket, pulling out a ring with a single key on it. I look up at him in confusion until he tucks my arm into his and walks me back to his motorcycle. Once we're beside it, he holds out a helmet toward me. "Remember, I'm driving."

I laugh at him like he's joking until I realize he's not. "Oh, I'm sorry, I agreed because I thought you meant you wanted to drive *my* car." I take one step back toward the safety of my nice, enclosed automobile.

"Nope. We're taking my bike and you're going to love it."

"But I have the directions to the law offices." I clamor for any excuse not to get on his deathmobile.

He lowers his brows, clearly recognizing my excuse for the lame attempt that it is. "I do know my way around Houston, Riley. Louisiana Street isn't exactly hard to find."

I try to think of another, more valid argument that doesn't just make me sound scared—and come up empty. Many law firms in Houston are located on Louisiana Street. Daddy's had been there since long before he went to jail. I haven't been by the office in a while, but Jordan's right, it isn't difficult to get there.

No matter how much I wish it were.

I glare at him as he steps closer, unlatching the strap on the helmet. He removes my dark sunglasses before pulling the helmet down over my head and securing it under my chin. The pressure on my bruised cheekbone makes me wince. I've covered it well using more makeup than usual for me, but the pain still lives beneath and nothing I do seems to be able to ease that part.

"What in the . . . ?" Jordan lifts the helmet gently from my head before putting his hands on the sides of my face and tilting my cheekbone toward the sunlight. His voice drops and I see something in his eyes that walks a fine line between fear and anger. "How did this happen?"

"It's nothing." I wave him off and try to step away, but he grabs my hand. Pulling it against his chest until I'm inches away and have no choice but to answer.

"It looks like someone hit you," he whispers softly, his eyes searching mine. "What happened?"

I groan. "It isn't a big deal—and she didn't punch me or anything. She just slapped me."

Jordan frowns. "Your mother?"

"Yes."

"Does she do that often?" Jordan watches me so close I can tell that he's looking for the lie.

"No," I answer him firmly. "This is the first time ever."

Jordan nods slowly. "Please call me if—"

I interrupt him. "It won't happen again." I sigh, grabbing the helmet. I try to pull it gently on by myself. Unfortunately, I can't seem to align it correctly and only end up hurting myself worse.

Jordan chuckles softly, but with my eyes blocked by the chin guard of the helmet, I can't even see him. His warm hands replace mine and he straightens, then gently pulls the helmet down into position.

"I take it you've never been on a motorcycle before?"

"No."

"You seem . . . nervous." He's putting it lightly and we both know it.

"It has all the power of a car without any of the protection." I gesture down to the metal monster next to us and sigh. "What did you expect me to do, pet it?"

"You're pretty cute when you're being difficult," Jordan says as he takes my keys out of my hands and sticks them in his pocket. His grin is so self-satisfied and his words such a weird combination of compliment and jab that it takes me a minute to come up with a response.

"You haven't even seen me be difficult yet." I decide I should probably just leave it at that.

"I'm pretty certain I have, but whatever it looks like, it wouldn't change my opinion." He speaks these words like they shouldn't surprise me, but they do, and as my cheeks flush red, I'm abruptly grateful for the helmet.

Once we're both seated on his black death trap, he turns the key and the bike roars to life. The engine revs so loud my ears ring. Jordan lets it idle, and the sound mellows to the point where I can mostly hear again. He reaches back and grabs my hands, bringing them tight around his waist. My nose fills with the strong, clean scent that is so Jordan. For whatever reason, the first reaction my body has is to melt against him.

"Riley, don't let go. No matter what," he says just loud enough for me to hear over the engine and my heart pounds in response as he lifts the kickstand and eases the motorcycle forward. Wrapping my arms tighter, I feel a little better knowing my instincts at the moment are from pure panic and not my confusing attraction to him. I force myself not to whimper as I close my eyes and lean my helmet against his back. Any playfulness from just minutes before is gone in the face of genuine fear. Motorcycles have always terrified me even from a distance. Being on one intensifies my distress more than I expect.

I cringe as he glides the bike smoothly out into the street, but when we reach the first corner and have to turn, the way it leans makes me squeeze myself even tighter against him. I feel him pat my hands as they grip the front of his shirt to reassure me. I try to relax because the tension is causing the muscles in my shoulders to ache.

Closing my eyes, I let the tension drain down from my neck, along my back and out through my legs. Once I release my muscles a bit, I'm shocked to feel the worries and fears that have tied me in knots for weeks start to melt away, bit by twitchy bit.

Wrapping one hand up and across Jordan's chest, I settle into the way our bodies shift together with the motorcycle's movements. We lean and curve as one, moving with the power and force of the rumbling engine below us.

It's still horrifying to think about how fragile and exposed we are, but in a way there is a certain desperate beauty to it. Right now, we live and die together. We're vulnerable together.

My hand curls into a fist and I look up as we start passing through shadow after shadow. We're getting close now, and the tall buildings of downtown Houston hide us from the sunlight. Between the shadows and the wind whipping past us, the temperature dips so fast that my skin prickles with an immediate chill. I snuggle closer to Jordan's warm back, for the first time not out of fear. I swear that being from Texas turns you cold-blooded sometimes. I don't handle temperature changes as well as a normal mammal should.

Jordan drives into a parking spot near the base of the tall blue building we're looking for, and I recognize another reason he prefers a motorcycle. Parking spots are definitely easier to come by in the city.

As he turns the key and cuts the engine, I'm blown away by the abrupt onslaught of city noises I couldn't hear before: cars honking, music from a café up the street, people talking. The deep rumble of the motorcycle had eclipsed all of that and more.

Pulling off his helmet, Jordan looks over his shoulder and smiles at me. "So? Did she grow on you?"

I make him wait for my answer. Taking a firm grip on the hand he holds out, I step off the bike and wait for my legs to stop trembling. Kind of a surprising side effect considering I've essentially been sitting still for the entire drive. When I fumble with the latch on my helmet, he reaches over and unclips it. Once I shake my hair down and free, I respond. "Better than expected. This beastly machine is a girl?"

"Don't you think?" He puts the kickstand down and stows our helmets in a container on one side of the seat.

I take a few steps up onto the sidewalk and examine the bike. It's all shiny chrome and black paint. He obviously takes care of it and it looks like Jordan to me now. He definitely falls under the masculine category. "I don't know." I shrug.

He gives me a pointed stare. "You'll hurt her feelings."

I laugh and rub my hand across the leather seat. "My apologies, very feminine bike. I didn't mean any offense."

"She forgives you." Jordan steps up next to me. "So, now what?"

I crane my neck up at the building and see nothing but mirrored windows looking back. That's one thing I don't like about skyscrapers. It feels like so many people can be looking down on you. You don't know who they are, and you can't even stare back.

"Now, we're going to talk to an old friend."

The elevator doors slide open and the tiny *ding* signaling our arrival feels absurdly loud in the quiet office. The reception area is empty. Curving letters glitter at me from behind the desk: *Law Offices of Smedley, Masters & Goldman.* The silver-and-black words feel strange and wrong now, like something is missing. Daddy is what's missing. It used to be Smedley, Masters, Beckett & Goldman.

It's early evening, but the lamp on the receptionist's desk is off for the night, and the reception area is empty.

Jordan grabs my elbow and jerks his thumb over his shoulder toward a lighted sign for the restrooms. "I'll be right back."

"Now?"

He gives me an exasperated look. "I didn't plan it."

I nod. "I'm going to look around to see if anyone else I know is still here tonight. Find me when you're done."

"Deal." He disappears quickly through the door.

I glance out the window in the reception area, marveling at how beautiful this city is from up here. What would our lives have been like if Daddy had never even been accused of this awful crime? How different would it be to visit him here in an expensive office in a beautiful downtown skyscraper—instead of in dark and dismal Polunsky? Daddy would have to deal with boardrooms and legal meetings instead of weekly visits and near-constant isolation.

That's a life we should've known, and every time I come here it feels like I'm peeking in on a parallel universe where everything in my life went right instead of horribly wrong.

I stick my head past the reception wall and take a look around.

Rows and rows of cubicles line the middle of the huge room. The outside walls are full of offices and shining boardrooms. The firm has obviously grown since I was last here. Mama told me it's more than double the size it was before Daddy went to prison. The firm had still been in this same spot, but back then they only had one quarter of the floor instead of the whole thing. Back then the cubicles didn't outnumber the offices twenty to one.

"Wow," I whisper to myself. There is movement in a room to my right, and Stacia pokes her head out.

"Riley?" She gives me a startled look before walking over for an awkward hug and then pulling me toward the room she'd been in before. It's a giant break room and she's making herself a coffee.

"What are you doing here, hon?" Her expression overflows with pity and I turn my gaze away, pretending I don't hate that look.

"I came to meet with Mr. Masters. We don't have long to do something before they're—they will—" I stop suddenly, realizing I've opened the door on my emotions too wide. I can't escape the thought that we are down to only seventeen days left—*seventeen*. I've always felt safe with the knowledge that Stacia truly believes Daddy is innocent and that she can be trusted to understand the pain I'm in. Still, the lump in my throat keeps me from speaking, and I silently curse myself and all my confused emotions.

Stacia pulls me in for another hug when she sees me break; this one is so tight it surprises me. "We're going to figure this out, Riley. We won't let them do that."

I hug her back and force myself to get a grip. "Do you really think you guys can do anything to help him?"

Stacia hesitates, her eyes damp. She truly seems to be hurting and it's nice to not feel alone in my pain. Then she squeezes my arm. "I think he's going to be—"

"Excuse me, ladies." A deep voice that sounds like pure warmth speaks from directly behind me, and I whirl around.

A smile steals across my face when I see Benjamin Masters standing in the doorway, but that's before I see his right hand bringing Jordan into the room behind him. The sleeves of Mr. Masters's expensive dress shirt are rolled up to the elbows, his vest is undone, and his tie hangs loosely around his neck.

"It seems I've found a . . . visitor," Mr. Masters states simply, but the hint of a frown on his face surprises me.

Jordan's eyes shift between me and the lawyer's hand on his arm. He seems like he's trying to ask me something. Maybe, *Should I run?*

I give a slight shake of my head.

"Mr. Masters, I didn't know you were still here," Stacia says, dropping her arm back to her side and looking from Jordan to the firm's partner in confusion.

"Yes." His eyes focus in on me, his eyebrows lifting as his gaze moves almost imperceptibly toward Jordan. "Well, here I am."

"I—uh—" Stacia begins, looking confused, but Masters interrupts her before she can get any further.

"I hate to interrupt your conversation, but would it be possible for me to speak to Miss Riley in my office, please?" He turns and guides Jordan back a few steps without waiting for her reply.

"Of course. Do you need me to call security?" All emotion is gone from her voice. She's switched straight over into business mode.

"Not necessary, but thank you." His voice comes from halfway up the hall now, and I exhale sharply. Mr. Masters definitely likes a bit of drama, but I'm happy to see he isn't going to jump the gun with this one.

With a quick wave and an apologetic glance to Stacia, I follow after them. Heading for the office of Benjamin Masters—brilliant lawyer, Skittles hoarder, and one of my favorite people in the world.

21

THEY ARE QUITE A BIT ahead of me, so by the time I stand outside the corner office with the words *Benjamin Masters—Partner* on the door, Jordan is sitting in a chair, and Masters stands with his back to him, staring out the window. Clearing my throat, I walk slowly through the open door.

Mr. Masters turns to face me without saying anything. Despite the deepening frown on his face, he opens his arms and I rush forward to give him a hug. He prefers to keep displays that make him seem "more human" out of sight of his employees. So I'm not surprised that he was less welcoming in front of Stacia. He says, "It's good to see you."

"You too," I say back, hugging him tight. And it is. It's always good to see Mr. Masters. He's the closest thing to a father figure I've had—outside of Polunsky. He always comes to the few school events I've been required to participate in, brings me very thoughtful presents on my birthday, and even took me out to celebrate when I got my driver's license.

He always says the exact same thing: "Your father can't be here yet, but I can. Thank you for letting me."

Mr. Masters doesn't release me as he whispers in my ear, "What kind of mischief have you gotten yourself into this time, Miss Riley?"

I whisper in response. "He's fine. He's with me."

Mr. Masters pulls back and searches my eyes, then his gaze moves to my cheek. He squints and grabs my chin before lifting it to the light and staring at the bruising that is barely visible there. He growls and it shocks me. I've never heard Mr. Masters make a sound like that. "If that young man did this . . ."

"He didn't," I respond immediately, pulling my chin from his grasp. When he just stares at me, I finally give him the truth in an effort to get Jordan off the hook. "It was Mama. We had a discussion . . . and we didn't see eye to eye on things."

Mr. Masters winces and shakes his head with closed eyes. "If this ever happens again, you come to me immediately. Understand?"

"I do."

He nods again before tossing a look over his shoulder and moving aside so I get a glimpse of Jordan sitting in one of the office chairs and eyeing Masters warily. "Do you even know who he is?"

I falter as I respond, "D-do you?"

"Of course," he scoffs, before walking back toward his desk and raising his voice to a normal level. "It's my business to know. I was very sorry to hear about what happened to your mother."

"Oh, thanks," Jordan mutters, shifting in his seat uncomfortably.

I hadn't expected Mr. Masters to know Jordan on sight, but I can't say I'm shocked by it. I take a seat in the chair beside Jordan, patting his hand as I pass since it seems he needs some reassurance. His normally olive skin has gone sickly gray.

Mr. Masters stands with his hands clasped loosely in front of him. I recognize the stance immediately: he looks like he does in a courtroom. Me bringing Jordan here has thrown him out of his element and so he's reacting in a way that makes him more comfortable. He's putting on his lawyer face.

We watch Mr. Masters stare out at the Houston skyline. It glitters back at him as the sun moves across the sky. It appears he's seduced by the view, but I know better. His mind is in here, noting the awkward shifting of Jordan in the seat beside me.

I've spent enough time with Masters and my father to understand men like them. Good lawyers are one part actor, one part confidant, and one part shark. Even more important to understanding them is to know that you can never predict when they might jump from one role to the next.

He doesn't trust Jordan, wants to protect me, and is trying to figure out why I brought him. It's a complicated dance he's trying to move gracefully through, while I just want to dive straight to the point. Just as I give up on waiting and open my mouth to speak, Mr. Masters jumps in and I know immediately that this had been the cue he'd been waiting for.

"You probably remember the first time we were introduced, but do you know when *I* first met *you*, Riley?"

"No, but you've known Daddy for as long as I can remember." I'm not sure where he's going with this. He could be about to drop something big on me, or he could be trying to make an impression on Jordan. So I keep my voice confident and my tone level—the way Daddy taught me to answer reporters when I was eight and the first one asked me what I thought of my "daddy being a filthy murderer."

He turns from the window and moves to lean against the desk directly in front of me. His smile is kind and warm, so I relax a bit.

"You're right, I have. Years before he went to jail, we were thick as the dew on Dixie. I met you on the day you were born." He folds his arms across his chest and leans back as though relishing the memory. It always strikes me as entertaining how much more often these kinds of sayings seem to come out in his language when he's in his lawyer mode. "David started with the firm just after your mama found out you were on your way into this world. He was the most terrified young father I'd ever seen."

No one has ever told me what life was like that long before the trial. And now, I don't dare speak for fear that he won't continue. My heart clenches up tight when he stops. Mama never likes to talk about it because she says focusing on what she lost would only make her sad all over again. Sometimes I wonder if she ever thinks about what *I* lost—about the fact that it wasn't *just* her.

I hope that if I don't say anything then maybe Mr. Masters will go on. My fingers grip the arms of the oversized leather chair, but I don't notice until the nail beds of both hands start to tingle from lack of circulation.

Mr. Masters chuckles. "You should have seen him. David looked like he was scared he might hurt you or your mama. Like you were delicate little flowers that he might break if he wasn't extremely careful."

The imagery is nice and I cling to it like a cozy blanket in my mind. Wrapping my thoughts up within it to hide from all the nightmare-inspired fears of my father as a murderer with blood coating his hands and rage spilling from his eyes.

"Now." Mr. Masters leans forward and the new glint in his eyes warns me before his words even come. "Can you explain to me why such a flower would bring the son of the man who put her father in prison into my office?"

"Why does who my father is matter?" Jordan jumps in before I can respond.

Mr. Masters crosses his arms over his chest and leans back, turning his eyes to Jordan. "How could it not? Everything you're invested in is everything we've spent over a decade fighting against. Isn't it a son's duty to defend the honor of his father's position?"

"Yes. Especially when there is every chance that he was right." Jordan glances my way and I give him a quick shake of my head.

This is a game from Mr. Masters, and I'm not afraid to play it . . . if I can just get Jordan to be quiet and let me. He leans back in his chair, eyeing my lawyer friend warily.

Taking a breath, I try to remember more tips Daddy taught me so long ago. Panicking is bad, but letting your opponent know you are panicking is infinitely worse. Convincing your opponent you have the upper hand is the *only* upper hand to be had in many situations. Just as I'm about to open my mouth to respond, Jordan speaks up again, beating me to it, and I sigh in exasperation.

"We need details from her father's case. Shouldn't she have access to his file?" Jordan's words spill out over one another and he keeps looking at me and nodding like somehow if we both nod enough then Mr. Masters will be forced to agree with us. He both sounds *and* looks panicked—perfect.

"As a minor she has no right to that file without signed parental consent. Does she have that?" Mr. Masters doesn't even wait a beat before pouncing. He places the palms of his hands on the desk to either side of him. His stance is totally relaxed, his shrewd gaze anything but. Inclining his head only a few inches forward, he still manages to make Jordan swallow hard and look away when he asks softly, "And I don't believe we've been introduced—not formally, anyway."

"Jordan Vega, meet Benjamin Masters," I say before Jordan can dig himself any deeper. "Jordan likes spending time at the mall, building race car tracks with his little brother, and getting in over his head while trying to help people he shouldn't. Mr. Masters likes being sneaky, playing mind games, and can really be helpful if we *give him a chance.*"

Jordan blinks at me, then back at Mr. Masters, but this time he keeps his mouth shut.

Masters's grin turns a little wolfish and he chuckles before extending his hand down to Jordan. "Charmed, I'm sure."

As Jordan reluctantly shakes it, I decide it's time to cut straight to the point. I stare directly at Mr. Masters. "I need your help. I have to find the truth before it's too late. I know that what I do may not change a thing, but whatever happens, I *need* to find out for myself."

He watches me for what feels like forever and I try not to blink. Finally, he nods. "Okay. But will you explain why someone who claims not to trust cops is out spending time with the son of Chief Vega?"

"He's trying to help me," I respond. When he sees me glance his way, Jordan gives me half a smile that I'm sure he means to be reassuring, but it only makes me feel guilty for even letting him get into this mess with me.

Mr. Masters straightens and walks around behind his desk, taking a seat. He begins moving papers off his desk and into different piles. One of the folders I see is clearly marked with the name *DAVID BECKETT*. I slide forward in my chair, wanting to see more. A big red sticker is stuck to the front of the file—it holds the perfect word to describe Daddy's current situation: *PRESSING*.

Once his desk is relatively sorted, Masters leans forward. "I, of course, can't let you take it, but what do you want to know?"

I reply with the first question that comes to mind. "What was Daddy like before he went to prison?"

"David was a different man back then . . . ," Mr. Masters starts.

I get an instant chill at what those words could mean, but shake it off as Mr. Masters continues. "He was relaxed, much happier."

"Did you like working with him?"

"Yes." He hesitates, then speaks carefully. "He was always a hard worker, very devoted to his clients."

"Only telling me the good things won't help me; you know that." I raise one eyebrow. Jordan sits forward in his seat beside me, now engrossed in this question-and-answer session.

"No one's perfect, Riley," Mr. Masters responds, his voice softer now. "I assume you know about Hillary Vanderstaff? And how he always spent a bit more time with female clients and co-workers than men?"

"Hillary Vanderstaff?" I remember the name, but little else. "Isn't she one of the victims?"

"Oh . . ." Mr. Masters's face falls and he closes his eyes slowly. "Maybe this is something you should ask your parents about."

"If my parents were willing to tell me, I'd already know." I groan as I wait for him to go on.

"She was one of the victims—and a previous client of your father's. She is how they tied him to the victims."

A sudden flash of clarity hits me. "Right, she was the one they falsely accused him of having an affair with. Was she his client at the time of the murder?"

"No, he represented her in a case almost one year before." Masters is very focused on his desk. He straightens Daddy's file before looking up.

"A year? And *that's* all the link they had?" My voice is incredulous. That tie-in is tenuous at best.

He sighs and his shoulders droop forward. It strikes me that for the first time since I've known him, Masters doesn't seem to be putting on a show. "I don't want to be the one to tell you this."

My heart, my lungs, and my stomach all seem to lock up in response. I'm terrified of what he's going to say next, and it must show in my face because I feel Jordan's eyes on me.

In the silence I press my teeth together so hard that it hurts, afraid that I can't trust myself to speak. Scared that if I open my mouth, my words may betray me by telling him the absolute truth that is burning in my soul—that maybe deep down I truly *don't* want to know. If I open my mouth, I might beg him to please tell me another sweet lie instead of the bitter truth so that I can continue to live in oblivion.

Truth is for the brave, and I'm not sure I fall into that category anymore.

"The affair was real. Your father was cheating on your mother with Hillary." His eyes fill with pity. My ears seem to ring with his last word. I sit perfectly still, gripping the chair arms tight. I close my eyes and try to understand how the lies of everyone I ever trusted had come back to bite me again.

22

"THEY LIED. THEY LIED TO ME," I repeat, this time just trying to be certain that I heard him right. Then I turn on Mr. Masters. *"You* lied to me."

When Mr. Masters doesn't say any more, I jump up from my chair and hold my hand out for the file. The lying isn't the worst thing that happened here. If what he's saying is true, then Daddy betrayed our family.

Mr. Masters just looks at me. He doesn't move. "Miss R—"

I rip the file out of his hand. My fingers have gone so cold that I almost drop it. My ears ring strangely loudly and I almost wonder if other people can hear them. What Masters is saying doesn't make any sense. Not Daddy. He wouldn't do something like this to us . . . would he?

No. If I'm supposed to believe, I have to see proof of it for myself.

As I open the folder on the desk and my fingers move, my body starts functioning at a more normal rhythm again. "Why this Hillary person?"

"Hillary Vanderstaff." Mr. Masters's voice is barely a whisper as

I flip through, looking for a victim profile sheet that bears her name. "I don't know why. She was very beautiful."

Jordan turns his eyes on Mr. Masters, his expression reflecting a darkness that surprises me. "You've been lying about him cheating for over a decade. Why would you cover for him like that?"

"Her father asked me to stick to his story long ago. I assumed that Amy had agreed it was the best choice. It wasn't my business to decide otherwise. Telling Riley the truth now is not a choice I make lightly." Mr. Masters draws himself up to his full height and I can hear a hint of the courtroom theatrics come back into his tone. "She says she wants the truth. In order to have any chance at finding it, she needs all the facts."

I finally locate the correct grouping of papers and draw them out. The picture attached is different from the one I'd seen online. She's beautiful here, smiling and vibrant. Farther down the sheet, I find a paragraph outlining the evidence of their affair, and my heart sinks. They've listed out dates, times, and lengths of many phone calls; receipts of purchase; and a catalog of various gifts. And at the very bottom, it lists twenty-two letters between them and the words *copies attached*.

Taking a deep, shaky breath, I flip to the attached papers. The first is written in flowery feminine writing and I deliberately don't read a word. When I move on to the next one, one glance tells me everything I need to know. I don't want to actually read anything my father sent to his mistress. My stomach sinks and I close the file. There is no doubt. That is Daddy's handwriting. I'd know that better than anyone.

Apparently, I wasn't the first girl he'd written letters to.

Handing the file back to Mr. Masters, I fight to keep my voice steady. "How can this possibly help Daddy now?"

It's clear from the look in Masters's eyes that he's having second thoughts about telling me. He looks like he wishes he could make this all better, but he can't.

He massages his forehead with his fingers. "I've been wondering for a long time if this affair could give us proof of innocence instead of proof of guilt. Hillary was the final victim back then. If they were together during either of the other murders, maybe we can find some kind of documentation to provide him with an alibi."

I frown and walk back over to slump down in my old seat. "I can't believe that if she'd been with him that he wouldn't have mentioned this sooner. We're talking about his life here."

"Your father's family life was not—healthy—when he was growing up. He cares very deeply about protecting this family ideal that he believes you have, maybe more so than any of us know. When I found out about the affair—" Mr. Masters clears his throat, but I can see a flash of fear in his eyes before he continues. "Admitting to the affair himself during the trial was just something he was unwilling to do."

"He never admitted it?" My voice is so soft I see both Jordan and Mr. Masters lean forward to hear it.

Mr. Masters sighs, looking both smaller and infinitely sad. My stomach roils in fear of hearing any more things I'm not prepared for tonight. "You've seen the file. The prosecution had compelling evidence that your father had an affair, and not a short-lived one. They didn't need David to admit anything."

Daddy always seemed so devoted, so loyal. Up until this moment, if I'd been forced to pick which parent would eventually cheat on the other, I would've chosen Mama without hesitation. It's hard to accept the idea that this situation has flipped on me completely.

Mr. Masters walks around the desk, pulling a chair up next to mine and holding my now frigid hand in both of his. "But unfortunately, men who cheat aren't an unheard of breed, and most men who've cheated don't suddenly become murderers. This fact ties him to one victim, but as far as they could find, he didn't know the others. There was no evidence left on the victims and no way to irrefutably tie him to being at any of the crime scenes."

"But he had no alibi . . ." I whisper in response.

"True." Mr. Masters grinds his teeth together. "And they used that to their fullest advantage."

A new thought occurs to me and I can't decide whether to be protective of Mama or angry at her. "I assume Mama knows the truth?"

Mr. Masters gives me a troubled look. "You know your mother, Miss Riley. She's tough to read. She never talked about it. She deliberately avoided the trial whenever she knew they were going to discuss it. I even saw her bring a book out if she was there and it unexpectedly came up."

"Wait. What do you mean?" I shake my head in confusion. "She has to know, right? Even if she pretends she doesn't, she *has* to know the truth."

He shrugs. "Somewhere inside she must, but denial is a powerful beast when used by the right master. And God knows your mama has become proficient at looking the other way over the years."

I'm silent in response. There is nothing to say. This conversation with Mr. Masters has confirmed my fear that both of my parents are complete strangers to me now—possibly unstable and dangerous ones at that.

"What have you heard about this newest murder?" Jordan speaks up from beside me. When I glance over at him, the clear worry in his eyes tells me that now I'm the one whose skin is extremely pale.

"I'd imagine, while this case is ongoing, your father would have much more information on it than I do," Mr. Masters responds with a sharp edge. "But since I'm assuming that he isn't sharing that information with you, I will tell you that I heard from an insider about a breakthrough today."

I whip my head up. "Breakthrough?"

"With the original victims, there was a detail deliberately kept out of all media coverage. And it wasn't mentioned much at the trial because it didn't help the state's case. There were souvenirs taken from each victim." The voice that has comforted me for much of my life suddenly sounds sinister with those words.

I shudder, asking reluctantly, "Souvenirs?"

"Yes, a trophy of sorts. But nothing too terrifying, my dear." Mr. Masters pats the back of my hand. "It was always a piece of jewelry. With Hillary it was a necklace, with Sarah Casey a ring, and with Maren Jameson it was a watch."

"Oh," I say. This is news to me. I'm certain I've never heard this detail.

"I brought it up during trial because it was a big flaw in the state's case that they were never able to find the trophies." Mr.

Masters speaks louder and I can hear the puzzle and intrigue in this case drawing him in like a moth to the flame. "If David was the murderer, how come they never found them? The state presented witnesses who claimed he seemed nervous and skittish the last couple of days before Vega showed up with his warrant. They said that he knew they were closing in, and he got rid of the trophies."

I see Jordan nodding slowly out of the corner of my eye and send him a withering glare.

"What?" he asks, but his expression looks guilty, and he mutters after I turn away, "It does make a certain amount of sense . . ."

I ignore him, waiting for Mr. Masters to go on. "He's right. It was a worthy argument—until now."

My eyes widen, and Mr. Masters answers my unspoken question before I even have a chance to ask it. "The newest victim also had a souvenir taken, a pair of diamond earrings."

I suck in a quick breath. "And since they never revealed that information to the public . . ."

"It's not likely to be a copycat," Jordan whispers softly. This has been a lot of information to process and my mind is still whirling from it, but I feel a distinctly different sensation from earlier today rising in my chest.

I feel hope.

Mr. Masters pats my shoulder before climbing to his feet. Walking around his desk, he slips Daddy's file into his briefcase. He hooks his index finger under the suit coat and lifts it off of his chair, draping it across the expensive leather case.

Turning to face us, he places both hands palms down on the desk with a soft thump. "This is what's going to happen. I'll answer all of your questions, Riley. Any question you have, anytime. And I'll keep you in the loop on anything new I uncover in my research to prepare for any further appeals on your daddy's case."

"You will?" I move forward to the edge of my seat, barely daring to hope that someone is finally willing to tell me everything.

"Yes. You aren't a kid anymore, unfortunately." Mr. Masters gives me a sad glance and continues, "But I have a condition. You come to me *first* with your questions. And you talk to *me* before doing anything stupid. No more sneaking around crime scenes or anything remotely like that. Do we have a deal?"

I nod and get to my feet, walking over to give him a hug. "Thank you."

"This isn't going to be easy, but I think you're strong enough to handle it. Whatever happens, you deserve the chance to find your own truth." Mr. Masters turns his gaze fully on me and a genuine smile curves up one corner of his mouth. "God knows it can be hard enough to find that in the courtroom sometimes."

"I'd also like you to promise me something," Mr. Masters continues, giving me a pointed look. "You need to come stay with me for a few days if you and your mama have any more *discussions*. I'm certain your daddy would stop that immediately if he were there to watch out for you. I owe you both that much."

"We won't—" I feel my face redden and slowly raise my hand to my bruised cheek. "It's never happened before."

Jordan sends me the same concerned glance from earlier, and I simply nod. "But okay, I can agree to that."

"Good." Mr. Masters looks from me to Jordan and I have a hard time reading his expression. "And keep an eye on that one."

I lean against the arm of my chair and face Jordan, chuckling at his offended look. "I will."

Mr. Masters puts an arm around my shoulders and walks me out with Jordan in my wake. Back down in the lobby, Mr. Masters gives me a quick squeeze before shaking Jordan's hand. He whispers something into Jordan's ear before winking at me and then walking briskly away.

As we make our way through the now rapidly dimming streets of downtown Houston, I notice that Jordan seems deep in his own thoughts. I can't complain, because I am, too. Mr. Masters has an ability to throw people off balance, which is part of what makes him such an amazing lawyer.

"Are you still happy you decided to come with me?" I ask, surprised at how nervous I feel about asking.

"Of course. Why would you ask that?"

He watches me closely as I answer. "I don't know. It must be uncomfortable for you when people treat you less like you're you . . . and well . . . more like you're me."

He frowns. "What does that mean?"

"He acted like you weren't trustworthy simply because of who your dad is."

Jordan's expression turns playful and he looks me straight in the eye. "Maybe I can win him over. It seems like only a little more than a day ago that you treated me the exact same way."

I laugh. "Probably was."

Jordan keeps walking, seeming content to go back to whatever he was thinking about. I can't keep myself from asking anymore. "What did he say to you in the lobby?"

The thoughtful look returns as he answers. "He said if we continue like this, one of us is going to wind up getting hurt—and that it better not be you."

"Okay, that's awkward." I shake my head, trying not to feel embarrassed by the assumptions Mr. Masters obviously made. "He doesn't know what he's talking about, I'm sorry."

Instead of accepting my words like I expect, Jordan stops walking and stares at me before moving slowly closer. I freeze in place as his warm fingers touch lightly across my bruised cheek. My whole body flushes with a sudden heat.

His eyes meet mine and my heart races at all the emotion I find there. "What if he's right?"

Then Jordan pulls me against his chest and holds me tight. It takes me a moment, but I hug him back. I feel the worry coming from him and wonder if he finally understands that he's in over his head in this quest to help me.

Pushing that thought aside, I allow myself to enjoy him while he's still here and melt closer into his arms. I've never felt so safe.

Then I realize that I may be out of my depth with Jordan, too—but in a completely different way.

23

"FIRST STEP: ICE CREAM," I say, changing the subject to one I feel more equipped to deal with. I pull myself gently out of his arms and lead Jordan down Louisiana Street toward a Cloud 10 vendor on the corner as the sun sets on the horizon. The shining buildings around us glint red in the light of the dying day. Texas can be a beautiful place, and Houston is no different. It's gorgeous, but below that lurks a subtle, eerie tone for me that will forever be unsettling. My past here is too broken to see the beauty without any tinge of pain.

I order myself a scoop of Lavender Milk Chocolate as everything we learned in Mr. Masters's office swirls around in my head.

"Sour Cream with Banana Jam, please." Jordan orders without consulting the menu on the cart in front of us.

I grab my purse, but before I can even reach inside, he's pulled cash out of nowhere and is paying.

"Wait, you didn't need to—"

Jordan grins and takes both of the desserts from the vendor. "I'm not saying this is a date or anything. What's happening here is me holding your delicious treat hostage until you tell me what you're thinking." He gives me a sly smile and an attempt at an evil laugh before tucking my dessert behind his back.

I can't help but return his grin as I follow him to a nearby bench and we sit down. "It's very hard to take you seriously as a Bond villain when the leverage you're holding is ice cream."

"A good villain works with what he's got."

"Well, as long as we're agreed that this isn't a date . . ." I grab for my ice cream and he lifts it out of my reach.

"Oh, when I take you on a date, you'll definitely know it." There's no way for me to mistake his meaning this time, although I see a hint of nervousness deep in his eyes.

I raise my eyebrows, both incredulous at his confidence and a little surprised he would just assume I would go. When my speeding heartbeat pretty much declares my excitement about the idea of an official date, I tell it in my head to shut up. "*When*, huh? That's pretty confident of you."

"Yes. When." He gives me a firm nod like there is absolutely no room for arguing this point. Then he changes back to the original subject. "For now, though, information first, dessert later."

"I don't know. Everything he said . . . it's a lot to digest in a short time." I deliberately don't look at Jordan. In all honesty, I don't have a clue how to feel. I haven't had time to really think it through yet.

To his credit, Jordan doesn't look like he buys that as an actual answer for a second, but he does hand over my promised dessert and doesn't pressure me further. When his eyes meet mine again, there is more concern than playfulness there. "Fine, just answer this then. Are you okay?"

"I think so. We're talking about something that happened when I was six—and then everyone has lied to me about it ever since—but it still makes me see everything differently." A fresh wash of disappointment comes over me, and I take a bite of my ice cream, which tastes so amazing it actually does make me feel a little better. Cloud 10 may be my favorite thing about Texas. Still, I don't feel ready to look at Jordan right now, so I keep my eyes on the sidewalk between my violet sneakers.

"I can't imagine that it wouldn't," he says simply, taking a bite of his own ice cream but keeping his eyes on me.

I sigh and say the thought that bubbles in the back of my mind constantly. "We're down to seventeen days now, Jordan."

"I know." He responds quietly before surprising me by slipping one arm around my shoulders and squeezing me lightly against his side. It only lasts for a minute, but somehow just having him here helps me find a piece of hope to cling to.

I clasp the cup of ice cream tight in my hands, my fingers cold even in the warm evening air. "Thank you for coming."

"I just want to be sure that you *really* want the answers you're looking for. No one would blame you for preferring not to know, considering the time you have left with your father." He turns his gaze from the office buildings around us down to me. "I already told you, Riley. I am all in with you on this. No matter what."

"Okay then. I don't just want the answers. I *need* them. There's no turning back now." I swallow my nerves along with another spoonful of ice cream. "So I guess we're in this together."

The sun sinks below the faraway horizon and the streetlamps come to life, casting us in an eerie glow. I can't tell if it's because of the creepy lighting or because of the task we're facing, but Jordan's smile has taken on a grim aspect when I meet his eyes again.

Even in this unsettling atmosphere, his response reassures me the way it seems only Jordan can. "I wouldn't have it any other way."

I spend much of Tuesday alone. Looking through my notes and Daddy's old letters, I keep trying to wrap my head around the idea that he could possibly still be innocent of the murders . . . but guilty of betraying our family all the same. Cheating may not carry a prison sentence with it, but it's still something that's difficult to forgive. It's a decision he made that could've broken our family. I don't know how he could feel like the best answer was to convince everyone I trusted to lie to me about it. And I'm starting to feel like I don't know him at all.

Some of the things Mama said during our fight suddenly make more sense, but I'm still furious at her for taking part in Daddy's lies. We'll have to have a long talk the next time I see her. I'll still be going to visit Daddy on Friday, of course, even if I have to keep it from Mama, but we're both dealing with a lot right now, and I need to handle all of this chaos better if we are going to have even the slightest chance to heal our family again.

I don't see Mama all day, and although she responds to my texts, my calls go straight to voice mail.

I had clung tight to Jordan the entire way home Monday night. The motorcycle is definitely growing on me. And as much as I'd like to deny it, anything that requires me to get *that* close to Jordan without any need for excuse or explanation seems like something I could get on board with.

When he dropped me off at my car, Jordan opened my door, but before I could climb in, he pulled me against him for an abrupt, tight hug. He kissed my forehead and whispered, "Everything's going to work out, Riley. I promise."

Then he'd climbed onto his black bike and disappeared into the night.

I don't know how he feels confident enough to make a promise like that, but it helps me even if we know it might be a lie.

We made plans to see each other on Thursday, but I feel pathetic that I miss him already by Wednesday morning. We've texted a little, but he's taking Matthew to visit their abuela today, so I know I won't hear from him again until tomorrow.

I try not to think more about it as I make myself a bowl of fresh fruit. When my phone rings and the caller ID shows Mr. Masters's number, I pick up immediately.

"Hello."

"Hi, Miss Riley." His slow drawl begins, as always, with the pleasantries. "How are you doing on this beautiful day?"

"I'm okay." My nerves make me blurt out exactly what is on my mind. "Do you have any updates on the case?"

"No, I'm afraid not." His voice becomes a bit harsher and I'm instantly on edge. "But there is something I need to speak with you about."

"Oh . . . okay. What is it?" I sit down at the table with my fruit bowl but don't eat anything yet.

"Your mama told me about your visit with your father after the hearing. She told me what he said." His tone bites at me. My body feels chilled all over.

I sigh, willing him to understand. "Then you also need to know that he said later that it was a lie. He said he'd lost hope and wanted us to be free to move on . . . that's all."

"Hush. No need to get defensive." He clears his throat and I hear pain in his voice for the first time. "I promise not to give up on him. Not until someone proves to me, without a doubt, that he's guilty. And if that hasn't happened in nearly twelve years, I don't expect it to happen now."

I release a shaky breath of relief. "Thank you."

He pauses briefly before continuing. "Don't thank me yet. I want you to do something for me now."

"What's that?" I stir a red grape around in my bowl as I listen.

"Consider not visiting this week." These words come lightning fast, like he's not entirely committed to saying them and he needs to get this out now or never.

I don't answer. I don't know what to say. I drop my spoon with a clatter and roll my eyes. "What did she do to convince you to take her side?"

Complete silence stretches out on the other end for long enough that I look at my phone to be certain we weren't disconnected. Then Mr. Masters's voice cuts through the quiet like a red-hot sword. "She did nothing, young lady. You aren't the only one struggling at the moment. You know better than to believe that. Luck has bitten your family too many times over the last decade and you need to start sticking together."

He's never spoken to me quite like that before and it shocks me. I whisper back quietly, "You're right. I'm sorry."

"Very well then," he replies, much gentler this time. "Sometimes distance gives us perspective. My advice is what it is. Take it or leave it. I'm just working on turning that luck around for all of you."

"I promise to think about it." I swallow hard, already knowing that my words are a lie. It isn't that I don't trust Mr. Masters to try to do what he says. It's simply one single word in his plea that made up my mind for me—the word *luck*. Daddy has never had luck go his way.

Chance is not our friend. And karma is our enemy.

I hate all the terms people use to explain some hidden force in the universe that's intended to balance the scales in favor of the good or the righteous. According to everything we've been given so far, our family doesn't deserve any balance. We don't deserve any help.

So screw all of them. Screw chance, fate, karma, luck, providence, and everything in between. With only fifteen days left, I'm certainly not waiting around for them to show up now.

"Actually, instead of me not going"—I talk faster, as it sounds like he's getting ready to end the call—"what if we went together?"

His end of the line is silent for a few seconds before he responds, but I can hear the curiosity in his voice. "What exactly do you have in mind?"

24

EVERYTHING ABOUT THIS VISIT to Polunsky feels strange. It isn't like I've never been for a visit when Mr. Masters was also there, but it's been a while. It's a Wednesday, and we are sitting here waiting for Daddy. I'm not sure I've ever been to Polunsky on a Wednesday. Plus, we aren't in our normal visitation room. This room is saved for privileged discussions between lawyer and client. There is no physical contact here, but we will have more privacy. The room is longer, not much wider. There are still the same dingy white cinder-block walls. I chew on my nail and ask myself again if bringing Mr. Masters and Daddy together is a good idea.

The best I can hope for is that watching the two of them might give me new information or insight into the case that I haven't had before. And at worst, I still plan to visit Daddy on Friday, so I get to sneak in a bonus visit. Which is not normally allowed, but since I'm coming in with Daddy's lawyer during his regularly scheduled visit, and Warden Zonnberg likes me, they're going to let me get away with it.

I nudge Mr. Masters lightly with my elbow as he flips through a couple of papers in his file. "I don't think I'm going to bring up his—" I choke on the word *affair*. I'm still processing this new information and I don't feel like I'm ready to hear Daddy defend himself in this arena yet. Plus, I don't want Mr. Masters to be punished for telling me. The last thing I want is to let my emotions get the best of me and storm out again. Not when he has so little time left.

"Indiscretion?" Mr. Masters fills in a gentler word on my behalf and then reaches one arm around my shoulders to give me a quick hug. "This is your show, Miss Riley. And that's your business when you want to bring that up. I just hope this accomplishes your goal."

"Me too. I guess I mostly just want to watch the way he interacts with you. See if he's telling you the same things he's telling me." I don't know exactly what I hope to learn from this, but I'm here now, so I might as well see it through. I hug Mr. Masters back and the guard opens the door and leads Daddy in.

Daddy doesn't look surprised to see me, and there is something wary in his eyes as he watches me step away from Mr. Masters and take my seat. The guard secures him to the table and reminds me that touching isn't allowed in this room. Emotions fight within me as I search his face. As always, part of me feels happier just to be near him, but now that part is bombarded with so many other conflicting feelings. Worry because he doesn't look like he's sleeping well. Dread because the countdown to his impending execution is always present in the back of my mind. And a significant amount of anger at knowing this man cheated on Mama, betrayed our family, and then lied about it.

Daddy waits until the guard walks out and closes the door before giving us a somewhat cautious smile. "We haven't done this in a while."

Mr. Masters looks up from the papers and nods. "Riley wanted an extra visit, and I accommodated her."

The concern on Daddy's face fades away at that. "Oh, I'm glad to hear that. Thank you for letting her come with you."

Mr. Masters nods without looking up. He must've found whatever he was looking for in his file because he closes it and sits back in his chair. He smiles, but it doesn't quite reach his eyes. "Things are coming along well with the investigation into the other case. I would even go so far as to call it hopeful."

Daddy's expression has gone serious and he's staring so hard at his former law partner that I wonder if he's forgotten that I'm here.

"That's good. Any word on the new evidence?"

"I spoke with Chief Vega yesterday—" Mr. Masters begins.

"What did he say?" Daddy is so eager he cuts him off while I'm sitting here thinking about how bizarre my world has become. It's so strange to hear them talking about Jordan's father.

"He said that they don't have evidence that specifically points to this being a copycat case—at least not yet." Mr. Masters leans in as Daddy releases a big puff of air and his smile returns.

"I must caution you though, David. Don't get your hopes up until we know for certain where the investigation will lead." Mr. Masters sits back and crosses his arms over his chest. "You are too good a lawyer to fall into a trap like that."

"I know. You're right." Daddy's smile turns wry and he winks at me. "But come on, Ben, relax a little. It seems like something drastic would have to happen to change anything at this point."

I find myself smiling back at Daddy for a moment before I

remember all the things I *haven't* yet confronted him about, and it slides off my face.

"Speaking of which." Mr. Masters's tone takes on an icy edge, and he inches forward like he's about to pounce. "I understand you told Riley a different story two visits ago."

The grin drops from Daddy's face like a dead weight and he casts a hard glance at me. My stomach turns sour and I can actually feel all my blood rushing to my head. I turn on Mr. Masters, my mouth half open because I want to yell at him or tell him to stop, but I'm so shocked that no words come out. Mr. Masters throws me a split-second apologetic glance before moving his full attention back on my father.

I watch him and realize he's gone into full lawyer mode. This is a standoff—and Mr. Masters is trying to get answers for me in the only way he knows how. He's putting Daddy on the stand right here in this visitation room. Some of my outrage fades, but I still wish he'd discussed this with me first.

"I'm not sure what she told you . . ." Daddy's words are carefully chosen, his voice soft.

"Assume she told me everything," Mr. Masters replies.

"When did she tell you?" Daddy seems to be trying to figure out where to start, but Masters doesn't allow him to get comfortable.

"That isn't your concern here," Mr. Masters says, actually waving a hand to the side, dismissing Daddy's words like an annoying fly.

"She's *my* daughter. Everything about her *is* my concern." Daddy's voice hovers somewhere between anger and pleading. He is losing his composure and I can see it. He feels threatened and cornered. Isn't this what I wanted? Still, I feel less sure seeing this look on his face.

"You told her that you were guilty. That you had killed those women." Mr. Masters doesn't seem to know how to relent, and he only pushes harder. "I assume you're going to say now that this wasn't true."

The color is slowly draining from Daddy's face. His voice is soft and his eyes turn to me. "It isn't true. I promise it isn't."

Mr. Masters raises his voice now, drawing Daddy's attention back on him. "Then *why* would an innocent man say something like that to his only daughter? Why would you want Riley to believe you were a murderer when you were executed?"

Daddy opens his mouth to respond, but his eyes are still glued to me. Begging me to believe him. I'm torn and so I just freeze. I do nothing.

"Because I was trying to set her free." Daddy scowls at Masters now. His voice is a low growl. "Isn't that what you've wanted me to do with my family for a long time? Let them go? You've already tried to take my place with my daughter."

Mr. Masters takes a quick, surprised breath, and when I shift to face him, he clears his throat, ignoring Daddy's question. "How would Riley believing her father is a serial killer set her free?"

Then Daddy's tough façade crumples, pain showing clearly on his face. "Even if she thinks I'm the most horrible monster to ever live, at least she wouldn't be stuck here in Texas fighting an unwinnable fight. Riley has been stationary for her whole life. She's had no father, no good friends, and she's trapped in a state where everyone despises her because of the crime they already decided that I committed a dozen years ago."

The room is silent now and all I can hear are Daddy's ragged breaths. When he looks up, his eyes go straight to me. "I hoped that finally pretending to be the monster everyone has decided I am would let her move on and escape this place. If it could, that would be worth anything to me . . . even if it meant destroying myself in her eyes."

My throat closes up and I have to force myself not to cry. Instead, this time, I will save him.

"No more," I finally say, my words quiet but firm.

"I'm done," Mr. Masters says beside me. I'm surprised when the look on his face seems pleased. "Sorry, David. If what you said to Riley somehow gets out, I need to know you can handle being questioned on the stand about it."

Daddy closes his eyes and regains his composure before nodding. "Of course, I understand." He's not looking at me and the tension in the air has diminished, but it definitely isn't gone.

"I'm sorry this is so hard, Daddy." It's all I can think of to say, the only thing I can say to him right now with perfect honesty. There may always be lingering doubts in my mind when it comes to believing anything he says. There are still many things that remain unsaid between us, but for right now, I just want to help him somehow.

I reach my hand across and place it palm down on the table, but he doesn't take it. His hands are chained below, so he couldn't even if he wanted to, and I know he doesn't want either of us to get in trouble for breaking the visitation rules. Still, the look he gives me tells me he loves me and he's sorry for everything we've both been through.

For today, that is enough.

25

JORDAN'S FATHER IS DOING some paperwork from home on Thursday, and I have no clue what Mama's schedule is like these days, so Jordan and I meet up at the library closest to my house.

We sit at the table in the back corner of the history section, staring at a picture on my laptop of a lovely blond woman. Images flash through my mind again of the nightmare I had over a week ago featuring Mama as the victim. I swallow hard. I'm relieved to be certain that no matter what Daddy may or may not have done in the past, he did *not* murder Valynne Kemp. Someone must've snuck closer to the crime scene than the police usually allow or maybe the person who found her body took it. It's a close-up full-body shot of the way they found her at the crime scene. It was posted on a social media site. We found it by searching under her name; this one wasn't attached to any news article.

The way her body is posed. Exactly like the pictures of others I'd gotten a glimpse of at Daddy's trial. I feel a chill seep down through my body to the bottoms of my feet. She looks so outwardly peaceful, but if you peel back the layers and look closer, there is so much destruction beneath the calm surface. According to the news articles we'd read so far, the damage done to Valynne's body was nearly identical to that on the earlier victims of the East End Killer.

Everything appears serene in the picture, everything but the dark collar of bruising on her neck. Nothing appears to be out of place. Her hands are folded neatly over her stomach. The picture makes it look like being strangled was the only out of the ordinary thing that had happened in Valynne's otherwise very normal day. Even her hair spreads out softly around her head, a shimmering blond background that makes the angry bruises on her pale neck stand out in even starker contrast.

I remember vividly from the trial, after they showed a similar picture, the prosecution went through image after image. Each was filled with pictures of bruises, cuts, and burns on the skin. They're completely hidden by the clothing in the first photograph. Those women were beaten and tortured extensively—all before they'd been strangled.

The first time they went over what happened to the victims at trial, Mama hadn't been prepared with the headphones and coloring book she always brought with her later. She had made me cover my eyes, but the prosecutor explained it in far more detail than my young mind needed. I still remember the X-rays. I'd been too young to understand how to read them, but the prosecution described the many broken bones. He said most were fresh breaks from the hours before their deaths. I remember peeking between my fingers at one particularly gruesome shot of a rib broken in two places.

My mind gets stuck on thoughts of what horrific pain that woman would've been in. How terrifying it must've been. Had she been relieved when the killer finally strangled her? At what point does death change from something you fear into something you wish for? After the fifth broken bone? The tenth? After you can't take a breath without absolute agony?

My fingers start to tremble before me. The motion snaps me out of it and I blink. When I raise my eyes, I find Jordan watching me, his jaw tense.

"Sorry," I say softly, and my voice sounds as emotionally drained as I feel. I'd never believed it could be *this* hard to look at the information and actually try to think about how the details could indicate Daddy's guilt. I don't know what I expected, but at the moment everything that I normally rely on for strength feels mangled, raw, and useless. Like someone ran my heart through a meat grinder and then shoved it back into my chest.

"You don't have to be sorry, Riley." Jordan puts one warm hand over mine, rubbing his thumb across my knuckles. "You're tougher than I've seen anyone give you credit for. You are strong enough to handle looking at all of this and truly consider whether you think your own father could've done it. Don't *ever* feel like you're weak."

I stare at him, a little stunned by his words. I've always felt like the people around me think I'm weak. Is this really what Jordan sees in me?

"So, you've spent twenty minutes reading through all the details we could find on Valynne, and I looked at Hillary Vanderstaff." He goes straight back to work before I have a chance to say thank you, to respond, to hug him for seeing me that way.

Clearing my throat, I try to jump right back in, too. "Right, Hillary, okay. So we'll take turns. You ask me questions about my case. I'll ask you about yours. We'll compare notes and see what similarities and differences we've found." I shuffle my notes into some semblance of order.

"First question, where was Valynne's body found?" Jordan asks.

That isn't one of the details I have to look up. I was there. "East End, by the corner of Barlow and Prairie, in an alley behind a pharmacy."

"Who found her? What time of day was she found?" He leans back in his chair and rubs the knuckles of his right hand under his chin. I'm struck by how much he looks like Chief Vega in that moment. Instead of making me want to hit him or run away, like I expect, the thought brings unexpected warmth to my chest. It surprises me so much I completely forget what he asked.

"Um, ask me again?" I say finally, after pretending to look for the information to hide my embarrassment.

Jordan gives me a confused half smile, but then repeats himself without an interrogation, and I'm grateful. "Who found her and at what time? And what time do they think she died?"

"A delivery guy found her just after seven a.m. And the answer to your other question hasn't been released." I sigh and put my notes down. Maybe this is pointless. It's so hard to figure out what I think about everything with so little information. I look over at Jordan. "Same questions about your case."

"Okay, Hillary was the last of the three East End Murders from before your father went to prison. She was found in Mason Park by a jogger at six in the morning." He flips through his notes as he speaks, and I lean forward. Closing my eyes, I press my forehead into my palms and try to compare the details to my case.

"Why a park?" I muse quietly, massaging my temples gently with my fingertips.

"What?"

I sit up and frown at him, thinking out loud. "Well, why a park? An alley like where Valynne was found is more hidden. It's a place where they might not be found for a while. Was she under a bush or somewhere out of the way in the park?"

He examines one of his papers before answering. "No. It says she was actually just a few feet from a popular jogging path."

"So, why a park, then?"

Before I say another word, Jordan is flipping through to other pages in his notes. He finds what he's searching for quickly, flips to a different page, and starts scanning through it.

"What are you—?"

"Give me a sec, I'm checking something." He finds two more papers, then finally looks up at me and says, "Not why a park, why an alley?"

"What?" I go quickly through our conversation in my head and still don't understand what he's saying.

"All three earlier murders before Valynne are in more public places: the park, a neighborhood path, and a busy skateboarding park near an outdoor mall. The park isn't the one that stands out, the alley from the most recent murder is." He watches me for my reaction. This is an indicator of a copycat and I need to recognize it as such. He's waiting for me to go all in on this method of thinking, and that will mean trusting him to fight for my father.

I can try to do that verbally at least.

"That could indicate a difference in preference for the killer."

The words taste bitter with a tang of betrayal in my mouth. I want to take them back, but I bite my tongue and force myself to wait.

"It could be. Or it could be that being dormant for so long has made him grow timid. After all, watching your father be punished would make most people more cautious about being caught," Jordan says.

The bitterness disappears, and all at once my shoulders and chest feel lighter than they have in a very long time. Not only is Jordan keeping his promise and arguing for Daddy's innocence, but he's good at it. His argument is very reasonable, one I might not have considered myself.

Keeping my eyes down on the files so he won't see the intense relief in my face, I say, "Good point."

"Riley . . ." Jordan looks like he can't decide whether to continue on with his thought or not.

"Go ahead," I say, bracing myself for whatever he doesn't want to say.

"Did you have any suspicion at all that your dad cheated on your mom?" He winces as he says the word *cheated*, and so do I.

"I believed their lie." I feel deflated just saying it.

"What about what Mr. Masters said? Do you think your mom might actually believe the lie, too?" His voice is low now, like even the walls might hear us.

"I've been wondering that same thing." I fold my arms on the table, lay my head on them, and sigh. Memories of Mama's voice ring in my head from the far distant past. Words like, "They're lying about him, sweet pea," and "Your daddy wouldn't even cheat at chess, let alone anything else."

Of course, at six years old, I hadn't even understood what this kind of cheating meant. I hadn't even thought it was an important thing at the time. But Mama had to know about the evidence. And if they had presented the firm proof that I'd seen in the file, was she lying to me all along about what he'd done? Or was my mother really *that* naïve?

The more I think about it, the more I think there's only one real answer. *She isn't, she wasn't, she never could be.*

Mama is smart, tenacious, hardworking, and tough. The idea that she really didn't know after seeing that evidence at the trial just doesn't fit her at all.

So *why* was she still so loyal?

"If you don't want to talk about this, I understand." I feel his fingers lightly brush through the back of my hair. "I'm sure they went through it all during the trial, though. Do you think she just didn't believe them?"

"No." My stomach feels unstable. "I think she lied to protect him."

"Why would she do that?"

"I don't know. It seems like my mother, my father—everyone I trust—all they know how to do is lie to me," I say with a shaky voice, not even caring how pathetic it sounds. Sitting up, I look at the picture of Hillary that Jordan had printed out. It sits on top of his notebook.

I stare at the wispy bangs across Hillary's forehead. I both resent her for her part in Daddy's affair and feel terrible about what happened to her. Then a distant memory from the trial comes floating back. We'd been sitting behind Daddy in our normal spot. The lawyers for the prosecution were talking and I heard them say Hillary's name.

Mama had leaned down, smiled, and whispered, "Some of the things they say aren't for little girls to hear, okay?"

I looked up at her and nodded. Then she slipped a pair of giant headphones over my ears and adjusted them until they mostly fit my head. She pushed a button and my ears filled with a song by the Beatles.

She put one arm around me and gave me a coloring book and crayons. Music so I wouldn't hear, and something to look at so I wouldn't see.

But she didn't have on headphones. And her eyes never strayed down to my coloring book. Who was she trying to protect by pretending none of it was real? Was that moment the start of a lifetime of lies she would send in my direction? Does she need psychological help? Or rather some kind of truth serum for every time she speaks to me?

Suddenly, I'm on my feet and gathering my stuff into a pile.

"Riley?" Jordan stands up and starts doing the same thing. "Where are we going?"

"To my house. We're not accomplishing anything without new information," I answer quickly. "And since she's avoiding me and won't answer any of my questions, maybe Mama has a journal or a diary or some other way we can get into her thoughts."

Jordan follows me out of the library without comment, even though he looks like he might have plenty to say about this plan. This time, I'm glad he keeps his thoughts to himself.

I have enough doubts about invading Mama's privacy without any additional guilt.

26

THE LAST THING I EXPECT to find when I come flying in through the front door is Mama sitting at the kitchen table. Apparently, me coming home unannounced has the same effect on her because when she sees me, she gets up so suddenly that her chair legs screech backward across the floor.

I freeze in my spot and Jordan looks from me to my mother with a panicked expression. I glance at my watch and see that it reads three o'clock. Too late to come home for lunch—not that she ever does—but way too early to be home for the day.

Why is she here?

Mama has a deep frown plastered across her face. She doesn't speak yet, but instead throws a dish towel over the open box on the table in front of her before moving it down onto the ground beside her chair and retaking her seat.

"Should I go?" Jordan's athletic muscles coil inward, ready for me to say the word. His dark eyes are wide as he watches me, poised to bolt in any given direction if I tell him.

My first instinct is to shout *Yes!* and start pushing him toward the front door, but I don't. Instead, I take a deep breath and shake my head.

"No. You should stay." My whole body is shaking, but I manage to give him a firm nod. My hands ball into fists at my sides. I can tell from the alarmed look in his expression that he can see the raw fury that's boiling up inside me.

"Riley." His eyes are half pleading, half worried. "Are you sure you want—"

"Yes, I'm sure," I answer, with resolve as strong as the steel cages that hold my father. For the first time in a while, I *am* sure. I have questions for my mother and I'm not at all afraid to ask them.

Because right now, I am getting the answers that *I* need—no matter what.

"I didn't know you'd be home this early." Mama's voice is soft, her eyes are on the table. Even though I know it's probably mostly in my mind, something about her has changed for me now. She was strong. She had no weaknesses before. Now she is something else . . . an unknown.

My heart jumps to my throat as I see her reach out for the coffee mug in front of her. Her movements are wobbly and she's struggling to not fall out of her chair. It takes me a moment to put that together with the two empty liquor bottles on the counter. I've very rarely seen Mama drink and now she's at home in the middle of the day, completely wasted? When I gasp, she looks up at me and knocks over the mug. What spills out is far too clear to have any actual coffee in it.

Jordan moves immediately, rushing over to help her clean up.

I feel so small, so humiliated that I could disappear at any moment. It isn't bad enough that this friend—this boy that I'm beginning to care far too much about—knows all my secrets from the past. Now he has to make new dark discoveries with me? My father, the one-time admitted killer. My mother, the drunk who bruised up my cheekbone.

Me, the girl who lies to him at the mall, who drunk-texts him in the park, and the daughter in a family that does nothing but hurt each other.

Mama watches Jordan with bleary eyes and blinks a few times before jerking her mug out of his hands. "You. Why are you here?" she snarls.

Jordan stops moving, looking from her to me in confusion.

Coming forward in his place, I take the mug and put it in the sink. Mama's eyes never leave Jordan. They're filled with pure hatred that I've never seen on her before.

After a few seconds, the hatred fades to confusion and she slowly climbs to her feet, using me to balance like some piece of furniture that she doesn't actually see.

"You . . . you're too young." She takes a step backward, but when I try to pull her into her kitchen chair, she won't move any closer.

Releasing her, I sigh and move over to Jordan. I do the only thing I can think of to show her that he isn't a threat and he isn't his father, like she appears to think. I stand next to him, and then slip my hand into his. He jerks his head toward me in surprise but then tightens his grip. The warmth and feel of his hand around mine seem to lend me the strength I need.

"I know what you're thinking. This isn't Detective—or Chief—Vega. This is Jordan, his son. He's a friend."

Mama glares, looking from Jordan to me. I feel Jordan's eyes on me, too, and he moves his thumb softly over the back of my hand.

"I need a drink," Mama finally groans before shuffling around us to take her seat at the table.

"I think that's probably the last thing you need," I reply softly, and she whips her eyes up to me. She opens her mouth to speak, but before she has a chance, I cut her off. "Mama, what's going on? Why are you home? Why are you drinking?"

Her cheeks flush and I see the emotions on her face start with anger and morph into remorse and guilt. Mama's voice cracks when she whispers, "Riley, I got fired today."

"What?" Her words don't make sense. "Why?"

I grip Jordan's hand tighter and we take seats at the table with her. I sit next to Mama, trying to understand how this could've happened. Yes, Mama has lost jobs before, but this one seemed so steady. She's been there for a while and she works so hard. How could she have been fired?

"I've been missing a lot of work lately. When I should've been at the office, I've been meeting with Mr. Masters or Stacia to ask questions. I even went to talk to Vega." She puts her head down on her arms. "I hoped I could make him see, but all he would say was that he was looking into it. I know what this has been doing to you, Riley, and I wanted to find a way to make it easier on you somehow, but instead I've lost my job . . . again."

Then I reach down and lift the towel so I can see the contents of the box beside her. It holds pictures of the two of us, a purple stapler, a file of papers, and a silver nameplate from her desk.

I curse quietly and release Jordan's hand so I can hug her.

"Language, young lady," Mama snaps before wrapping her arms tight around me. In that moment, she looks more like herself than she has since the day Valynne Kemp was killed—and I'm surprised how incredibly relieved I feel to have the real Mama back, for however long she stays. When she pulls away, she looks like she's composed herself a bit, but I still see tears in her eyes as they flit over to Jordan. "If you know who he is, why is he here?"

"He knows, Mama," I reply clearly. She can make me feel bad about anything else she wants, but I will not let her make me feel bad about the only person I've ever let get close to me. "That night I was drunk, I told him about Daddy confessing."

"I haven't told a soul," Jordan jumps in quickly, trying to reassure her.

Mama stares at me in shock like my words caused her physical pain. Then she scowls menacingly at Jordan. "And what's he making you pay to keep this secret?"

Jordan's muscles stiffen beside me and I rush to his defense. "Nothing, Mama! He's not like that. He's been helping me, that's all."

Jordan's voice is slightly darker when he speaks again. "And I've decided I'm never going to tell anyone, so you can relax about that."

I glance over at him, my eyebrows raised.

"It isn't my secret to tell," he murmurs, reaching out to squeeze my hand again under the table. I grip it when he starts to move his hand away, weaving my fingers slowly into his. His eyes are on Mama now and they stay there.

"Fine." Mama folds her arms over her chest and leans back in her chair. She is less openly hostile, but she definitely isn't friendly. "I just hope you don't suddenly change your mind."

"I won't." His tone is firm, leaving no room for any further questions.

I turn back to Mama, thinking that now, with her guard down, might be the best time to get the answers I need from her. I try to decide on where to start.

I finally spit out the most important question my brain can settle on. "How many secrets do we have, Mama?" I watch her face contort with a bit of fear before settling back to normal.

"What do you mean?" she asks evasively. I remember what Mr. Masters said about her denial. Maybe that's her go-to stance when facing truths that she can't handle. She protects herself externally from anything that can hurt her, even if she knows better on the inside.

"Why didn't you ever tell me the truth about Daddy cheating on you?" I whisper, trying to brace myself for the answer, but then realizing there is no way to do that with a topic like this one.

Mama's face immediately falls, and watching it feels like a punch to the gut. Up until that instant, some part of me hoped that there might have been some misunderstanding. That Mama would sort it out and explain how all the evidence I'd seen was some sick private joke, and we'd laugh. But then, maybe that's just me trying to hide behind denial, too. Perhaps it's a family trait. Now that I've seen her expression, the regret and pain on her face, I know for certain that my instinct was right. She knows the truth. She isn't crazy or deluding herself, but she *has* been deliberately hiding this from me all along.

I slump down low in my chair, holding tight to Jordan's hand like an anchor in a storm. I feel so confused. I've always believed my parents—*always*. Now, within the last two weeks, I've caught them both in their lies and it's turned my world upside down. I've never been able to depend on anyone but them. Now I can't depend on anyone but myself.

How do I find the truth in a den of liars?

"I just—I thought you probably knew, hon—" Mama starts, but I interrupt her before she can dig herself a deeper hole.

"No, you didn't. Do *not* feed me any more lies!" I expect my words to come out as a shout. Instead they're a hoarse whisper. "You knew I didn't know, because you made sure I didn't, Mama."

Her expression is rapidly flipping through a variety of emotions: indignation, anger, sorrow, guilt, frustration, and finally defeat. "I was trying to protect you, Riley. You need to understand. You were so little, and it's so hard because we know Stacia. If we want to get your daddy out of this mess, we need her help—"

"*Stacia?*"

Mama's mouth closes.

"Daddy's assistant? The one we've had over for dinner? Talked to? Laughed with?" My voice creaks with a desperation for her to say she meant something else—someone else—*anyone* else.

Mama's skin pales to the color of the white kitchen cabinets behind her as she realizes she's just dropped a bomb into the center of my world. And now there is no way for her to stop it from going off. Distantly, I feel Jordan's hand frantically squeezing mine under the table like he's trying to give it CPR.

But I may never recover from this kind of destruction.

My urge to argue that this couldn't be true fades as I realize with a sinking feeling that it makes perfect sense. How they always "worked" late together. How she has been just as committed to proving his innocence as we were. She'd even been to visit him at Polunsky every week. He'd told us that she was assisting him with his case. He said she was the go-between for him and Masters, but maybe they'd just been carrying on the emotional aspect of their affair this entire time.

"He cheated on you with Stacia?" I repeat, feeling the weight of Jordan's worried gaze glued to me. I'm glad I'm already sitting down, as my thoughts feel like someone replaced my brain with a blender.

"Oh, God." Mama lowers her head slowly to the table. A muffled sob escapes before she continues. "I never told you because I was trying to protect you."

"From what? The truth?" I ask, my voice cracking with frustration.

"From the fact that someone we love can still hurt us so much." She lifts her head and I see tears streak down her face as her eyes plead with me to understand, but I don't. Protecting me because I was only six? Okay, I can see that. But I'm not six anymore, and I haven't been for a very long time.

"I found out he'd cheated with one of the victims from the case, Mama. I know you were all lying about Hillary. But from what you're saying, he cheated on you more than once. You knew about it. And one of his mistresses ended up dead? This person *can't* be the man I thought he was, but *you* knew the truth," I snap. "Why couldn't you protect me by telling me who he really was? By not letting me believe that the man I looked up to was a hero? Or for the love of God, Mama, doing what any *sane* person would've done by moving us to another state and changing our names?"

Her eyes widen and she stops crying. "Being a cheater doesn't mean he's a killer. Riley, what are you saying? Is that what you would've wanted me to do back then? You were so young. Would you have wanted to not know your father at all? Would you have wanted to not visit him or ever see him? Would you want us to spend our lives pretending that he's already dead?"

My heart aches at the mere thought, but I pause rather than reassure her. If there is anything I've learned lately, it's that my heart isn't exactly trustworthy. I glance at Jordan and the sympathy and kindness in his face lend me strength. Still, I can't make my voice rise above a whisper when I answer. "That probably would've hurt less than this."

Mama clucks her tongue at me. "Riley, you're acting like everyone else when *you* should know better. You're saying we should've tr-treated him like we assumed he wasn't innocent."

I'm quiet because I don't know how to respond to that anymore. She goes on, her speech starting to slur more with the emotion of our conversation. "No one c-can put him at *any* of the crime scenes, Riley. Not a single one. No one can even tie him to two of the three victims. He was at the office alone when it happened, so he has no alibi, but he did that kind of thing all the time. They never foun—found any of the so-called souvenirs he was supposed to have taken."

"I know all of this, Mama," I say softly, but she keeps going.

"Mo-most of their evidence is completely circumstantial. There were even times when . . ." Her eyes well up again and she looks utterly heartbroken. "There were times when I actually wished that he'd b-been with Stacia those nights because then she could've been his alibi. Do you know how sick that makes me feel?"

In that instant, I start to hate Daddy just a little bit.

27

"MAMA, DO YOU REALLY STILL BELIEVE HIM? Can you still believe that he's innocent after all he has done to you?" This time my words are quiet but clear. I stare straight at her, watching in a way I never have before for the slightest flinch, blink, or hesitation. Something to signal me of any worries or doubts, of any flat-out lies she's been telling me.

"I did"—Mama lowers her eyes to the table—"until you told me he confessed. Now I don't know what to think."

"Mama, why did you stay loyal to him through all of this?" Releasing Jordan's hand again, I reach for Mama's fingers, but she balls them up into fists so I grip her wrists. "Why would you let him do this to you? To us?"

It takes a few seconds before she releases a long, slow breath, and she looks endlessly sad. "I thought I was protecting you."

I can't take the same answer again. Anger bubbles beneath my skin until I can't sit anymore. I shove her hands away and stand up from my chair. "You weren't protecting me, you were protecting *him*. If you really cared about me, maybe you could've helped me with things that were actually killing *me* inside, like how lonely it is to have zero friends, or dealing with absolute jerks at school and in our neighborhood, or knowing how to cope with losing my father. We're only two weeks away now. *Two weeks*."

I can see the pain I'm causing in her eyes, but I've been waiting too long to say this and trying to stop now would be like trying to dam a river with barbed wire. "Never mind. You aren't capable of helping anyone. You always pretend you're so strong, but now I know why. You do it because you are *weak* and it terrifies you to admit that."

The room has gone blurry from my own tears. In some still-rational corner of my mind, I can't believe the words that keep spilling out of my mouth. Mama stares at me in silent shock until a soft cry of alarm escapes her mouth.

"Riley, stop." Jordan's firm voice shocks me back to sanity—and I wish it hadn't because I don't want to see the pain in Mama's face. He reaches up for my hand and I jerk it away without thinking.

"You're right." Mama gives a soft shake of her head and I see a sense of peace in her eyes for the first time in a very long while. "About everything, you're absolutely right."

Mama leans back in her chair and looks down at her hands before taking a deep breath. "But the lying ends now. I'll tell you everything, Riley. I promise. I want you to know, because I see that all those things I did trying to protect you are only hurting you."

Her entire body seems to tremble, and I run to her, throwing my arms tight around her and burying my face against her shoulder. After a moment, I hear the tinkling of glass. Looking up, I see Jordan picking up the empty bottles off the counter and grabbing the mostly full kitchen trash bag as he moves toward the back door. "I'll take this out," he says quietly.

He sends me a tentative smile and I mouth my thanks before he heads out to the garbage.

Mama watches him with a thoughtful look on her face. Then, without a word, she turns to me. "You need to understand why I did what I did, Riley. Why I stayed with him and remained quiet after I found out he was cheating. Your father wasn't the only one who made terrible mistakes."

My hands go cold, but I clutch hers tightly, afraid to interrupt her in case she stops talking. Jordan, who'd entered just as she said her last sentence, freezes in the doorway.

Mama continues. "You were two. It was before your father ever cheated. We were so happy . . ." She opens her mouth a few times, but nothing comes out.

I grab her a glass of water, waiting for her to compose herself a bit.

"I had to work really late one night at a restaurant I managed at the time." She drinks a long sip of water and then takes my hand again. Jordan has silently closed the back door and moved to lean against the counter, but I can see from his face that he's listening as intently as I am.

"Daddy always told me to stay the night or call him if I was too tired to drive, but I didn't." Her tone quivers. I'm so used to seeing Mama as impenetrable that *this* is terrifying. I'm filled with a sudden, desperate urge to escape the end of her story, to simply run out the door.

"I just wanted to be in my own bed. I was stiff and exhausted from the long night of work." Guilt begins to drip like heavy rain from her voice and I dread what's coming next. "I knew you were asleep and I knew if I called your daddy he'd have to wake you up to come get me, so I got in my car and drove."

She seems willing to stop there, so I prod her a bit. "What happened, Ma—"

"I fell asleep, Riley. They tell me I rolled the car, went through a barrier and down a hill. By the time I woke up after the accident, I'd been out for several days. Your father was furious, and he would never speak to me about what I had done." She hesitates and then plows forward, tears filling her eyes. "The baby was already gone. You . . . you were s-supposed to have a little brother."

I sit back in my seat in shock and stare at her. I vaguely remember Mama being in the hospital when I was very little. I wasn't sure if I'd visited her there or just heard my parents mention it. I'd known she'd had a car accident, but nothing else about it. A brother? I have a brother who died and I never knew about it. The first image that comes to my mind is little Matthew. But this time I picture him with Mama's shining blond hair and Daddy's smile. A lump forms in my throat and I can't speak.

"The nurses told me he was terrified he would lose me, too, but by the time I woke up, your father wouldn't even talk about the baby with me. I guess it was easier for him to just pretend I was never pregnant. Even after that, though, David never mentioned leaving me. When I tried to apologize, he'd walk out of the room. In my head, I had to mourn the baby, Riley. I named him Andrew." She whispers the name gently, her voice cradling him like her arms never could. Her tears have dried up now, but the devastation on her face is plain and raw. Mama laughs quietly to herself, but it's a sound of pain instead of joy. "I'm not sure if I've ever said his name out loud before."

"Oh, Mama." I slide out of my chair to kneel on the ground beside her, wrapping both my arms around her waist as tight as they can go. "It was an accident. It's not your fault."

Her sobs come back more intensely than before. She pats my head and I hear Jordan move quietly into the living room. I appreciate him at least trying to give us a little more privacy, even though I *really* don't want him to leave.

"I'm so sorry, honey," she chokes out. "I really wanted you to have a sibling."

"It's okay. I don't blame you," I whisper softly into Mama's shoulder.

Her arms squeeze me tight. She kisses the top of my hand as she murmurs, "No one has ever told me that."

I'm filled with a sudden fierce desire to protect her and with anger at Daddy for so many things. He's her husband. He's supposed to care about her and protect her. Instead, he blamed her and shut her out.

When I sit back, Mama looks over. "That's why I didn't leave him or divorce him when he cheated, Riley. Because what I di— what I did cost us so much more."

Her face is puffy and tear-streaked, her eyes full of nightmares I've never even known existed. I relive the awful words I said in anger and regret all of them. She isn't the one who hurt us. Daddy is. She didn't betray our family. She needs my help as much as he does—and deserves it more. Mama isn't the guilty party here; she's been a victim in every way.

I won't let that happen anymore.

After a few more tearful hugs, I convince Mama to drink more water. Then she goes to the bathroom while I grab a blanket and an extra water bottle to put by her bed. She wants to rest for a bit, and I think that's the best plan for her right now.

The moment the bathroom door closes behind her, Jordan is beside me. He reaches his arms around me and cradles my head against his chest. I tighten up instinctively, but my heart aches like it's been ripped apart. Though Jordan's arms make it feel like it might someday heal.

So I stop fighting against myself, I stop fighting against what I want. Instead, one at a time, I carefully wind my arms around his back. I hold on to him, close my eyes, and stop caring about when he is going to change his mind about me. Instead, I cling to him, and Jordan clutches me even tighter, whispering against the top of my head words that ease the pain in my soul bit by bit. He says things like "You're not alone" and "I'm not going anywhere."

These would be simple words of comfort to anyone else, but they're also words that no one has *ever* said to me. I wrap myself up in their sound and am only brought out of it when I hear the bathroom door open again. I withdraw slowly from his arms, and Jordan's eyes meet mine—full of worry, full of comfort.

I remind myself to thank him for this later, but then realize that the *Things to Thank Jordan For* list is getting a little long. Maybe it's time to stop adding things to the list and just start saying thank you.

"Thank you," I whisper softly. He smiles and bends forward to kiss my cheek. My hand touches the spot his lips just were. Then I walk away and head down the hall to help Mama get settled in her room.

28

MAMA LOOKS WOBBLY WHEN SHE COMES OUT into the hallway, so Jordan joins me immediately to help steady her.

My head is still reeling from hearing everything she's been through. She's lived a life where she had to choose between the man she loves and literally everyone else. In a similar situation, would I be that strong? Have I inherited my stubborn loyalty from her?

Apparently I didn't get any sort of loyalty or fidelity from my father.

She's been backed up against a wall time and time again. No wonder she's falling apart. How long can anyone be expected to live under that kind of strain without being able to show so much as a crack in their otherwise unwavering faith?

I run to the bathroom for a cool rag as Jordan has taken on most of the job of supporting her. On my way back, I stop to listen when I hear her speaking to him.

"I know exactly who you are." Her words slur, but they're simple, and there is no question what she means. I stand with my feet frozen in place, torn between waiting to see how Jordan handles this situation and hurrying in to help him get out of it.

"I know who you are, too." His voice is light, but I can tell that he's uncomfortable.

"Why are you hanging around my daughter?" Mama's bluntness makes me suck in a quiet breath of surprise. She isn't messing around. Southern hospitality is her motto, and she never talks to people this way.

Jordan doesn't answer her for so long that I wonder if he felt offended and has left. I take two steps toward the doorway and then freeze up again when I hear him say words that make me feel lightheaded.

"Because she's both amazing and stubborn in all the best ways." He doesn't sound nervous anymore, more like he's searching really carefully for the right answer. "Because I want to help."

Silently, I lean my back against the wall. My heart burns and flutters and I can't help but smile.

When Mama responds, her voice is significantly kinder, but her words still make me cold. "You just make sure you're prepared to deal with the fallout before you drag her down with you."

He repeats, "Fallout?" like a question, but I get the distinct impression that he knows exactly what she means.

"Don't play dumb with me. I know you're smarter than that," Mama says, but then her voice softens so much I have to inch my way to the end of the hall to hear her. "Riley better not get hurt when your father finds out you've been spending time with her."

My mind latches onto those words and I don't move. It isn't like I haven't had similar thoughts myself about Jordan's dad being furious if he finds out Jordan's been hanging around me. But somehow hearing someone else say the same thing makes it more real—more terrifying.

Mama doesn't give me any extra time to think about it.

"Riley, did you get a cool cloth? My head is starting to pound," she hollers, and I hear footsteps too heavy to be hers walking toward the hallway. Panicking, I quietly move back a few feet and then come jogging just as Jordan steps around the corner.

"Got it." I hold the cloth up, fighting not to let guilt or confusion about what I'd overheard show in my expression. The deep frown that creases his face is erased the moment he sees me. I know then that he won't realize I've been secretly eavesdropping, not when it seems like he's so busy hiding his own fears.

The thought makes me penetratingly sad in a way that I can't shake.

"I'll just wait out here," Jordan says, pointing over his shoulder toward the living room.

I move in to where Mama sits up in bed, closing the door behind me. She grabs a couple of ibuprofen pills from her nightstand, and she reaches her hands out for the washcloth and the water bottle, muttering, "I'm sorry, honey."

I feel terrible. I want to kick myself for calling her weak. I had no idea she was hiding secrets like these. "You don't need to be sorry, Mama. The only thing you should apologize for is not telling me this was all going on so I could help you."

She still won't meet my eyes.

I wrap my arms around her. "I'm so sorry for calling you weak. I was wrong. But I can't help you, or even understand, if you don't tell me."

Mama hugs me back and gives me a teary smile. "I know. When I look at you, I still see the tiny girl whose feet swing a foot off the floor when she sits on the courtroom benches. I know you aren't little anymore, but parents aren't supposed to accept that defeat easily. I don't want to put any more on you than you've already had to deal with. You—you were right that you've had too much and I don't want to give you anything extra to carry."

"I'm fine, Mama." I smooth down one side of her blond hair. Then I decide that saying these things isn't really helping either of us. "Well, okay—no, I'm not fine. And neither are you. And neither is Daddy. But for now, we're all doing the best we can, and that's okay. Right?"

Mama laughs. "You sound like a therapist. Maybe we should be calling today a breakthrough."

I groan and then smirk. "Don't tell anyone about this, then. I prefer for most people to think of me as a dangerous misfit. If people think I'm unpredictable then their expectations are considerably lower."

"Fair enough." Mama kisses my cheek, but I can see her eyes starting to droop. She slides down against her pillow, and I don't even have enough time to walk slowly to the door and close it before she is slipping into oblivion.

As I head back into the living room, I look out the front window.

"Everything okay?" Jordan whispers, coming up to me.

"Yeah. Thank you." I don't turn around, but he's so close I can smell his scent and feel the warmth coming off his body. And we just stand in the silence together.

I'm not sure why Jordan isn't talking. Maybe it's because he's afraid to wake Mama. But in her state, we could probably throw a concert in here and she wouldn't wake up. Or maybe he's staying quiet for some other reason.

I don't really care why, I'm just so happy he's here.

After everything I just learned, my mind still spins, and I like the comfort of this silence.

I move and Jordan follows me toward the front door. I pick up the bag we used to carry our notebooks back from the library. Pulling them out, I walk into the kitchen and place them on the table. Then we just stand, looking at each other. I'm exhausted. I feel like everything from the last few weeks has landed squarely on my head and it's just too heavy for me to stand up straight beneath it all anymore.

Jordan studies me and then asks a question I don't expect. "What do you need?"

I look up at him. The table separates us, but he's only a couple of feet away and somehow it feels like a massive chasm compared to when he held me earlier. What I want, more than anything else in this moment, is to be closer to him, but I'm obviously not going to say that. "I don't understand what you mean."

"Yes, you do," he responds immediately, and his eyes feel like they're staring a hole right through me.

I put my hands on the back of the chair in front of me, staring down at the worn wood. "No, I don't."

He takes a step closer and his voice drops lower. "Riley, what do *you* need?"

Something about the way he's talking and moving and looking at me ignites a spark that only makes my desire to be close to him a million times stronger. In contrast, the fact that he seems to know exactly what he's doing makes me feel like I'm being manipulated, and it kind of ticks me off.

Moving around the chair, I inch up so close to him that he fills my senses with everything that is Jordan to me. I'm not sure if it's his cologne or what, but it smells warm and spicy. It's the kind of scent that I wish could be made into a large, soft blanket that I could wrap myself up in. When I'm just as close to him as I can handle without touching him, I look up into his face and ask, "You want to know what I need?"

He nods, and from this vantage point I see the muscles on his throat constrict as he swallows. I hope it's a sign that maybe I have as much of an effect on him as he has on me.

"I need answers, Jordan." I watch his eyes and carefully judge his reactions to my wording.

"To what questions?" He doesn't move or change his position, but his attention is fully on what I'm saying now.

"I heard what my mom said, about the fallout when your dad finds out you've been spending time with me."

He recoils like I've punched him in the gut, taking a step backward. "I thought you overheard, but I wasn't sure."

"I've mostly tried to stay out of your issues with him." I consider explaining why I've changed my mind, but instead just finish with "I'm sorry for eavesdropping."

"No, it's only fair. God knows I'm neck deep in your family problems at this point. It would be hypocritical of me to refuse to talk about mine." He leans against the edge of the table. "It's been really hard . . . since Mom died," he continues, his face looking haggard. Jordan wears his emotions well, but at the mere mention of his mother, he instantly goes from normal to beaten down.

"I noticed that the pictures of her are gone from your house . . . ," I start, hoping that giving him a place to begin might help.

"My father can't handle even looking at her." He slides down into the chair with that sentence. "He says he deals with death all day long and he doesn't want to face it when he gets home."

I wince, knowing exactly how much that hurts. I slip into the chair closest to him, but I don't speak for fear that it might slow him down.

"But I miss her. Matthew misses her. My brother is so young that I really need to make sure he doesn't—I *can't* let him—forget her." He folds his arms across the table and rests his chin on top of them. In that pose, he suddenly looks just like a bigger version of Matthew.

"That makes sense." I wish I had some way to comfort him.

"So I keep talking about her. I keep finding the hidden pictures and hanging them back up." Jordan turns his eyes on the table. He traces one swirl in the wood with his thumbnail when he goes on. He's visibly steady, but his voice wobbles, betraying the emotion below the surface. "Did you know . . . did you know she was killed by a drunk driver? He drove straight into her. They both died on impact."

My heart hurts for him as I watch the muscles in his neck and jaw clench and relax again and again as he fights for composure. So many things about Jordan make more sense when I understand this pain that pulses just below the surface. My entire being fills with sadness for him and for Matthew. What an awful thing to have happen. My fingers ache to reach out and soothe him, but I know there is nothing I can do to take away that kind of pain. No matter how much I may want to.

"I'm so sorry," I say, feeling useless. "How long has it been again?"

Jordan raises his eyes to look at me for the first time since we started this conversation. "Five months and twenty-four days."

He's still counting, just like I am. He counts up from the night his whole world changed. I count down to the day that the same thing will happen to me.

His voice drops so low I can barely hear it. "My dad was the first officer on the scene. And he couldn't do anything to save her."

My throat closes up. For the first time ever, I'm flooded with intense sympathy for Chief Vega.

"This is just one reason I feel like I *need* to be able to help you." His voice is even lower than normal. It sounds rough and it takes me a minute to understand his words. "Ever since my mom—ever since we lost her, Dad and I can't stop fighting. But I know—I know without question that she'd be furious at us for that. I feel so guilty knowing she'd be mad, but I just can't let our family forget her."

"I understand why you can't let that happen," I say softly, "but I don't get what that has to do with me."

He pauses for a moment, fighting through an obvious wave of pain. Then he takes a deep breath, and when he speaks again, there is a hint of desperation. "I need to feel like I can make things better somehow. I couldn't help her. I couldn't save her. You can't understand how much I need to feel like I matter right now."

The emotion in his voice is so raw that I'm filled with an

239

immediate instinct to protect him somehow. But as much as I want to understand him, his words don't make sense. Of course he matters. All I see in his life are people who need him. Why doesn't he see that?

"You matter to a lot of people. Matthew and your father love and need you, Jordan." I speak the words softly.

"Matthew *needs* a mother." Jordan looks up at me and his eyes are wet. "Since he's lost that, he needs a nanny—someone to make sure he's loved and clean and fed. It doesn't matter who it is if it isn't her. But that isn't what I'm talking about, Riley. I want someone to care that *I* exist, not because of what I can bring them or do for them, but because of who I am. I need someone to need me around because I am uniquely me and I'm exactly what this person needs. My mom needed me. My dad—my dad doesn't *need* anyone."

Seeing this amount of pain in his eyes tears me apart. I'd always thought he helped me because he could somehow see how badly I needed help even when I couldn't convey it, but that was only part of the truth. As badly as I need him, he needs me, too. We heal the broken pieces of each other *because* we're so opposite. We have both nothing and everything in common and I've never felt like someone could understand me the way he somehow does.

I tentatively lift one hand up to his cheek. I graze the tips of my fingers across the lines in his brow and they relax. As I brush my knuckles down the right side of his face, I'm surprised by the shadow of stubble I find along his jaw. The muscles fall slack and he closes his eyes, inclining his head toward my hand. I gently touch his eyelids with my fingertips, and slide the edge of my nail gently along his long, dark lashes.

Finally, I move my thumb down and hesitate for just a moment before lightly pressing it against his full lips. Jordan's lips are soft but firm, and my heart races when he kisses my thumb. I look up and realize his eyes are open again. The heat in them could make a Texas day in July weep from envy. I'm suddenly self-conscious and I start to pull my hand back from his face, but he catches it. His eyes never leave mine, but he softly turns and presses a kiss on the inside of my wrist.

Tingles of pleasure shoot up my arm and through my body. Then he turns my hand over and kisses the back of it before lowering it to the table and holding it lightly between both of his.

"Anyway, *if* my dad gets mad because I'm spending time with you, it will be more because of me than because of you." He squeezes my hand again and then gives me a pointed look. "Just let me worry about that, okay?"

I give a soft sigh, but I can't even imagine disagreeing with him right now. "Okay."

"Any more questions?" His smile is just rueful enough to make me laugh. And I know one thing for sure: Jordan is *needed* far more than he knows. Because despite our different pasts, there is no one else that I would want with me when I uncover my family's hidden truths.

29

I SIT AT THE TABLE with Mama on Friday afternoon. The dark circles under her eyes have lightened a bit since this morning, but it's fair to say that her hangover has mine after the park incident beat by a long shot. She was browsing through potential job openings; now her laptop sits forgotten in front of her as she stares at me in confusion.

"Why do you still want to go?" she asks with a tone that says she wonders if I've lost my mind.

"Because I want to confront him. I want the chance to ask him why he would do such awful things to our family. I want to understand what the hell he's been thinking," I say as I stuff my sunglasses and phone into my purse with much more force than necessary.

Mama closes her laptop. "Then I'm going with you."

"No," I respond so fast her eyebrows shoot up. "I think I need to face this on my own. Plus, seeing him right now is probably the last thing you need."

Mama looks slightly offended. "I can handle him."

"Please, Mama." I reach out and grab her hand. "Just let me do this alone."

She hesitates a moment more before answering. "Okay. Let me

know if you want me to pick up some ice cream for after. We might need it."

When I walk out to my car, I see a folded-up paper stuck under my windshield wiper. I can tell immediately from how tightly it's folded that it isn't a flyer and I sigh. Great. These kinds of secret messages are always super friendly.

Even bracing myself, my shoulders cave in a bit as I carefully open up the paper. I'm so tired of being surrounded by this kind of crap all the time. My eyes go first to the dark lines in a drawing at the bottom of the page. I can't make it out at first, but when I realize I have it upside down I feel a little sick.

As I turn it over, the details become clear. At the top now is a drawing of a man in an electric chair. Jolts of electricity zing through his body and his eyes bug out of his face. This isn't even the worst thing I've seen, but the timing makes me furious. Then I finally look down at the bottom half of the page and growl under my breath as I study it.

This one is much more direct. It's me this time—a common theme; I'm his daughter so obviously I should be punished, too—my brown hair is stringy around the caricature depiction of my face, a hangman's noose tight around my throat.

Crumpling it up, I look at the houses in the neighborhood around us. I think I spot the movement of a curtain or two, but nothing I can be sure of. Mama usually tries to watch out for them first and get rid of them before I see.

But this one was left on *my* car, with *my* picture on it—being *hanged*.

This one feels personal. I stick it in my jacket pocket, send a heated glare for a moment at each house in sight, then get in my car and drive away.

I only make it three blocks before I come up with a plan.

I still want to go see Daddy, but this time, I'll take Jordan with me. It had been Jordan's idea to come with me to see Mr. Masters, but maybe he'd been onto something.

After all, I am only abiding by one of the universal truths that Daddy taught me about chess—get your opponent off balance with an unanticipated move and you'll force them to backpedal and change their plan. Push them out of their comfort zone and you can control the game.

Daddy is obviously more deceitful than I've ever given him credit for. Knocking him off his game may be the exact thing I need to do to get a closer look at the truth.

Now I just need to convince Jordan to go along with my plans.

I call him on the Bluetooth Mr. Masters had installed in my car while turning around to head toward his house. He answers on the first ring. "Hi. Just a second." Then I hear the sound of him walking and a door closing behind him.

"Your dad is home?" I ask, hoping this won't get in the way of what I want to do.

"Yep," he says, but his tone is much more relaxed now than it was before.

"Feel like escaping for a couple of hours right now?"

I can hear the smile in his voice when he answers. "Absolutely."

"Good." I hesitate to explain where we're going, but I decide that springing our destination on him later might not be the best of ideas. "I think you should come with me—for a visit."

When he is silent for a few seconds, I know I don't need to explain further. He knows *exactly* what I'm talking about. So I move straight into the next step, convincing him that it's a good idea. "Maybe we can surprise him. Shock him enough that he might reveal something he hasn't before."

I deliberately don't clarify that I'm hoping he'll be honest about his affairs and maybe finally reveal his true alibi. I'm hoping he won't give me any more information that could indicate his guilt. God knows I've seen enough of that already.

Jordan still hasn't spoken, and I worry he might be upset at me for even suggesting this.

"Jordan?" I speak his name quietly, kicking myself for not having this conversation in person so I could see his reaction and read the emotion in his eyes.

"I'm in," he answers so quickly and quietly now that I'm not certain I heard him right.

"You are?" Considering the situation, it seems smart to double-check.

"Yes. Don't sound so surprised. I just hope it goes the way you think it will. My dad is heading my way. Where should I meet you?"

"The park." I can't help but feel like this conversation is ending too quickly. I feel like there is more I should say, but I don't have a chance now. "I'll be waiting. Come as soon as you can."

"See you soon." And his end of the line goes dead.

I'm at the park within ten minutes. I park at the end of the lot, then close my eyes and rest my head against the steering wheel. I know this is a terribly risky idea. Ever since the phone call with Jordan, I feel like this whole scenario could be one giant mistake. What if Daddy gets furious at me for even bringing Jordan and refuses to talk to us? What if this is one of the last times I get to see him and it goes horribly wrong? What if Daddy says something to Jordan and Jordan decides I'm not worth the baggage that I come with? What if—

Rap—Rap—Rap—

I throw myself back against my seat, eyes wide. Jordan is standing next to my door, his face split between warring emotions: half an apology and half stifled laughter.

I catch my breath and then wave him around to the passenger side, jamming my thumb into the Unlock button harder than is necessary. He's still chuckling when he climbs in but he follows it with a quick "I'm sorry, Riley. I didn't mean to scare you."

His dark curls fall forward against his forehead as he fumbles under the front of the seat, looking for a latch to slide it back. His knees are crunched into my dashboard, his body looking disproportionately long in my passenger seat. I try to think of who sat in it last and then realize that it was me. Mama and I went for groceries this morning and we took my car, but Mama drove. I'm five feet seven inches and Jordan has a good six inches on me. I sit back, laughing quietly to myself as he keeps searching under the front of the seat for the latch that I know is on the right side.

He whips his head up and his warm eyes glint at me in the afternoon light. "I hope you're enjoying yourself."

"Very much." I smirk. "You scared the crap out of me. This feels like swift and sweet karma."

He shifts to face me and bangs his knee against the dash, wincing. "For knocking on your window? I didn't even try to sneak up on you. You just weren't paying attention. This is hardly fair." Then he reaches to the far side of his seat, finds the right lever, and the entire seat shoots all the way back.

Jordan stretches out like a cat and then smiles. "Much better."

I turn the key and put the car in gear.

He grabs for his seat belt and raises his eyebrows at me. "So, you're sure about this?"

"Not even a little bit."

My phone rings next to me, the number unknown, so I answer it. "Hello."

"Hello, Miss Riley."

"This came up with an unknown number instead of your normal one," I say.

"Yes, sorry about that," Mr. Masters says quickly. "Just trying to be cautious. I may get you a different phone to use for a while as well."

"Is that really necessary?" Jordan asks when there is a pause in the conversation.

I sigh at the silence on the other end. "Sorry, I should've mentioned. Jordan is here with me."

Mr. Masters speaks directly to Jordan this time. "Don't dig up more snakes than you can kill, Mr. Vega. You've seen the evidence in this case. If we assume that the killer is, in fact, not in jail already and he or she finds out that you two are poking around, which of the three of us most resembles one of his victims?"

Jordan's eyes widen and dart over to me before he swallows hard. "Fair enough."

I frown and try not to show the sudden biting chill that slithers down my spine. "I'm not even blond, and I'm too young—not his type."

"No, but sometimes anyone who's in the way will do just fine." Mr. Masters's voice lowers and he waits for his words to sink in. "In all your haste to find your truth come hell or high water, you should try to remember that and be careful."

I don't say anything until Jordan gives me a pointed stare and I roll my eyes. "Noted." Then I decide to change the subject. "I've learned some new information. I'm not sure if you already know about it."

"What did you find out?"

I open my mouth to answer, but then hesitate. Everything Mama told me still feels so raw and personal, it's hard to make myself repeat it.

Mr. Masters doesn't seem to need an explanation for my reluctance. "Miss Riley, now isn't the time to start chewing your bit." His tone is kind, but there is a slight edge of impatience behind it.

Jordan watches scenery outside his window, but when I glance his way, he meets my eyes and gives me the tiniest nod of encouragement.

"Okay." I speak up. "I'm not sure if this has anything to do with Daddy's case, but I found out something about my parents last night."

I can hear Mr. Masters frown through his voice. "Like?"

"It's about an accident Mama was in." I listen for a reaction, but there is none. "Apparently she was twenty-three weeks pregnant at the time. The baby—my brother—died in the accident and it doesn't sound like Daddy took it well."

Mr. Masters's voice sounds distant when he says, "Thank you for telling me. Anything else?"

"Yes. I talked to Mama about the affair, but apparently she thought I was talking about his affair with Stacia, not Hillary." I hold my breath, but everything on the other end sounds calm, no reaction. I'm not sure if that means he already knew or that he can hide his surprise well. I decide to just come out and ask. "Did you know about that?"

"I suspected." His voice is cold and hard. It's so strange to hear from him. "You've been busy. Is there anything else I should know about?"

"Not yet." I listen closely, anxious in case he decides not to tell me the information he promised.

Mr. Masters doesn't say anything else, so I clear my throat. "And your update?"

He waits like he's unsure whether to really tell me the rest. "I believe your father might have hidden something in our offices, but I haven't found it yet, and I'm not sure what it was."

"He hid something? Like what? Why do you think that?" I glance over at Jordan, but he looks as confused as I feel.

"It's half a hunch and half based on old memories." Mr. Masters's voice has dropped down low, like he's telling us an important secret. "I remember him staring at a wall panel when we were in his office during a meeting once. And when I came back later, he was pushing around the corners of it—like he was trying to get it to move."

"Well, have you checked that panel?" I ask as my mind tries to sort out what this could mean.

"It's been almost thirteen years since that happened. I didn't even think about it until recently—"

I cut him off. "How could you have never thought of it before now?"

He gives an exasperated sigh. "Miss Riley, have you forgotten that I'm a criminal defense attorney? If I start snooping without my clients' permission around every case, it's just as likely that I might find something incriminating to my clients as something that could help them. Sometimes it's smarter to forget details like this one."

"Oh." This brings me up short. "So why are you looking into it now?"

His voice softens. "You need the truth. You deserve it. And I'm going to give it to you if I can."

I'm filled with gratitude. "Thank you."

"Don't thank me yet. It's been so long now that I'm not certain I remember which side of the room he was on, let alone the specific panel," Mr. Masters says, sounding frustrated. "To make it plain: I'm working on it and hope to have answers soon. Even if I find this hidden panel, though, it could be anything—from a key to solving this case to a journal of his escapades with his mistresses, or something much worse that we wish we hadn't found. In any case, it could help us find the truth that you're after."

I feel ill at that last thought and don't speak.

"I'm sorry to be so blunt, Miss Riley, but I thought you'd want to know." Masters listens for a response even though he didn't technically ask a question.

"Thank you, Mr. Masters. Apparently my father had far more secrets than I gave him credit for," I murmur quietly, keeping my eyes glued to the road in front of me. "Please let me know if you find anything. Good luck with the panel."

"Thank you."

"Oh, and I need a favor." I bite my lip, hoping that he'll say yes.

"Such as?"

"Can you call Polunsky right now and have them leave a one-day pass at the front desk for me to bring in a visitor?"

He's quiet for several seconds, and then he starts laughing. "Oh, Miss Riley, after what we did to him on Wednesday, are you sure you want to go in there and start a ruckus like this plan is bound to do?"

I glance over at Jordan, who is staring out the window, his jaw clenched.

"I've seen him when he's prepared, and I've seen him with you. Now I want to catch him off guard a bit." I try to make my voice sound as sure as I want to be.

"Well, showing up with Vega's son ought to do it." He laughs one last time. "I'll call the jail as soon as we're off the phone."

"Thank you."

"Not a problem." Masters doesn't hang up. His voice muffles a bit and it sounds like he's moving. "But be careful, young lady. Something about this whole mess is crooked as a barrel of snakes."

Before I can say a word, he jumps in with his final advice. "Do me a favor. Don't trust *anyone*." And the line goes dead.

30

THE VISITING ROOM AT POLUNSKY is no more than eight feet long, but I can't hold still. If anyone had asked me an hour ago who was more nervous for this visit, I would've said Jordan, but on the drive it's like all the anxiety seeped out of him and found its way into me. Jordan sits at the table, his hands clasped in front of him, looking totally relaxed.

Only a few twitches from him hint at the truth. His hands clasp so tight that the skin beneath his fingers stands out white next to the rest of his olive complexion.

We tried several times during the drive out here to come up with a plan for our visit. What questions did we want to ask? What should we do? How do we best convince him to answer?

But we gave up when we realized that we don't have a clue if he will even stay to talk once he sees Jordan. If we can't anticipate how he'll react to Jordan's presence, how can we hope to guess how he might respond to our questions?

The guard opens the door and leads Daddy in. His face is tense from the moment he enters, but when his gaze lands on Jordan, it's clear that throwing him off balance is a tame way to put it. His eyes go so wide they seem to bulge out, and he actually stumbles over the guard's foot, landing with his shoulder against the guard's chest. Even though it is immediately obvious that this was an accident, the guard reacts as though Daddy just pulled a knife.

He grabs onto the front of my father's jumpsuit and slams him hard against the doorframe. The guard shouts directly into Daddy's face, "Don't move!" Which seems redundant since the force of being slammed against the frame has obviously knocked the wind out of his body.

Jordan comes suddenly to his feet, eyes wide. I slide quickly over, grab his shoulder, and gently push him back down into the seat. "Be still. If you do anything it will only get worse."

We'd learned that the hard way over the years.

The guard turns Daddy around and shoves his face against the wall with enough force that his cheekbone starts to swell immediately. I want to shout at the guard, to scream and claw his back. Anything I can do just to make him stop, but I've tried that before. I was escorted out of the building, and Daddy wound up in the infirmary.

I've spent years trying not to focus on the problems with prisons, but it's impossible not to recognize how messed up it is. Daddy has lost fifteen pounds in just the last year. He's been served rotten food or not received his meals at all. The skeletal body he has now barely resembles the pictures of him before his arrest. He'd been healthy and strong and now he's becoming sickly and weak. Which only makes it easier for the guards to "keep him in line" like this. Guilty or not, people are people and shouldn't be treated worse than animals.

The guard checks his pockets for anything my father might be hiding. The only thing he pulls out is a picture that shows Daddy and me when I was little. I'm sitting on his shoulders and he looks up at me with a wide grin on his face. I've never seen that photo before.

The guard starts toward the garbage and Daddy moves to take it back. "Please, no."

"Against the wall, inmate," the guard growls. This time he holds the picture up in front of Daddy's face and then rips it in half. My heart suddenly feels the same rip.

Jordan grabs my hand on the table, squeezing it in an effort to comfort me, but when I see Daddy's gaze focus on the motion, I immediately push his hand away. The fierce and protective anger in my father's expression is something I've never seen before. For the first time ever, I'm a little glad that he's wearing handcuffs and am nervous for the guard to remove them.

The guard finally eases up, spins Daddy back around with his back against the wall, and gets right up in his face. "Don't—touch—the—guards."

Daddy lowers his eyes, looking completely submissive. It works to mollify the guard and he pulls his key out to unlock the cuffs. When he's free, Daddy steps toward me and gently reaches for a hug. After the look he gave us when Jordan grabbed my hand, I'm nervous, but with the guard still watching, I go for it.

Once I'm in his arms, Daddy whispers in my ear, "What do you think you're doing?"

I don't know how to answer yet, so I just move back toward the table. As soon as we're seated, the guard exits, closing the door behind him. I see him throw Daddy's picture of us into the garbage outside. I can't help but wonder if, by bringing Jordan to this visit, I might be doing something similar to my actual relationship with my father.

Shoving aside that awful thought and the guilt that comes with it, I sit awkwardly beside Jordan and across from Daddy. They stare at each other openly, Daddy with obvious malevolence, Jordan with something bordering on defiance.

This is going downhill even quicker than I'd thought.

"So, I guess I don't need to introduce you two . . ." I give a sputtering laugh.

"It's nice to see you again so soon, sweetheart, but when they told me I had two visitors today, I'd been hoping your mother had come," Daddy mutters, looking only at me. Apparently his next option for dealing with this is to pretend Jordan isn't here.

"She isn't feeling well." I cut myself off before I end up spitting out anything less true.

Instead, I try to ease into the discussion we need to have. It was the entire reason that Jordan came with me, after all. "Jordan is trying to help us." I phrase it in the best way I can, hoping maybe Daddy will soften a bit with this knowledge.

He looks directly at Jordan with clear skepticism. "He is, huh?"

Jordan responds before I get a chance. "*He* is trying to help *Riley*."

I hurry on before he can say anything that will be harder to defend. "Yes, he is. I've been trying to understand what happened back then, Daddy." Then I lower my voice and go on. "Jordan came with me to see Mr. Masters. We found out some information about the newest murder."

"That's . . . interesting." Daddy's eyebrows shoot up and he leans back in his chair. His eyes dart back and forth between Jordan and me as though he's trying to figure out this situation. It's clear that he thinks Jordan got the info from his dad, and I decide not to correct him.

"Yes," I continue with more confidence, and let a little of the anger I've been feeling lately show through. "Now, I need to know if you were with Stacia on the night of one of the murders—and don't try to tell me that she left early because I know there are times when she stays late but clocks out early. I've asked the security guard if she's in the office in the past and he says she clocked out, but when I call her cell, she tells me she's still there. Were you together on the night of Hillary's murder? I know you were having affairs with both of them. Were you with Stacia when Hillary was killed?"

Daddy's mouth literally drops open and his eyes are completely focused on me now. "W-why are you even reading about the case or looking into all of this, Riley? I told you not to do that."

"That doesn't matter, Daddy. You stole that option away from me when you told me . . . what you did." I glance at the back of the guard through the door, but Daddy's eyes widen and go directly to Jordan. He stares straight back at Daddy, making zero attempt to hide the fact that he knows exactly what we're talking about.

"You told *him*?" Daddy's pitch drops and he glares at me. "You foolish, foolish girl."

"And I told him that you said it was a lie and why you said you did it." I straighten up my spine and scowl in return. "You're the one who put me in this situation, Daddy. Jordan is just trying to help me find a way out of it."

Daddy is silent, but he continues to glower from Jordan to me and back. Jordan looks like he really doesn't want to be here, but I can tell from one glance that he wouldn't leave me even if I asked him to.

"He didn't answer your question." Jordan's voice is low and deliberately quiet, but it draws a growl from Daddy anyway.

And I'm tired of my father treating me like I'm the only one around here who can be questioned. "This visit isn't about what I'm doing now, though, it's about what you did back then. And he's right: you never answered me." I fold my arms and rest them on the table. "Were you with Stacia?"

Daddy groans, and then his shoulders droop slightly. "I cheated on your mama because people make mistakes and I'm no better than that. I was mad at her for something and it felt like the only way I could make her hurt, too. It was stupid. I was stupid. That affair ended long ago, though, and the only reason I even see Stacia anymore is because I trust her to help me with this case. She's smart, and she feels like our affair somehow landed me here. Don't ever speak to her about this because she'd be horrified, but yes, I cheated, and I regret it."

I feel slightly lighter somehow to finally be hearing what sounds like the truth. I push for more information. "Were you with her the night Hillary was killed?"

"No, I wasn't." Daddy hangs his head down and I feel my hope deflate. "I wish I had been just so I could've prevented all of this, but I wasn't. I told them the truth when I said I have no alibi."

"None?" I ask, feeling desperate. "Not for any of the murders?"

Daddy lifts his face and meets my eyes, his expression full of remorse and regret. "If I had, why wouldn't I have used it back when I was arrested? Believe me, honey, I wish I had someone who could vouch for me. I wish I hadn't spent so much time in my office alone." He reaches his hand out and takes mine. "I wish I'd spent more time at home with you, with your mom."

The room fills with a quiet sadness in the wake of his statement. I look over at Jordan and am hurt to see him still staring at my father with such skepticism. An intense urge to fix something, to make it better for my father, overwhelms me.

"It's going to be okay." He looks up at me, his eyes filled with nothing but despair. "There are many things with this new case that indicate it isn't just a copycat. The killer knows too much for it to be that simple."

Jordan's skeptical look gets darker, but I ignore it, pushing forward. "We have Mr. Masters trying to help in any way he can. He thinks he may be able to find something else that could help. He's going to look—"

Jordan nudges me softly with his elbow in a symbol to stop, but I think that maybe Daddy could make our search go faster if he tells us where the secret panel is.

"He thinks you might have a panel or some kind of hiding place in your old office," I whisper quickly, knowing it's too late to go back now. "Do you think you might've put an old journal, or movie stub, or *anything* in there that could help?"

Daddy looks puzzled. "I don't know what you're talking about. He must be confused. There isn't a panel like that . . . and why is he even involving you kids anyway?"

My heart plummets. "There isn't one?" Somehow, between

Stacia not being an alibi and the fact that there is no panel, this single conversation has ripped big chunks of my remaining hope away. I can tell from the concerned look that Jordan gives me that he can see it in my face.

"No, there isn't. I'm sorry." Daddy releases a giant puff of air, and he gently squeezes my hand, which has gone limp in his. "But you two really just need to sit back and wait for this case to sort itself out. You already said the evidence points to it not being a copycat."

My father glances pointedly at Jordan before finishing. "I'm sure that even *Chief* Vega will have to come to the same conclusion at some point."

Jordan's face reddens and he opens his mouth to respond, so I cut him off before he can.

"I hope he will soon, but I'm not giving up." I release a tense sigh and look over at Jordan, who has resigned himself to fuming silently beside me. "We should probably go."

Daddy looks reluctant to agree, but finally says, "That might be best."

We climb to our feet and the guard opens the door to watch us. I hug Daddy again and he whispers in my ear. "I know I'm just an old guy in prison, but maybe choose who you spend time with a little more carefully."

I whisper back, "He's better for me than you think."

This doesn't appear to make my father feel any better. And when Jordan steps forward and extends his hand, Daddy looks at it for a second like it might bite him before finally shaking it.

"It was nice to meet you, sir," Jordan says, obviously trying to be cordial. "I really do hope we find the *truth*."

It would be hard not to notice the edge Jordan puts on his last word and it's clear that Daddy didn't miss it either when he grunts in response. Daddy walks to the guard with hands extended to receive his cuffs. "Drive safe, Riley, and be careful who you choose to listen to."

31

MY NIGHTMARES HAVE GROWN DARKER to match my life. The storm outside howls again, even louder this time. It sounds like something hunting for vengeance. The power is out, and I know Mama was here only a couple of minutes ago. I walk through the dim hallways calling her name, but there is no answer.

In her room, her bed is made, but I see the lamp on her nightstand has been knocked over. I move to pick it up and jump when a roll of thunder crashes outside.

My heart pounds loud in my ears as I try to catch my breath. I tell myself that it's just a storm, that I don't have to be afraid, but the hairs that stand up all over me don't seem to listen.

I lift the lamp up and as I place it back, another lightning bolt shreds the sky outside and I notice something strange. The side of the nightstand looks like it has a hidden drawer I've never seen before. It is barely cracked open, so I pull it out and see a shimmering light reflected back from inside.

Pure curiosity drives me to reach in, and I lift out a necklace and a watch. My skin flashes hot to cold and I can't breathe. They look just like the description of the jewelry that had been taken as trophies from the East End victims.

Searching the drawer, I see the ring and earrings sparkling up at me. I drop the pieces I'm holding and back myself up into the corner, needing to put at least a couple of feet between me and the trophies a serial killer took from his victims. My mind is a whirl of confusion, trying to sort facts into any sort of order. Does this mean Daddy is guilty? Have his trophies been here with us the whole time?

No, because *Valynne's* earrings are in there. That means—

"You really shouldn't be in here, Riley." Mama stands in the doorway, her face shrouded in shadow.

"Mama . . . no . . ." My voice is a whimper and I cover my face with my hands.

"It's okay, darling. I don't want to hurt you . . ." Her smile seems to turn my heart to ice. "I'll only hurt him."

Glancing to the opposite corner where she is pointing, I can barely make out a hunched male figure. He isn't moving. The cloudy sky outside opens for a moment and I see it's Jordan. His skin is pale and a deep cut on the side of his head has bled down his face and across his shirt.

I move toward him, but Mama flies to intercept me and I scream. The lightning cracks across the sky. The thunder drowns out any other noise.

And then I'm sitting up in my bed. A real storm outside rattles the windows. I'm sweating and panting and my heart feels like it may never slow down again. Grabbing the water bottle off my table, I take a deep drink and just try to make everything in my body calm the freak down.

I've had awful dreams about Daddy, but this is the first one about Mama—at least where she wasn't a victim—and it's left me thoroughly traumatized. I pick up a magazine and spend the rest of the night flipping through it instead of trying to sleep. Every time I start to drift off, a picture of Jordan bleeding fills my mind and I jerk myself back awake. I'd rather be totally exhausted all day Saturday than risk going back to anything remotely like that.

With so little sleep, Saturday has already been a long day. If I hadn't fallen asleep on the couch while I was trying to read through my notebook this afternoon, I probably wouldn't be able to function right now. We only have twelve days left—twelve. The countdown itself is suffocating me slowly. If it continues like this, it feels like I could die before we ever get to Daddy's execution date.

It's after eight o'clock at night when I arrive at the park. I'm a few minutes late and Jordan is already waiting for me. He has a wide smile when he sees me pull in. I'm a little surprised because he hadn't been exactly happy with me when we'd left Polunsky yesterday. He'd said he wasn't mad, but he definitely wasn't normal.

I think about bringing the notebooks out with me. That is what we're meeting to discuss, after all. We're running out of avenues we can look into ourselves, and I need his help finding a new plan to pursue next. But I figure we might want to stay under the parking lot light or in the car anyway. It will be fully dark soon, and I don't see us trying to read our notebooks on the grass in the dark.

I open my car door and climb out. His white teeth are a stark contrast to his olive skin, and I feel my cheeks burn slightly thinking about his lips against my wrist two nights ago. It takes all of my energy to keep from kicking myself. I will not act like some swoony, ridiculous girl, whether or not Jordan makes me feel like one.

I don't know what we have going on between us at this point. The only thing that matters is that he makes me happy at a time when I shouldn't be. Summers are usually an improvement over the school year, but with everything going on in the last few weeks, this one would have been a nightmare without Jordan's help.

"How was your day?" I ask casually as I lead the way over to the swings. In the blood-red light pouring off the gorgeous sunset, both of us look a little flushed. Then I wonder if it's actually from the sunset at all.

He chuckles as he follows me. "Neighborhood football again—does that answer your question?"

I throw a tentative look at him over my shoulder. "If you really used to like it, maybe you should go back someday?"

"Fine, maybe I will—if you promise to come see a game." His brown eyes spark with the challenge he knows I might not accept.

I groan, but then have to admit that deep, *deep* down, I would kind of like to see Jordan play. "Fine. One game is all I'll commit to, and I can wear a hoodie and big dark sunglasses so no one recognizes me."

"Deal. I'd hate to ruin your rep." He grins wide. "At least it wasn't as bad tonight. I dropped two passes, but I actually had fun. Our end of the street won."

When we get to the swings, he takes a seat.

"Do you always drop passes? Maybe you shouldn't go back after all," I half tease.

"No. If I dropped passes all the time, I wouldn't have been on the team, let alone a starter." His eyes drift back to the sunset before us. "I was just distracted today."

"Oh." I try to decide whether I feel bad that helping me may be what's affecting Jordan's playing, but he interrupts me.

"How's your mom doing?" he asks, giving me a concerned look.

"Improving, and she has an interview for a good job lined up on Monday. That should help. Thank you for yester—actually thank you for everything these last—"

He doesn't even let me finish. "No need to thank me. I'm just glad she's okay. Are you?"

I try to think of a response, but just end up shrugging. I really don't know what the right answer to that question would be. He seems to understand, because he doesn't press me. We swing in silence, watching the sunset together, and I realize this might be the most at peace I've felt in a very long time.

I let my swing twist back and forth a bit, and something falls out of my jacket pocket. Before I get a chance to grab it, Jordan reaches out and picks up the paper I forgot I'd put in there.

"What *is* this?" He unfolds it and gets too good of a look before I jump up from the swing and rip it from his hands.

"It's nothing. It doesn't matter." I hold the paper behind my back, hoping he'll just drop it.

Jordan's face looks like a summer storm heading over the horizon, and I know immediately that hiding this from him isn't an option anymore.

"Was that drawing of—give it to me." His calm voice is a startling contrast to his angry expression.

I groan. "It's fine. This really isn't a big deal." I bring the paper forward and try to smooth it out. He stands up from his swing and I hold it out where we can both see. I look again at the crude sketches of Daddy in the electric chair and me hanging from a noose. Seeing them in the fading evening light sends a fresh chill through me. Jordan holds entirely still for several seconds.

"Riley?" Jordan hasn't lifted his eyes yet. He sounds horrified. "You've received more than one note like this?"

I crumple the drawing a bit and drop it onto the ground. "Yes. I've gotten them off and on for years. At school in my locker, sometimes on the front porch, but this one was left on my car. People are stupid sometimes. It's just something I've had to get used to. Don't worry about it."

By the time I finish, the storm in his expression has turned into a full-blown hurricane.

"This isn't *nothing*, Riley. Who would draw something like this? Doesn't having this kind of hostility all around you scare you? It damn well scares me. Why didn't you tell me?" His stare borders on violence. "I thought you trusted me. I thought we were . . ."

His words hang on the air, heavy and dense with implications. They make me want to beg him to finish his thought. What *did* he think we were? What could we even have the potential to be, considering our fathers, considering their history?

But he won't finish. He's waiting for an answer from me. And I honestly have none.

"Yes, it's scary. It's terrifying, but if I let myself be scared by every idiot in this city who has a paper and a pencil, I'd never sleep." My voice shakes now that I allow myself to say these words out loud.

I haven't let messages like this scare me in a while, but that doesn't mean I don't still worry that next time it won't be just a threat in a drawing or on a note.

The anger in his face turns to fear, and then I see sadness that hurts me deeper than I knew it could. "Do you still not trust me? After everything?"

I sit back on my swing and sigh. "Maybe I should've told you, but what good would it do? Like I said, this isn't a new development, and I don't want us to get distracted. We have twelve days left. We're running out of time, Jordan." My voice has a distinct note of panic to it at the end that seems to reach through his emotions. He watches me with a silent frown as I twist in my swing until I'm fidgeting and just wishing that he would speak.

Eventually, I wrap my arms across my stomach, trying to protect myself from his disapproval, which stings worse than it should. "This is too important to me; you know that."

"*You* are too important to *me*! You're more important than a case or a truth or anything else!" He turns away from my shocked expression, leaving me trying to get my heart to stop pounding in my ears. Jordan picks up the paper and scans it again before shoving it in his pocket. He turns to face me, then steps over, lifts my hands off the chains, and pulls me to my feet until I'm standing in front of him.

"Trust me, Riley." The worry I see in his eyes is plain. The hurt he's feeling is fresh.

"I do trust you—" I begin, wanting to reassure him, but he stops me.

He grabs my hand and pulls it in against his chest, clasping it tight between both of his. His eyes plead with me to understand what he's saying. "Believe me that I won't hurt you. I won't disappear. I'm not going anywhere."

The heartbeat that I feel beneath my knuckles is as steady and earnest as Jordan's voice. I want to believe him. I want all of his words to be true, but saying that it *is* true, saying that I do believe him, leaves me open and vulnerable in a way that terrifies me. Only one thought keeps me from saying what he wants me to say.

Not everyone chooses to leave me, but they still do.

"I'm not saying that I won't disappear until we figure this out. I'm not saying I'm here until we find out if your father is guilty or innocent," Jordan gives voice to my fears. Then he brings my hand up, kisses the inside of my wrist again, waiting until I meet his eyes. And then he says the words that I never thought I would hear anyone say. "I'm saying I don't care if your dad did it or not. I don't care because it doesn't change how I feel about you. I'm saying you never *have* to be anything more than just my friend, and I'll still be here to help you. I'm saying I'm here for you as long as you want me around, Riley—*no matter what.*"

When he looks in my eyes, I believe him. In spite of all my parents' lies and the fact that I just found out my dad is a cheater. In spite of the fact that everything between us started out balanced on a finely woven tangle of lies from both sides. In spite of all the reasons my mind gives me not to get any closer to him than I already am.

My heart wants to believe him, and although my heart has given me so many reasons not to trust it, somehow I still do.

"I believe you," I whisper, reaching my free hand out and brushing his soft, dark hair out of his eyes.

"You do?" He looks like he isn't sure he believes me and I can't blame him.

"I do." I pause, searching for the words I need to say in return. "I promise, but you have to trust me, too."

A smile tugs at the corner of Jordan's lips. "You make me nervous."

"What?" I laugh.

His smile fades, but his gaze holds mine. "This whole situation scares me. This—what we're doing—it could be dangerous. I'm scared that someday I may say something stupid to drive you away—and it would lead to you winding up dead somehow. I couldn't take that again." His face is full of the same emotions I've tried to hide from others: anger and sorrow, grief and pain, desire and desperation.

"What do you mean—again?" My fingers itch to reach out for him, but I force them to remain by my sides until I get the full explanation.

Jordan winces and presses his chin into his chest. I can tell he hadn't meant for that word to slip out. Several seconds pass and I wait, biting my tongue, holding my breath.

When he finally looks up to answer, it feels like a knife going through my heart to see his eyes so full of pain. "I've never told *anyone* this . . . but my mom called me on the night she died, before she left the hospital. She said my dad wasn't there to pick her up and she was going to be late. I—I was selfish and I made her feel guilty because it was going to make me late to hang out with some friends. It's my fault that she borrowed someone's car and left right away instead of waiting. It's my fault she was driving that night. All mine. Now . . . I can't *ever* take that back, Riley."

Without thinking long enough to second-guess myself, I reach up and brush the fingers of my right hand against his cheek. He leans his head into my palm and closes his eyes tight against the onslaught of emotion. I try to reassure him. "You had no idea, Jordan. It was just a mistake. People make mistakes all the time."

"I told her that her schedule was ruining my life." He whispers the words, and his breath is hot against my wrist. "Those were the last words she ever heard from me. The last thing I can ever say to her."

"She knows you better than to focus on that." I've seen flashes of something painful that he's been hiding, but I never dreamed he'd been keeping something like this buried. Something this painful, this poisonous—it can eat you from the inside out. It can turn you into someone else, and I can't let that happen to Jordan. I bring my left hand up and place it on the other side of his face until he opens his eyes to look at me. "She wouldn't want you punishing yourself for what you said. You know that, don't you?"

I move my hands down to his neck, watching the shadows play across his cheekbones. His eyes hide nothing from me now. He is haunted and damaged and in pain, so much more than I knew. He hides his secrets better than I ever have, but he isn't hiding them from me anymore. He's trusting me with something he hasn't told anyone else. Shouldn't I be able to put the same kind of trust in him?

"What about you?" he whispers, and his voice is rough as it breaks through the quiet.

I consider dropping my hands back to my sides, but I can't make myself let go of him yet. "What about me?"

"Do *you* know me better than that yet? Do *you* still want me punishing myself for not telling you who I was from the beginning?" He lowers his head so I can't see his eyes anymore. "I never meant to hurt you. That has *never* been my intention. I'm still so sorry, Ri—"

Suddenly, I can't stand to let him apologize again for something so stupid that I forgave him for a long time ago. I do what I've been trying not to think about doing every day for a while now. I kiss him. I pull his neck down, stand up on my tiptoes, and bring my lips up to his.

I've only kissed one boy before, and it was significantly different from this. During my years of perfected avoidance of people in general, I'd done such a superb job that the only guy I ever kissed was someone I met in a mall even farther away than the one where I met Jordan. It was a couple of years ago. We'd flirted, hung out together for one afternoon, and he knew nothing about me. I had told him my name was Buffy and he'd actually believed me. His kiss was kind of sloppy and he tasted like popcorn.

Jordan is completely different. He's obviously surprised, because he falls one step to the side, but it only takes him one soft kiss to recover. By the time I'm trying to decide if this was a mistake and if I should pull away, he slams that thought clean out of my head by kissing me back—and doing one hell of a job at it.

Jordan's kiss makes mine look like a finger-painted portrait next to a Picasso. He wraps one strong arm around my waist and the other around my back and up to my shoulders. His fingers tangle in the hair at the nape of my neck and he pulls me off my feet and tight against him. My hands, which were behind his neck, end up in his hair as my arms cling around his shoulders for support. His lips are soft, and each kiss makes my entire body vibrate with a need to be closer to him. The movement of his lips over mine seems calculated to steal my breath away, and it's clear that I'm woefully overmatched in this department. In chess terms, I'm a novice and he's the equivalent of a grand master. His arms crush me against him with blinding urgency, but his kiss seems to think it has all the time in the world. It is slow, sweet, and I never want it to stop.

I scratch the back of his neck lightly with my nails. He groans and I brush my fingertips through his dark, soft hair. He smells so good, but his kiss tastes even better. The fingers from the hand on my waist slide up across my ribs and it tickles. I laugh involuntarily against his mouth and he pulls back, grinning down at me.

"What is this? You're ticklish?" His eyes have a wicked sparkle to them now that makes me feel like dissolving into a puddle. "The incredibly tough and unbreakable Riley Beckett has a weakness?"

He tickles my ribs with his hands again and I wiggle against him, laughing and trying to escape. Then he moves his head down and snuggles his face in against my neck. I freeze as tingles zing through my body from head to toe. I can't find words to respond with anymore. Jordan chuckles low and soft as he drops a few kisses up my neck and chin, then kisses my lips again.

This time I pull back and rest my head against his chest before I lose my mind completely. My heart is racing, and I have to catch my breath, but finally I respond by carefully lowering a few of my own barricades.

"It would seem that Riley has more than one weakness." I look up at him with a self-conscious shrug. "How's that for incredibly tough?"

I hadn't thought it possible, but Jordan's grin spreads even wider and he lifts me off my feet again in a tight hug. "She seems pretty invincible to me."

I close my eyes and hug him back. For just that moment, I allow myself to pretend that there is no ticking clock, no truth to find, and no father sitting in prison—instead, it is just Jordan and me.

And *invincible* seems like the perfect word to describe this feeling.

32

I STOP STARING AT MY NOTES, stretch my neck from side to side, and look at the time on my phone. It's almost ten o'clock now. Jordan and I have been sitting in my car at the park, going over our notes about Daddy's case for more than an hour, and it doesn't feel like we've gotten anywhere.

"What are we missing?" I finally ask. "Is it crazy to think there may just be one fact somewhere that will tell us the truth?"

Jordan slumps forward and looks at the dashboard glove box in front of him. "I don't know, Riley." He hesitates for a full minute, looking torn before asking, "Do you want me to talk to my father about it?"

"No," I respond, perhaps too quickly, and Jordan waits for me to explain why, watching me closely. I don't say anything else because I don't want Jordan to talk to Chief Vega until we either have irrefutable evidence or we are almost out of time. Until then, I'd prefer the chief to know nothing about me involving his son in all of this. But I really don't feel like explaining that to Jordan.

"I don't want to either," he says after a moment. "But I want you to know that if you ask, I *will* do it."

"Thank you, but I don't think that's the best option—at least not yet." My phone rings and I pull it out of my pocket. The screen flashes the number for Mr. Masters's office before I answer.

"I'm surprised you're still at work this late, Mr. Masters."

"I'm sure there are a lot of things I do that would surprise you." A twitch of his humor actually comes through the drawl and I smile to myself under the parking lot lights. He continues, "Is everything okay? Is Mr. Vega with you?"

"Yes to both, and please no lectures. I'm glad you called, though. You told me to let you know if I found anything interesting—" I plan to go on, but he speaks before I get the chance.

"I want to know, and I have information for you, too, but I don't feel like it's safe over the phone. I'm not alone here." His voice grows muffled. "I think it's best if we meet in person. It has to be tonight."

"Okay. Should we come to your office?" I ask.

"No." His answer is immediate and he sounds like he's thinking. "That won't work either. We need to go somewhere we've never met before . . ."

"Okay . . ." I'm starting to worry about him. "Is everything o—"

"No, I'll explain everything when we meet. Mason Park is our best option. Meet me in thirty minutes. Write down this number and call me when you get there." His tone is brusque now, all soft edges gone, and my hand scrambles for a pen. I flip to an empty page in my notebook and jot it down.

When I finish I say, "Okay."

"Be extra careful. And don't be late." Then I hear a beep and he's gone.

"Hmm . . ." I say as I stare at the phone. Mr. Masters is

275

sometimes gruff, often stubborn, but he never makes me feel un-important. I feel a moment of stifling worry before I stuff the phone back in my pocket. When I turn away from the window, my face almost collides with Jordan's head.

"What did he say?" Jordan leans back a bit to give me a little space.

"He said to meet him at Mason Park in half an hour." I reach down for my keys. "That's nearly thirty minutes from here anyway, so I guess we better get going."

Jordan nods but I catch the slightest hint of hesitation and I raise my eyes.

"What?" I ask, starting the car, but not putting it in gear yet.

"Why Mason Park?" There is worry in his voice.

I catch on to his question immediately, but I don't know the answer. "He said it was our best option. Isn't that the park where Hillary's body was found?"

"Yes." His face is grim as I pull out from my space beneath the parking lot lights. It's weird to think that we're heading back to the place where the body of my father's mistress was found.

Well, *one* of his mistresses, anyway.

Drawing one shaky breath, I grip the steering wheel tightly in both hands. "He was weird and it worries me. I guess we'll have to ask him when we see him."

Mason Park is massive. It sits on over one hundred acres in Hous-ton's East End. Right in the middle of it sits Brays Bayou. My daddy used to talk about bringing me here when he got out—back when he still talked about that like it was something that could happen.

276

It's nearly ten-thirty by the time we get there, and the lights throughout the park seem like pinholes through a black paper, fighting hard but never able to push back the penetrating darkness. The trees hang thick and heavy around the bayou, and the branches cast shadows across the ground like webs of a giant spider just waiting to ensnare us.

I reach for my phone as soon as we've closed and locked my car. My hand dives into my pocket to retrieve the torn-out page of my notebook where I'd jotted down the number Mr. Masters gave me.

I'm not sure if it has to do with the way Mr. Masters ended our call earlier or just the bad vibe I'm feeling, but my tense body wants to finish this meeting and get out of here as quickly as possible. Dialing the number, I wait with my hand gripping the phone tighter than necessary as it rings in my ear.

Mr. Masters picks up after the fourth ring and his drawl is back and slow as ever.

"Good evening, Miss Riley."

"We're here. Is everything okay? This is a pretty creepy time and place to meet." My voice strains and I fight with the same worry that has been plaguing me the whole way here. Daddy has been the one who has watched out for me from behind bars. Ben Masters is the man who has always been anywhere I might need the extra support, and I've never truly thanked him for it. As much as I want Daddy to survive, I must make sure Mr. Masters comes out of this unscathed, too.

One thing we know for sure, the murderer of Valynne Kemp is still out there. Whether they are a copycat or the original East End Killer, they're dangerous. It's unlikely that person would be happy with all the digging around that Mr. Masters has been doing lately.

"Trust me when I say that here and now is the only place I thought we could meet safely. Don't worry, but be careful." His voice takes on a decidedly softer tone that I don't hear from him as often lately, but it calms me down. "I'll tell you everything when you meet me."

"Where should we go?"

"Come to the grove of trees between the soccer and baseball fields," he whispers, softer now. "And Riley? You brought Mr. Vega with you as well, right?"

"Yes." I lift my eyes to look for Jordan and find him standing behind me, leaning in close enough that he can hear everything.

"Good . . . good," he murmurs without explaining any further. "Make sure no one else is following you. See you soon, Miss Riley."

"See you soon." I hang up and stick the phone in my pocket, taking a quick glance around us. This end of the park is empty this time of night; the crickets near the bayou chirp in an off-balance way that makes my nerves feel raw. When I turn to face Jordan, his expression matches the grim feeling that has settled over me.

"Why can't we meet him in the middle of a hot, sunny afternoon?" I say quietly to Jordan as we start walking toward the Mason Park Community Center, which is near the sports fields. Shadows move across the ground in the distance, close enough to be seen, but far enough that I can't make out any details. I can't help but feel like someone is watching us.

Jordan scoffs and shakes his head at me. When I give him a

look, he frowns and says, "Your Mr. Masters does seem to have a bit of a flair for the dramatic."

"He does." I smile softly to myself. "I just hope that's all this is."

"Me too," he answers immediately.

"Do you know specifically where they found Hillary?" My voice sounds tight and Jordan leans closer before shaking his head quickly.

"They said it was near a popular jogging path, but didn't give specifics on which one." He frowns and looks down at the path we're on. "There are so many in this park, it could've been anywhere."

My eyes immediately scan each path in the park around me. In the darkness, each one looks more frightening and ominous than the last. Every branch seems to be an arm reaching out; every howl of wind through the branches could mask a distant scream; every minute we are here feels like it brings us an inch closer to Hillary's fate.

I quicken my pace and pull my jacket tighter. "The sooner we can finish this and get out of here, the better."

We walk past the empty sports fields, their lack of light and life making them seem dismal and lonely. It's odd how these reminders of happy times somehow become incredibly depressing the instant the crowds leave and the lights go out.

Every movement and sound draws our attention with each tense minute that passes. I glance over at Jordan and see his gaze shifting from side to side with nearby sounds, with the rustling of a branch.

He catches my eye and attempts to smile. "Isn't this the part in the scary movies where everyone dies or we find a skeleton or something?"

"Don't worry, I've seen this one. It's usually the girl in the bikini who dies first." I gesture toward my jeans and purple striped T-shirt. "We should be safe." I try to play it off, pretending I'm not as scared of what we could run into as he is.

Jordan puts on a brave smile, too, then shrugs. "Don't be too sure, Riley. You don't know what I'm wearing *underneath* this." He points to his dark blue jeans and red shirt, then winks. A surprised laugh bursts from me at the imagery.

"Excellent point." I squeeze his hand and think I see the grove we're looking for up ahead. I whisper the rest. "Although, if you *are* wearing a bikini under that, I think there may be an entirely different discussion for us to have."

We both freeze when I hear a woman's voice yelling up ahead, but I can't make out what she's saying. My entire body breaks out in a cold sweat, and Jordan instinctively steps in front of me. As we jog a few steps closer, I see two figures in the grove where we are supposed to meet Mr. Masters. From this distance, it's hard to tell, but they seem to be fighting.

My thoughts settle on one possible scenario: the woman is the next victim of Valynne's killer, and maybe if we hurry, we can stop him from killing someone else. I glance at Jordan, and can see he's thinking the same thing. We both break into a run.

Before we get to the grove, an earsplitting boom rends the air and Jordan and I dive toward each other, tumbling to the ground. My eardrums are vibrating and I keep staring at Jordan to make sure he's okay. He seems to be doing the same thing with me.

When we realize we're both fine, we crawl into the shadows of the nearest tree and peer through the branches as quietly as possible toward the grove.

Now there is only one figure standing—next to a large mound on the ground.

A gunshot? That isn't the East End Killer's M.O. My panicked mind searches for some other explanation as we move a few steps closer: a mugging gone wrong perhaps?

Should we run? Should we help?

Then pure fear slides through my veins as I realize that Mr. Masters should've been here already . . . that maybe he beat us here and one of the figures in the grove is him.

I hear footsteps and a woman runs into view. With her back toward us, I see a gun dangling from her fingers. Her entire body quivers. I gasp and grip Jordan's arm.

Even from this angle, I would recognize her frizzy hair anywhere.

She turns at my gasp and lifts the shaking gun in my direction.

"Stacia," I whisper, and Jordan immediately grabs my arm, trying to pull me back into the shadows behind him. I don't move.

Her eyes are distant at first, then they focus in on me. Her blouse hangs oddly to one side, and her jacket is ripped. She has something rectangular clutched in her free hand, but I can't make out what it is. She looks unkempt and wild in a way I've never seen her before, and she lowers the gun back to her side.

I hear people in the distance and she looks toward them. She pulls the rectangular package in against her chest before sprinting into the trees and toward the other end of the park. I watch her go, wondering if I should have stopped her and whether she was being attacked and needs help.

With my mind whirling, it's only when her back disappears into the trees that my thoughts settle on the form on the ground and my whole world lurches to a stop.

"No . . . no, no, no!" My words begin as a whisper and end as a shout. Jordan reaches out to stop me, but I break free, running over to the body on the ground and praying again and again in my head for it not to be *him*.

When I reach the form, I roll him onto his back. Everything in me seems to lock up in one instant as I see those familiar blue eyes gazing up at me.

Jordan is by my side immediately, pushing his hands into the bloodstained shirt, trying to apply pressure to the wound in the center of his chest.

I can't breathe. I can't think. How can this be happening? Stacia shot Mr. Masters? Why? *Why?*

Then the blue eyes blink and turn on me. Choking in a deep gasp of air, I lean down. "You're going to be okay. We'll get help." I pull out my phone and begin to dial 9-1-1 with shaking fingers, but Mr. Masters pushes the phone out of my hand and it falls somewhere in the grass behind me. He seems like he wants to talk, but blood trickles out of the corner of his mouth when he opens it.

"No . . . don't talk. Just wait until you're better." I sit beside him, hugging his head. "I love you. Please don't leave me."

Sitting back, I see a tear leak out the side of one of those blue eyes. Then they fill with an abrupt terror as he pulls me down again. Jordan still has his hands pressed against Mr. Masters's wound, but I hover close over Mr. Masters, brushing one hand across his forehead.

He draws another rasping breath. It looks like it causes him extreme pain, and I choke on a sob.

Then he utters the one word he's been trying so hard to tell me: "Run."

My head shoots up, and I look around us, suddenly feeling a very different sort of fear, but there is no one else. The commotion of people in the distance is getting closer, but it's only the three of us alone in this clearing. I lean back over this man who has always been there and whisper, "Shh. It's okay."

With a final shudder his body relaxes and his eyes become unfocused. By now the entire front of Mr. Masters's shirt and jacket are red with blood, and there is a rapidly spreading damp spot on the ground beneath him.

I kneel beside his head, a slow numbness creeping over me like the ocean tide on the beach.

"Mr. Masters?" I whisper, but there's no response. My own voice seems far away, and I move in a daze. On instinct, I do what I always see people do at crime scenes on TV. I press my fingers against his neck, trying to find a throbbing pulse—something to give us hope that he can be saved.

I feel nothing.

Jordan is covered in blood up to his elbows and his skin is deathly pale in contrast. He keeps putting pressure on Mr. Masters's chest and repeating his name. Finally, I reach out and grab Jordan's wrist.

"He's gone," I say, then I repeat it again until it sinks in for both of us. "He's gone. He was trying to help Daddy. He was trying to help me, Jordan. He came here to meet us, and oh God . . . he's gone."

My voice cracks, and Jordan finally looks up at me. Neither of us speaks. There isn't anything to say.

Suddenly there are flashlights and shouting people everywhere. Not people—police. I look for the phone Masters had pushed out of my hand. I didn't call them. Jordan is yanked to his feet and I see Chief Vega behind him. He grabs Jordan's face and looks hard at him. "What in God's name are you doing here?"

I glance in the direction Stacia ran and raise my shaking hand to point that way. "Stacia . . . she ran that way."

Vega looks down at me, his face a mask. Then he nods, releases Jordan, and starts shouting orders.

She really killed Masters? How could this have happened? Nothing makes any sense. I squint into the darkness but I see no movement anywhere in sight. My entire body is quaking even though I don't feel cold. In fact, I'm so hot I think I'm sweating. My brain and body don't appear to be communicating, and I can't figure out how to make them start talking to each other again.

I hear Jordan's voice from a distance as I smooth Mr. Masters's silver hair back off his forehead. "We didn't get a chance to call you. How did you know to come?"

"Mr. Masters called me fifteen minutes ago and said I needed to come. He said he thought you were in danger at Mason Park, and then he hung up." Another officer comes up, pulling Vega's attention away.

Out of nowhere, one of the chess games I played with Daddy

comes to mind. I'd thought I had him, and then he turned every-thing around on me in a completely unexpected move.

Always make your smartest possible move, and keep the endgame in sight.

Mr. Masters must've called the police just after he called me. Did he know Stacia was here then? Did he know how dangerous she is? He and Daddy are the smartest men I've ever known and some-how they'd both been cornered, trapped. We're running out of options in an increasingly deadly game, and now I have to face it without either of them.

Jordan kneels beside me. He keeps trying to close Mr. Masters's coat over the wound, but with the position of his body, it refuses to stay closed. I'm deeply grateful for the numbness that seems to be protecting me from feeling anything right now, because one of us has to function.

I smooth my hand over Mr. Masters's face, closing his eyes be-fore I climb up on my trembling legs. Chief Vega looks over at me and tells the person he has on the phone to hold on.

I turn and look him straight in the eye. "I w-want to help you. Tell me what you need to know."

33

"WHY DID YOU COME HERE TONIGHT?" Chief Vega asks
once he has me wrapped in a paramedic blanket and seated on the
front of his car.

"M-Mr. Masters asked us to meet him here," I answer, trying to
ignore the worried way Jordan is watching me from his seat in the
back of the ambulance. The paramedic keeps trying to clean the
blood off his hands—Mr. Masters's blood.

An intense wave of dizziness hits me, and I tilt on the car hood.
Chief Vega reaches out to steady me, but I place my hands on the
hood beside me and do it myself.

"Did he tell you why he wanted you to meet him?"

"Not exactly," I answer, my throat feeling and sounding raw.
"He said he had information about my dad's case."

I hesitate before continuing with a biting edge. "I'm pretty sure
you're familiar with that."

Chief Vega acts as though I didn't add the last part as he asks a
few more questions about whether Stacia saw us and if Masters
gave us any reason to think Stacia was involved.

"You said you saw two figures in the clearing before you heard the gunshot." He squints down at his paper before looking at me again. "What were they doing?"

"I heard her yelling, but I couldn't make out what she was saying." I think back on the image of the two figures fighting in the clearing. "They were struggling. Maybe fighting over the gun, I don't know."

Then I hear the gunshot again in my head and I flinch.

Chief Vega puts down his notebook. "Let's take a break. I'll get the rest of the answers at the station. Okay?"

"Okay." I'm grateful. I need a minute to process this before talking more about the end of Mr. Masters's life. It's too much.

The chief puts his hand out like he's going to pat me on the shoulder, but when I shrink back, he only returns it to his side. Without another word, he turns away and starts organizing the many officers who've gathered in the clearing.

Under Vega's command, the police swarm through Mason Park like honeybees in a field of wildflowers. They've taken so many pictures that I've lost count, and I watch them move Mr. Masters's body into a black bag. It's exactly like the one they put Valynne Kemp in. I haven't cried. I've barely blinked. Even though I can't see Mr. Masters anymore, I can't take my eyes off the lumpy contours of the bag. It feels wrong to stick someone who was vibrantly alive only a couple of hours ago into a black sack. It feels like he has already been discarded. Even though I know he doesn't care anymore, it makes me feel claustrophobic just looking at him.

Jordan comes to sit beside me on the car hood, but he doesn't speak. I tuck my feet beneath me because I can't stop thinking about walking over and unzipping his bag. Seeing him one more time. Letting this man, who has been there for me through everything, have access to the air that he can no longer breathe.

Eventually, I stop trembling, but my jaw won't seem to unclench. The paramedics—who have now declared us to officially be in shock—keep bringing me wool blankets and draping them over my shoulders, but I feel so overheated that I keep pushing them off.

Chief Vega has been in charge of telling what appears to be every officer in Houston what to do and where to search for Stacia. He questioned me after I basically ordered him to, but I'm not sure he's spoken to his son at all. Jordan's shoulders slump farther in on himself as he watches his father from a distance. He looks like a turtle trying valiantly to pull his head into a shell that has somehow become too small for him.

Everything about this feels so unreal. Mr. Masters's voice over the phone . . . he'd sounded terrified, and now I'll never know exactly what he'd wanted to tell us. Was it about Stacia and what she was capable of? Even his final word, *run*. From what? What did that mean? Did he somehow not know that Stacia had already left?

Now one of only two people who'd never left me is gone. The man who was more like family than my own family is dead.

Except for the pictures from the trial and the bag from Valynne's crime scene, I've never seen a dead body. Now I know what it's like to see the life drain from someone and the spark leave their eyes.

I shudder as a tiny sob escapes my lungs and it burns. The quaking begins all over again.

After about two hours of waiting, Chief Vega finally turns in our direction again. His skin is as pale as Jordan's. The main difference between father and son right now is that while Jordan looks

288

terrified and angry, his dad looks exhausted. "I'm going to need you both to come down to the station for a few more questions. Riley, I've called your mother, and she is going to meet us there."

I groan, looking at my watch and realizing I've definitely broken my promise about being home by curfew.

Jordan's hands ball into fists beside me as his father turns away. I hear him respond with a "Yes, sir" that is so vehement that it might as well have been a curse. Chief Vega's back stiffens, but he continues walking away without even another glance toward us.

Jordan and I are placed in separate rooms as we fill out written statements about everything we saw and heard at the crime scene. By the time I've relived and written down what happened, I feel like someone has squeezed me like a rag and drained all the emotion from my body. I hurt everywhere, but it feels like an ache so deep that it's burrowed below my muscle and into my marrow. The kind of pain I may never be rid of. Still, I feel like I did a good job of remembering everything. I'm not sure if I'm too rushed or if Jordan's far too detailed, but I finish long before he does.

I'm sitting alone in Chief Vega's office and looking out the window behind his desk. I'm so tired I just want to go home and pretend this night, this month, this lifetime never happened. My mind is absent as I stare into the darkness outside, until a navy blue Toyota pulls up and turns off its headlights. I sit forward, squinting because the car looks so familiar.

Then the door opens and a very wobbly Stacia climbs out.

I tense, wondering if I should duck down so she won't see me. She doesn't even look my way. Vega sent officers to her home and we'd heard someone over the police radio report in that she wasn't there. I'd thought maybe she'd made a break for it, but here she is.

I watch her stumble out of her car, obviously drunk and wearing heels that are so high I'm certain I couldn't even walk in them while sober. Her makeup is darker than I've ever seen it, and there are black mascara trails down her cheeks. She's wearing a sequined top with a multicolored scarf and she has on more jewelry than I've ever seen on her before. Compared to her normal appearance, this looks like an explosion happened while she was standing in front of a jewelry store.

Stacia looks more like she's getting ready to go clubbing than stopping by the police station after just murdering her boss in a park. I breathe out a small sigh of relief when I look closely at her outfit and can't see anywhere that she could be hiding the gun she'd run off with.

When she makes her way toward the station entrance and out of my sight, I get to my feet and move to stand in the doorway so I can see what happens when she comes in. She walks straight up to the front desk. Everyone is busy and no one is there, so she dings the small silver bell again and again until everyone stops what they're doing and looks over at her.

Chief Vega walks out of a room with Jordan directly behind him and when he looks at Stacia I know he recognizes her, because his hand moves to the butt of his gun and he keeps it there.

"Hello," Stacia says, putting one hand on her hip in a big and exaggerated motion. "I need some assistance."

"How can I help you?" Vega asks, taking a few cautious steps closer. I see other officers around the room take their cue from him and move in front of any civilians they are with. Several also put their hands on their weapons, and I see a woman in the back whispering quietly into a phone. My back stiffens and fear makes me take one slow step to back up toward the darker recesses of the office.

Stacia notices my movement and her face lights up. "Riley!"

I freeze, then step forward into the doorway again. "Hi, Stacia."

"Come here, sweetheart." She waves for me to join her by the front desk, and when I hesitate, her face crumples. "You should be front and center for this . . ."

She doesn't have a weapon and half the guns in the room could be pointed at her in under a second. Jordan's eyes meet mine and they plead with me not to go—he gives a stiff shake of his head. I look back to Stacia. If me standing beside her will get her to explain what happened tonight, then—for Mr. Masters—it's worth any risk.

I slowly walk toward her and Jordan tries to come after me, but his dad stops him. He whispers something back to Jordan that makes him stop fighting.

"I'm here." I stop a few feet away and try to look calm. "Why are you here? What do you want to tell me?"

"I know you saw me at the park so you know already—" A half sob escapes her chest before she smiles ruefully. "That I'm a killer."

My heart burns with pain and anger in my chest. The bizarre thought that confessions aren't supposed to be like this crosses my mind before I bite my tongue and wait for her to continue. She doesn't, so I say, "Why did you kill him?"

"Them," she corrects me immediately. "Why did I kill them."

"Why did you kill them?" I repeat, feeling sick to my stomach, but I force myself not to turn away or run.

"Because it helps me feel better when I don't feel—happy." Stacia closes her eyes for a second and I see Vega moving a few feet closer. When she hears his shoe squeak, Stacia opens her eyes and grabs a pair of scissors off the front desk. She holds them out toward me. Then she grabs me and wraps her arm around my neck when I try to step away. Every gun in the room is lifted to point at her.

"Let her go, Stacia." Chief Vega sounds perfectly calm.

She growls into my face and the hair on my body stands on end. She presses the scissors against my throat. "I thought you wanted to hear my story!"

"I do," I answer quickly. "I don't like scissors, but I'm not going anywhere."

Stacia calms down immediately and loosens her grip on my neck, pulling the scissors a few inches away from my skin. "Good."

"Who did you kill, Stacia?" I ask softly, careful not to move or even breathe very loudly. With enormous effort, I manage to keep my eyes toward Stacia and not on the silver sheen of the scissors she holds in front of my face or on the many guns in the room now pointed toward us.

"I knew since you saw me with Mr. Masters that I wouldn't get away with it. But if I'm getting credit for him, I want credit for the rest." She laughs softly and moves the scissors through the air like she is tracing an infinity sign. "I killed *all of them*."

My throat closes up and she suddenly looks less like Daddy's weird mistress or his assistant—and more like a dangerous psychopath who is waving a sharp object in my face. I start to tremble again before I lock up all my joints in an effort to stop it.

The next time the blade moves before my eyes, I flinch and she freezes, looking sad. Then she lifts the scissors to her neck and drops her arm so I can take a step away. I turn to see her touching the scissor tips to her earrings and then her necklace. She grabs hold of my arm. "Did you see?"

"Yes, very nice," I answer immediately, but then the earrings catch the light and I actually look closer at them. They're high quality and look very expensive. My hand covers my mouth and my eyes go wide. "Oh my God. A—are those Valynne Kemp's earrings?"

Stacia nods with approval like I've finally reached the right answer. "And . . . ?"

My eyes quickly scan her other jewelry, and I see she has a necklace that could be Hillary Vanderstaff's, a ring that could be Sarah Casey's—even a watch that isn't her usual one. It must be Maren Jameson's watch. Stacia has the trophies from all the victims, both the ones Daddy was convicted of murdering and the newest one. And she just wore them all into the police station. Could Stacia have been the East End Killer this whole time?

I glance over at Jordan and his father. They both have looks of complete shock on their faces. From the edge of my vision, I see an officer sneaking around the corner of the desk toward her.

"How did you get this jewelry?" I ask, forcing myself not to bite at the hope that dangles itself like bait before my nose.

Stacia looks at me like my question disappoints her, and she shakes her head. "I've always had it—ever since the nights I killed them. Vega is a fool, putting your daddy away when he had nothing to do with it. I hoped they would eventually figure out he was innocent, but they didn't. After he was arrested, I tried so hard to stop. But then I had to start killing again, to give them a clue." She looks at me and shrugs. The combination of madness and utter sorrow behind her gaze is terrifying. "I couldn't let them execute him for something I did. I guess we do crazy things for the people we love."

"Stacia, I need you to put down the scissors and let Riley go," Chief Vega says quietly.

Her hand loosens on my arm, and my instincts scream at me to move away, to run, but I'm so close to getting what I've always wanted that I can't back down now. *Why* did you kill them?"

She shrugs and says simply, "Because they looked like your mother. And she had your father, so I couldn't stand by without doing anything."

And then, as if she had heard her name mentioned, my mom rushes in through the door to the police station. Her hair is mussed and her coat is buttoned wrong. Vega had obviously woken her when he called, but I'm relieved to see she looks totally and completely sober.

Mama lets out a huge puff of air when she sees me, then her eyes go to the scissors pointed at my chest—and then up to Stacia.

Then the thing I least expect happens. Mama lets out a wild snarl and leaps on Stacia. She hasn't even hit her before Stacia drops the scissors in shock. Then Mama is on her and she punches Daddy's mistress twice before two officers pull her off and another takes Stacia back toward a holding cell.

Stacia yells out to Mama through her already swelling lip, "You know he always loved me more. You're just the woman that he refused to abandon. *I'm* the strong one. He's always known that."

Now that I don't have scissors pointed at me anymore, my heart resumes a normal rhythm and I feel like I might be sick. Did Stacia really kill all those women because she loved Daddy and couldn't handle the jealousy? I know she killed Mr. Masters because he found out. I was there to see it. What if she had just decided one day that killing replacements for Mama wasn't good enough? What if she decided it was time to go for the real thing?

My chest burns, and I have to force my breathing to slow down so I don't pass out. Jordan's eyes are full of worry when they meet mine.

Mama's knuckles are bleeding as she turns to the officers and asks politely, "Could you release me? I need to clean up this blood before I make a mess."

I grab some tissues from a box on the desk and bring them to Mama as the officers receive a nod from Chief Vega and step away. She dabs at a few drops of blood on her right fist, wincing. Then she wraps both arms around me tight. "You, my dear girl, have some serious explaining to do."

I laugh and hug her back. "Yes, I guess I do."

Chief Vega walks up and taps my shoulder with Jordan right behind him. "Are you okay? That was dangerous to face her like that, but very brave."

"I'm fine," I say, taking a step back out of Mama's hug, but she keeps her arm around my shoulder, and I'm glad. I need that strength to ask the question that I'm about to ask. "Does this mean—does this mean that my father will be released?"

Vega's jaw tightens and he doesn't answer for a few seconds. "That isn't up to me, but I will make sure all of the evidence and Stacia's confession are processed and presented before a judge first thing Monday morning. The rest will be up to the court and the district attorney's office."

My chest feels like it has a slowly filling balloon trapped inside it that he just popped. I can't say I'm surprised by his answer, and honestly a piece of me deep, deep down feels the smallest bit of relief. Maybe they'll just delay his execution and his release may take a while. That way I can figure out how to deal with the idea that my father may finally come home—only now I think of him less as an underdog hero and more as a cheating, lying stranger.

Chief Vega looks from me to my mom and then he lowers his voice. "I'm sorry I can't promise anything more. I will say that this case looks very different right now than it has in the past."

Mama looks down at me and forces a smile, but I see a tiny amount of anxiety behind her gaze.

And I wonder if she might be seeing that same anxiety in me.

34

IT'S MONDAY AFTERNOON. Jordan has been at my house for an hour, and we haven't spoken more than two dozen words the entire time. We're watching some old *Twilight Zone* episode we found online. It's kind of creeping me out and that's the only thing we've discussed. I keep worrying this could be what I've been afraid of all along. Maybe now that we don't need to talk about Daddy's case anymore, we have nothing else to talk about. My heart tells me that fear isn't true and Jordan deserves more credit than that. Maybe something else *is* bothering him—whatever it is, I hate it. What does it say about us if things get awkward and uncomfortable the moment we don't have a life or death question we're trying to find the answers to?

Mama calls me from the other room and I jump off the couch at the first excuse to get away for a minute. It's weird having Jordan and Mama around at the same time, but she set up some new rules while we were on the way home from the station Saturday night, insisting that we stop sneaking around.

"If you are going to date someone, you'll do it in daylight and under my nose, young lady. You'll do it proper or you won't do it at all," she'd said.

"Yes, ma'am" is still basically the only acceptable response when Mama talks to me like that.

I jog into the kitchen, where Mama sits at the table with the phone in her hands. Her skin is pale, and when I sit down, she grabs my hand. "I just received a phone call from Chief Vega."

"What did he say?" I'm not sure if I want to know.

"They received preliminary forensic results back on the scarf Stacia wore into the station," she answers, and her grip on my hand tightens. "They've matched it to all of the murders; it has DNA from five different people. They believe it was the weapon used on all of the women."

I don't know what to say. I can't speak and I can't seem to figure out what kind of response she is looking for from me. Finally, I come up with something truly profound. "Wow . . ."

"Chief Vega said that he and the DA had a judge issue an emergency stay of execution, and they have a hearing scheduled with the DA and a judge on Friday. If the results come back like they're expecting, your father's conviction will be overturned." Mama blinks a few times as if she can't even believe the words she's saying herself. "It sounds like—like he'll be exonerated, Riley. He may be released in less than a week."

I try to swallow but I can't, and I actually feel light-headed. No response I can give would be adequate. I'd honestly given up hope on ever getting Daddy exonerated. At some point over the last few years, I'd settled for just hoping that they wouldn't go ahead with killing him.

And now with this stunning news, I don't know whether to laugh or cry . . . or both at once. On the one hand, Daddy may be released from Polunsky. I won't have nightmares about his treatment, the food, or the other inmates anymore. I won't have to worry about him anymore.

On the other hand, I've learned so much in the last couple of weeks. I won't be able to forget it, no matter how hard I try. How can I go back to respecting and honoring him when I've learned that he's never been the man I've built him up to be?

Can I trust him not to cheat on Mama again? Can she?

What if she decides he can't come back here at all? Would that be better?

I tighten my grip on Mama's hand and put on a smile, vowing to myself that wherever Daddy ends up, I will make sure he never hurts Mama again.

And who knows? Hopefully he's learned his lesson from his time in prison. Eleven and a half years served for crimes he didn't commit should at least buy him a fresh start, right?

Mama still watches me, waiting for my response, so I say the only thing that is completely, one hundred percent true.

"I can't believe this is actually happening."

After an extensive reminder of the rules for having Jordan over, Mama leaves for her job interview. When I come back to the living room, I see Jordan poring over a page from his notes on the East End Killer case again. I'm certain the only reason Mama hasn't taken our notes away already is because she doesn't know where I hide them.

He's studying something so intently that he doesn't even realize that I've come back. Something about Jordan waiting until I leave to pull out the notebook rubs me the wrong way.

"Hey," I say quietly, and he jumps. Seeing him close the notes immediately only increases my irritation. "What are you doing?"

"Just double-checking a couple of things." He's deliberately vague as he watches me, then he tries to change the subject. "Want to watch more of this show?"

"No," I answer softly, knowing that with Daddy coming home soon, we're going to have to sort this out sooner or later. "Is there *anything* that can convince you that he didn't do it?"

Jordan sighs and hangs his head. "Are *you* convinced?"

"Yes!" I answer immediately, deliberately avoiding taking any time to think. "She had the trophies and the murder weapon. She confessed!"

He whispers so softly that I barely hear him. "So did he."

I flinch, feeling like he smacked me. "I never should have told you."

"No." Jordan looks up now. He keeps his words quiet, but I see a steely resolve in his eyes. "You should have told *everyone*."

"You're just biased!" My voice feels like it's rising in volume and I can't stop it. Daddy's possible release has me scared and excited and angry, and Jordan is providing me with the perfect punching bag to take all those mixed-up emotions out on. "He may have done a lot of awful things, Jordan, but he isn't a killer."

"How can you *know* that? How can you even believe you *really* know him after everything we've learned?" He points at me with the corner of his notebook, and I rip it from his hands.

"Apparently, I know him better than I know *you!*"

Jordan reaches his hands up and pushes his hair out of his face. I can see his frustration growing, but I don't care. Can't he see that the last thing I need is his questions on top of my own right now?

He looks me dead in the eye, and I see something else in his face now. Fear. "What if you don't know him at all? What if they release him out on the streets and he hurts someone else? What if this time it's your mom . . . or *you?*"

"I guess we'll find out soon, because your dad called to say that he'll likely be released next week!" I spit out the last word so hard that a dark strand of my hair swings in front of my face.

My words obviously shock him because a full twenty seconds pass before he replies. "This isn't some game we can keep playing anymore, Riley."

I jerk back. "This has *never* been a game to me."

"I know it isn't—I just meant—" He groans and I can see several emotions behind his expression. Then he seems to decide to go a different direction. "So you're telling me that the moment the courts start believing he's innocent—now you suddenly think the system isn't broken anymore?"

"And you suddenly think it is?" Cynicism drips from my tone as I throw my hands up in the air and turn away. Every argument he uses on me, he could just as easily say to himself. How can he not see that? "You were there when Stacia confessed, too. You saw all the evidence she had—"

"Think about what we saw, though. She is clearly unstable, and also desperate to do *anything* to save the man she loves from being executed." He speaks slower, obviously trying to keep our argument from escalating out of control.

"Fighting within the law, even threatening a judge or something, I could see her going that far. But you're suggesting that she killed Mr. Masters and Valynne Kemp and now could very likely end up on death row herself?" I lift both my eyebrows. "You're giving her credit for an incredible amount of loyalty."

"Yes," Jordan says, giving me a pointed look. "Something your father seems to inspire in women all over Texas."

I draw in a sharp breath, bristling at the jab even though a voice deep inside tells me that he has a point. Before I dare speak, I bring my hands up and massage the back of my neck. The knot of tension there just keeps growing with this argument. "That doesn't make any sense. Why wait eleven and a half years if she's willing to do something this drastic? Why not just lie and provide him an alibi to begin with?"

This time Jordan falters. "I don't know. Maybe she didn't want to lie then, and seeing him in prison has made her desperate. I do know one thing though: my dad thinks she's lying. He thinks people will be in serious danger if your dad is released—and I believe him."

I just stare at him and then roll my eyes, not at all surprised to hear Chief Vega is following protocol on the release while secretly not believing Daddy should be back on the streets. I reply sarcastically, "And this is supposed to shock me?"

"Why did Mr. Masters even want to meet us? Have you thought about that?" When he says Mr. Masters's name, I flinch, but with a determined look on his face, Jordan just keeps going. He shoots off more questions so fast that it's obvious he's been wondering about them as much as I have tried not to. "Why did she kill him at all? What was he going to tell us, Riley?"

My voice drops lower now as a fresh wave of pain about losing Mr. Masters washes over me. "Maybe he was going to tell us that Stacia did it. Maybe she killed him to stop him from doing just that."

"And then just popped on down to the station to confess on her own? Why?" He presses on, like if he can just ask the question the right way, the truth will suddenly appear for me.

"She already told us that. She knew we both witnessed her killing him, and she decided that if she was going down for that one, she might as well come clean about all of them and save Daddy, too." I stare hard at Jordan, preparing myself for whatever he has coming next.

"Or maybe she killed Mr. Masters to stop him from telling us something else, and she succeeded. Maybe she knew she was going down for that death, so she might as well save your father in the process. Plus, she's a legal assistant for a criminal defense attorney. She has to know that, as a woman, her chances of actually being executed are far lower than his." His argument is part plea and part reprimand.

"You can't argue that she's unstable and then argue that she's reasonable enough to think all that through," I say. "You're grasping."

"Maybe so, but come on, Riley, you have to see that Stacia's story doesn't really fit every detail." I can see that my stubborn responses are starting to chip away at the composure he's trying so hard to maintain.

I sit down in the nearest chair with a groan. "No, but I'm sure you can educate me."

"She doesn't seem methodical or organized, but the killings *are*. Even the way the bodies were laid out matches the way your father lived his life—the mask of normal on the outside, broken and twisted on the inside." He shakes his head and sits down in the chair next to mine. "You have to see that."

"And a legal assistant who's hiding her taste for murder doesn't sound like that as well?"

"Can't you see that I'm scared?" he pleads. "If your father is released, he might hurt you, but I've seen him with you and I doubt that."

"Good." It's a relief to finally agree on something.

"But it's also possible that he'll come after the man who put him in prison in the first place." Jordan's voice is desperate to make me understand, but I can't. Not right now. "Setting aside innocent or guilty, your father still must be so angry. What if he decides to get revenge for all the years he lost? I can't let Matthew lose the only parent he has left."

The energy and anger has been sucked out of me and now this argument is just breaking my heart. "You've *never* believed he could be innocent. You still don't. Like father, like son—I shouldn't have hoped for anything different."

"And you never believed that he could really be guilty." Jordan's shoulders slump and I see the massive dark circles under his eyes. I can't face the idea that what we had may be gone forever. I can't look at him and *see* what trying to help me has done to him.

It hurts too much and I'm tired of all this pain.

"I think you should go now." I push the tears away from my eyes before he can see and get to my feet.

He stands up immediately. "Don't do this, Riley, please. I'm just worried. I'm scared that he'll—"

"Come on," I interrupt, and start moving toward the front door, waiting for him to follow me. When he doesn't, I say, "We were idiots to think our differences wouldn't rip us apart eventually."

He follows me, but I can see the arguments he's trying to formulate in his eyes as we walk and know that I need to get him out of here before I crumble completely.

"We're too different and we've always been too different. Seeing you can only hurt me now . . . and you said you wouldn't hurt me."

Jordan stands on my front porch, his eyes filled with pain and worry. He reaches out, his fingers grasping my hand as it falls limp in his. "I don't want to hurt you, Riley. I don't know what I would do if anything happened to you."

"Please leave me alone. You'll only make this worse." I shut the door before he can say anything else, then I get as far away from the front door as I can so I won't change my mind and try to take it all back. In my room, I close and lock the door, turn off the lights, and cry silently into my pillow until I fall asleep.

35

BENJAMIN MASTERS'S FUNERAL IS CROWDED with clients, secretaries, lawyers, judges, and cops. People from all sides of the law gather together and mourn him.

My black dress doesn't keep me warm enough even with the sunlight heating up the fabric. I tightly clutch the yellow flower Mama gave me to place on the casket.

We sit with the people from the law firm. They hug us and tell us they're happy about the news with Daddy's case. When we turn away they whisper about how Stacia "wasn't ever quite right." They say Mr. Masters must've figured out it was Stacia and decided to confront her. More whispers come next, calling him something none would have dared say to his face: "An old fool for trying to take on a killer by himself." It reminds me of some of the things they'd whispered about Daddy during his trial, and I have to grit my teeth not to respond the way I want to.

I want to stand up, turn to them, and then scream in their faces, *You don't know what the hell you're talking about! So would you please shut up?*

Mama and I both bring yellow roses to put on his casket. First, because Mr. Masters always argued that the yellow rose should be the state flower. Second, because they symbolize friendship and we both agree that our family has never had a better friend.

I stand over his casket and put my hand on the cold silver metal that is so unlike Ben Masters. His thick, warm drawl will always comfort me, and his quick wit and intelligence are impossible to contain in such a small box. I hate knowing he's in there, knowing we lost him—knowing *I* lost him.

Mama walks up beside me and wraps an arm around my shoulders. Bending closer, she whispers in my ear, "You have to stop blaming yourself."

I look up at her and my eyes fill with tears again. "He wanted to meet *me*, to tell *me* something, Mama. He wouldn't have even been there if it weren't for me."

"Investigating your daddy's case is what got him in trouble. And that's his job. This isn't about you, honey." She leans over and kisses my forehead. She smells like fresh flowers, and her eyes are clear. I've been watching closely, and I don't think she's had a drop to drink since the night she was fired. She was actually offered a job yesterday working as an executive assistant with a large accounting firm. She'll be starting next Wednesday. She's excited about it because the atmosphere is more relaxed, and she thinks she'll be able to be home more, which sounds pretty great to me.

Maybe everything will turn around for us now. Maybe we'll finally get that fresh start we've always needed.

I feel someone staring and search the crowd. Jordan's brown eyes watch me from a few rows back on the other side of Mr. Masters's grave. He stands next to Chief Vega. They're both among a group of other officers. The chief nods to Mama, but I can't take my eyes off of Jordan. He looks incredible in his black suit and it makes my heart jump around inside my chest. His eyes are full of all the things I want to see. They're warm and welcoming, and I can see even from this far away that he misses me, too. I want to run to him. It takes all of my willpower not to sprint over and wrap my arms around him.

In the three days since I asked him to go, it's been so hard not to pick up the phone and call or text him. I miss everything about him.

His father leans over and whispers something to him. Frowning, Jordan turns, and the spell is broken. I'm reminded of all the reasons our most important differences will prevent me from ever being with him again.

Dropping my shoulders, I stretch my back as I try to clear the longing out of my bones. I whisper to Mama, "Can we please go?"

She doesn't say a word, but I see her look up at Jordan before she takes my elbow and leads me toward the car. His eyes are on me again like a weight as I walk away, and my steps feel harder and heavier because of it. By the time we get to Mama's car, I'm trying hard to keep myself together. Once we're a few minutes into the drive, Mama looks at me with sadness in her eyes.

"You're sure this is what you want, honey?" Her words are soft, but the fact that she's speaking them means a lot. I told her when she came home on Monday that I wouldn't be having Jordan over anymore, and she hadn't asked any questions. Instead, she just gave me a hug.

"I know he'll only confuse me right now."

Mama nods and keeps driving, but she reaches over and holds my hand as she does it.

On Friday afternoon, when I would normally be heading out to Polunsky, I'm in a courtroom instead. Mama sits beside me, clutching my hand. I know that everything Mama's heard from Chief Vega and the new lawyer tells us that this should be pretty straightforward, but I've never been in a courtroom without being terrified. The family-of-the-victims section is conspicuously empty today, and I don't know if that's because they feel bad about all the time that's been stolen from Daddy—or perhaps because it's still impossible for them to look at him and not see a murderer.

It may be that way for most of Houston, to be honest. Far more attention in the media is given to a man's guilt before he's declared guilty than to a man's innocence after he's been cleared. David Beckett's guilt had rated as a front-page story for months. The meeting to declare him innocent after nearly twelve years in prison only got a single paragraph near the bottom; the rest of his story was continued on the fifth page. Now it's Stacia's story that dominates the media's attention.

It won't go to trial. She'll go straight to sentencing, because she signed her confession.

If she hadn't signed and it had gone to trial, it's weird to know that I would be sitting on the side with the victims this time around. Mama and I—along with his full-grown daughter, who now lives in Canada—are the only family Mr. Masters had.

I wish again that he could be here with us. Mr. Masters would know what to do with everything we are facing. I desperately miss him always taking the time to prepare us for what we might see and hear.

Now, there is only one thing we can do. We have to prepare for the worst and hope for the best.

And the best is what we get.

It's shorter and sweeter than any time we've ever spent in a courtroom. It feels like a dream. The crowd is full of smiles instead of hostile stares. A new judge declares Daddy cleared of all charges and offers the apologies of the court and the State of Texas. After my father shakes a few hands and starts to head our direction, strangers with microphones stop him to ask questions like, "How does it feel to finally be going home?" Daddy is all charm in his suit and tie. I don't remember ever seeing him in a suit and tie, except in pictures from before. His old suit hangs loose on him now, but anything is a massive improvement over the prison jumpsuit.

Maybe they'd give us one to burn.

Daddy kisses Mama and me on our foreheads and hugs us tight. He walks with one arm around each of us as we head out of the courtroom. I'm blindingly happy and at the same time so confused. My mind keeps getting stuck on things we've never ever had to worry about before. Is he hungry? Should we stop and get him food? Is there any restaurant he likes in particular? I've spent time with my father every week, and we've never discussed this. I'm thrilled to see Daddy outside of Polunsky, but at the same time I feel like I know so little about this man before me.

We walk out into a hot, sunny day and Daddy stops, drops his hands from our shoulders, and turns his face up to the sky.

As we stand and watch him, Mama shoots me a nervous smile.

It's such a whirlwind, I feel like my brain may never stop spinning in the wake of it. We sit awkwardly in the car on the way home. Mama drives because Daddy needs to renew his license. I'm in the back. I don't remember the last time I sat in the backseat. I can't find one of the seat belts and once I do, it's stiff and uncomfortable.

"We need to stay here for a few weeks while things get finalized, but then we could go anywhere we want. We can make a fresh start." He watches us both with a hopeful expression.

Mama looks like she's considering it, but her tight smile isn't hard to make out even from the backseat.

"Mama just got a new job . . . ," I start.

Mama says at the same time, "Riley seems like she's finally settling in here a bit."

Daddy frowns for an instant before he shrugs. "We can wait a bit then. I need to fill out the compensation paperwork anyway."

"What's that?" I lean forward a bit to hear him better.

"Since I was wrongly convicted, the state will pay money to make up for what I've lost."

I'm shocked that the state of Texas feels like they can possibly put a monetary value to something like twelve years of a man's life. "How much do they think ripping you away from your family for twelve years is worth?"

"Almost one million dollars." Daddy glances back at me and shrugs at the stunned look on my face. It's like he's been through too much to hold on to his anger.

But I'm still angry. It's cost me so much, too, and the great state of Texas won't be paying me a dime. I shake my head and fall back against the seat. Crossing my arms over my chest, I mutter, "There isn't enough money in all of Texas."

Daddy turns around and catches my eye. "No, but it's a start."

Mama clears her throat twice before jumping in with the next topic. "I think you need to understand, David, things can't immediately go back to the way they were before."

She told me on the way to the courthouse that she'd be saying all of this and asked me how I felt about it. I'd only hugged her and told her I was proud of her.

So while she talks, I focus in on Daddy, trying to gauge his response.

His face is suddenly guarded. "What do you mean?"

"I mean that you're welcome to come home with us—"

He sputters, "I—I'm *welcome* to come home to my family?"

"You need to understand. We may know you from across a table for an hour or two a week, but in our own home, you're a stranger to us now." Mama's words come fast like she's afraid if she slows down they won't all make it out.

He's not saying anything anymore, but his expression has an odd kind of blankness to it.

"You can't expect everything to be the same. We've changed. Riley is so grown up now." She smiles back at me, before her jaw becomes firm when she looks at the road in front of her again. She looks decided as she finishes. "We're all different and we need the chance to get to know each other again. You can sleep in our guest bedroom for now."

Daddy rubs his hand across his forehead. A vein stands out on the side of his neck, but then he relaxes. "Then that's what we'll do. Whatever makes my girls comfortable."

I stare out the back window for the rest of the drive. Exhaustion lulls me into a sort of trance, and my mind is so busy trying to make sense of this new world. Mama, Daddy, and I are all vastly different people since the last time we were in the same house together. Can we even fit in it now? Will everything break apart once we walk through the door?

Will our family break now that we're finally together if the dream doesn't turn out to be everything we'd hoped?

Once we pull into the driveway, I see a few neighbors have put signs out on our lawn and they mill about on our front porch. The signs are the opposite of the messages they've been sending Mama and me for years. They say, "Welcome Home!" and "Congratulations!" The neighbors welcome Daddy home with open arms and it's all I can do to not roll my eyes in disgust. A few have left baskets of food or bottles of wine on the front porch to celebrate, and I wonder how many of them are driven by guilt about the way they've acted. I watch my parents walk beside each other as they talk to the neighbors, but they don't touch. This is definitely going to require an adjustment—and sleep. We should all sleep. A month's worth of exhaustion has caught up with me, and my whole body simply yearns for bed.

It feels like I haven't slept well ever since I kicked Jordan out of my house.

Walking to my room, I glance at my phone and see no missed calls or texts. My heart shatters all over again when I think of him, so I do my best not to. He's done as I asked, and other than the look we exchanged at the funeral, I haven't seen or heard from him since.

I miss talking to him, the way he challenges me to see things differently. The way he makes me laugh.

Jordan's voice is only a piece of what I long for. I miss his touch, his smile, his smell, his kiss—God, I miss him kissing me, holding me.

I've questioned my decision to make him leave a million times. Sometimes I'm just furious with him for bringing up the doubts that I'm trying to let go of. It felt like he wasn't just reminding me of everything that could go wrong, but he was also rubbing it in my face. Other times I feel like such an idiot that I swear if I have a brain cell left in my head at all it would be long dead of loneliness. Maybe I've made a huge mistake and now I don't know how to fix it or take it back. And Daddy being home only further complicates our situation.

As I turn off the light and walk toward the living room, my phone *dings* once and lights up from my desk in the darkness. I freeze, not sure if I'm strong enough to handle turning Jordan away again.

His text somehow makes me feel better instead of worse like I'm expecting.

Jordan: I promised I wouldn't leave you and I'm keeping that promise. Let me know when you need me.

Let him know when I need him? I groan to myself at the yearning that fills me just to be near him. I *always* need him. When I turn to face my doorway, Daddy's standing there and I jump.

"Oh. Hi." I stuff my phone into my pocket and smile at him.

"I didn't mean to scare you. I just wanted to see my daughter's room." His words are kind, but he doesn't look at my room at all. His eyes watch me too closely to see anything else.

"Well, this is it." I flip the light back on and gesture around at the walls that have been a light yellow since Mama and I painted them ourselves the summer after sixth grade. Looking around, I realize this place is filled with memories of Mama—and nothing of Daddy. He looks like a square block we're trying to fit into a round hole.

I sigh at the lost expression on his face as he finally looks at the room around me. I step forward, grab his hand, and pull him in toward my closet. Opening the door, I show him my stacks of shoeboxes, but he simply frowns in confusion.

"These boxes are filled with all the letters you wrote to me. I've never thrown any away—not a single one. There are more boxes in the attic," I state simply, and when I glance over at him, his eyes are watery. "This is the part of my room that has always belonged to you."

Daddy pulls me into a tight hug and seems too emotional to respond. I hug him back as tight as I can, closing my eyes and trying to memorize what he smells and feels like outside of a Polunsky jumpsuit. I'm determined to make new memories with my father that will never fade, even if I can't store them safely away inside any shoebox.

He kisses the top of my head softly and whispers, "Thank you, Riley. I'm so sorry for everything I've missed, for the lies."

"Let's just start over," I say back. "I'm happy you're home, Daddy."

He squeezes me again and then tilts his head as he sees something over my shoulder. Then he chuckles low and pulls back with a wicked grin. "Feel up to a game?"

I glance over at the corner where I keep my glass chess set. It's tucked to the side on a small table because it's been a while since I've had anyone to play with at home. Mama used to play, but once I started beating her consistently we both lost interest, and she became too busy with work. The idea of playing a game with Daddy, using real pieces, in my own bedroom, spreads warmth through my chest.

I grin at him. "Only if we can use this pretty one instead of the one we used at Polunsky. I've had more than enough paper cuts, thank you."

He moves to my table and helps me clear off the other things cluttering it. When we both sit down, he has a competitive twinkle in his eye. "Let the match begin."

36

"CHECKMATE," I WHISPER, almost in shock as I scan the board again to be certain I didn't miss anything. Once I'm sure, I raise my eyes to Daddy's. He's still staring at the board with a puzzled frown on his face, but when he lifts his eyes to mine, he smiles.

"Indeed." He examines the board again, looking slightly shocked. "You beat me."

It's our second game. Daddy beat me soundly in the first one. This time the result is the opposite. I see Mama standing in the doorway with a wide grin on her face and her eyes on me.

"Looks like you've finally met your match," she says to Daddy and he laughs almost to himself.

I suddenly realize I've been hogging him since he got home, and maybe Daddy and Mama need some time together, too.

"I'm exhausted, though." I don't have to fake the yawn, but I need to embellish a bit. "I think I need to go to bed."

Daddy comes around to hug me. "I guess you're too old to need to be tucked in anymore."

I laugh. "Maybe . . . but that doesn't mean you can't still do it."

• • •

After my parents tuck me in, I try to get comfortable, but my brain refuses to slow down. Sleep won't come. Just as I'm finally starting to drift off hours later, I hear them arguing. It's only an occasional raised voice, not specific words because they both seem to be making an effort not to let me hear. If I'd already been asleep, it probably wouldn't have woken me, but instead of sleeping soundly, I'm awake and now a spectator to a show that I'm not supposed to see. I creep out of bed and over to my door; I open it slightly and sit against the wall beside it, listening.

"How could you tell her something like that?" Mama says in the closest thing to a shouted whisper I've ever heard.

"I've already explained myself and apologized, Amy." His response is normal volume and I have to strain to hear it, but there is enormous tension in his voice.

"Fine." Mama sounds like she's finally releasing years' worth of pent-up frustration. "But you need to know, I'm stronger than I was before, David. I won't put up with the things you did back then anymore. If you cheat again, Riley and I will be gone forever."

"Don't threaten me," Daddy snarls and I almost jump up to stop them, but his voice drops back to normal almost immediately. "We both made mistakes, don't forget that."

Mama doesn't answer for a bit and I can hear the injured note in her voice when she does. "You wouldn't ever let me, would you?" Before he can respond, she goes on. "I'm sorry. I've said it a million times. Don't turn your back on me again, David. His name was Andrew, and I pay every day for what happened, but it was an accident."

They go on like this for hours. Arguing about anything and

everything in voices just low enough that I know they think I can't hear them. My dream for any future as a family becomes more and more trampled beneath each word. At one point the arguing slows.

"Riley has to be our only focus now." Mama sounds exhausted, and I wonder why they don't just go to bed.

"Always," Daddy answers, and my last thought before sleep overcomes me is that it's nice to see them agree about something.

At some point in the darkness of night, Daddy comes in and finds me curled up with a pillow beside my barely open bedroom door. I'm surprised at how strong he still is when he picks me up and carries me back into my bed.

"I'm sorry, Riley." He kisses my cheek, but I'm still too far from fully awake to respond. "I promise I will make this better."

By the time I wake up, it's late afternoon and the house is quiet. A note sits on the counter from my parents. Daddy went shopping for a car and some new clothes that will fit him better. Mama went with him apparently, which is probably a good sign.

After eating, showering, and checking my phone again for any other word from Jordan, I get ready and then pick up a book Mama bought for me a couple of years ago. She called it a "happy book." She thought it would be better for me than reading *The Count of Monte Cristo* again. I hadn't even read the back cover at the time, but I want to now.

Maybe it's about time I give "happy" a try.

The book is actually quite good, and by the time I look up again, the sun is heading for the horizon. I put the book aside, pick up my phone, and call Mama. Daddy doesn't have a phone yet anyway.

I hear her ringtone coming from the other room, and I go searching for it and find it on her bed. It's weird, but not unheard of. Mama has left her phone home a couple of times since she lost her job. She told me she wants to enjoy feeling untethered while she can.

Walking outside, I check our front porch swing just in case they'd come home but stayed out here for some reason. I feel uneasy, but push the feeling aside. After looking into details from murders for a few weeks straight, it's hard not to look at everything in my life with a little suspicion.

I head toward the mailbox, my eyes checking both ends of the street. In the distance, I hear the roar of a motorcycle and my stomach flops as I search for Jordan and his black bike, hoping against hope that he misses me enough to ignore my request and come back, but then the sound fades away and I feel like I lost him all over again.

I come back in with the mail and drop it on the counter. I spy my name on the second envelope and realize I didn't even look through the stack.

Pulling out the one with my name printed in clear block letters, I frown, and my anxiety grows when I see there is no return address.

I carefully rip it open and pull the letter out; I don't even have to read a word to recognize Ben Masters's handwriting. I stumble toward the table and sit down. My heart aches from his loss all over again, and I flip the envelope back over to check the postmark. The date is from Wednesday, four days after he died. Did he arrange for someone else to send this before he came to meet us on Saturday?

I read the first two lines and my heart feels like a sledgehammer pounding against the walls of my chest.

> Miss Riley,
>   I hope I've already told you this is coming and to ignore it. If not, then something went very wrong and you're in tremendous danger.

My eyes fly to the bottom of the page and I see Mr. Masters's handwriting growing more and more rushed as the letter goes on. My fingers grip the paper tightly as I stand, instinctively walking to the living room and locking our front door.

I read on.

> I'm certain I'm being followed. Tonight, while searching your father's old office, I found the panel I've been looking for.
>   I'm so sorry to tell you this, my dear Riley, but behind the panel I found what I feared most. I found jewelry, the very trophies from the murders your father is accused of committing.
>   He is guilty. There can no longer be any doubt. He murdered those poor women. His confession to you may be the only truth he's told any of us in years.
>   Behind the panel I also found a few wedding photos of your parents. They had red X's through your mother's face and lines across her throat. I'm including them so

you can see for yourself. He wrote terrible, horrifying things on those pictures. I recognize his handwriting, Riley. I have no doubt that he wishes to harm her.

I'm so very sorry to have such terrible news. Please understand that the only safe situation for your mother is for your father to remain locked away.

I'm bringing the jewelry to you tonight so you can see the pieces for yourself. Then I'd like your friend to call Chief Vega so I may discuss what I've found with him. If I don't meet you, please give the chief this letter as soon as possible.

I believe Stacia has been sucked into your father's plot and he may be using her to meet his needs outside of the prison. That's why the office isn't safe to meet. Nowhere is safe. I chose Mason Park because it's the one place that I think may keep her away. I think the site where your father left the body of his previous mistress haunts her. She doesn't want to follow us there... at least, that's what I'm counting on.

Make certain this truth is told, and be extremely careful of Stacia. Tell your mother. Tell Chief Vega. Tell everyone, Riley.

Your father must not be allowed near your mother. I've spent years as a criminal defense lawyer, and I've never seen anyone more skilled at deception or more dangerous than he is.

You are a daughter to me and always will be. Don't allow yourself to think you are anything but brilliant,

*courageous, and kind. In the sight of things that would've
made others crumble, you stand tall. Don't forget who
you are and that I love you.*

*You are nothing like him, Miss Riley. Do not ever
doubt that.*

*By your side always,
Ben Masters*

I can't move as I read the letter again and again. At the back is a smaller envelope with the photos Mr. Masters mentioned. Daddy's handwriting looks harder and more jagged than in his letters to me, but it's his all the same. I stare at one with Mama's head scribbled out. The words *She must die* are scrawled across the bottom.

My feet feel like lead and my head can't seem to stop spinning. This can't be right. It *can't* be right.

I keep reading it, hoping to find the line that proves this to be some kind of cruel hoax.

I keep reading it because somewhere in my soul, I already know that it's true.

Mama . . .

Dropping the envelope, I scramble for my phone and my keys, and I head out to my car. I don't know where I'm going, but I can't just sit here. Knowing that I can't call Mama, I call the only other person I can think of—Jordan. It rings only once.

"Riley? I was just going to call you."

"He did it, Jordan," I choke out around the raw fear that seems to have formed a ball in my throat. "He killed those women and now he has my mom. I think he might hurt her."

There is a moment of shocked silence before he answers. "I'm parked on the corner of Adams and Seventy-Second in the East End. Come to me right now."

"I was going to go to the police and tell them he has her. Tell them we have to find my parents." My voice is shaking so badly I just hope that Jordan can understand what I'm saying. I rub my palm against my forehead in confusion at the stoplight, trying to figure out what way I should turn.

"That's what I'm saying, Riley. Your parents are *here*." Jordan is speaking so fast that I struggle to make sense of what he's saying. "Don't worry about the police. I'll call my dad right now and tell him. I'll call you right back."

"What? Jordan?" I stammer, trying to understand why he is with my parents.

Then there is a *click*, and I jerk back the phone to see the words *CALL ENDED* printed across the screen in big red letters.

I force myself to take slow, deep breaths even though I'm flying down the freeway at speeds my car has never seen before. I almost hope a cop turns on his lights and starts following me.

I can lead him straight to my father.

Why on earth would Jordan be with them? Maybe if he's there then Mama will be okay. I cling to that bit of hope and try not to think about how many hours my parents have been alone together today.

My phone rings and I pick it up immediately. "What the hell do you mean you're with my parents?"

Jordan answers without missing a beat. "I've been driving myself crazy, Riley. I miss you. I was worried about you. And I wanted to make sure that your father wasn't coming after my dad."

I want to say the same things back to him, but this isn't the time for all of that. I want to save those words for later, when I can hold him tight. When all my insides aren't twisted into a tight knot because I *know* that Mama is safe. "Why are you with them?" I spit out each word.

"I was in the park this morning, Riley. I saw them drive by and hoped it was you in the car with your mom, but it wasn't. It was him, so I followed them . . ." His words trail off softer at the end of his last sentence.

"You did what?" I hiss as I turn with screeching tires onto Adams. I'm just a few blocks away now.

"I know you believed he was innocent, but I just couldn't make it all fit." He stops for a minute like he's unsure whether I want to hear the rest. "I wanted to make sure he wasn't going to hurt anyone else."

I spot his bike and pull to a stop behind him. I don't even respond, I just end the call and slip my phone into my pocket. I'm out of my car almost before the engine completely cuts off. Jordan sees me and the look on his face says he isn't entirely certain how I'm going to react.

In my mind, there is only one possible thing to do.

I run to him, throwing my arms around him and knocking his body against the back wall of the alcove he'd been standing in. His warm body begins to calm the trembling in mine that wouldn't seem to stop. He pulls me in so tight against him that I can't tell where I end or he begins.

Jordan smooths my hair with one hand and buries his face against my neck. "Shh, it's going to be okay."

"Thank you." My face is pressed against the warm black T-shirt he's wearing. "Thank you for watching them."

"You're welcome." He kisses my cheek and then I pull back, grabbing hold of his hand. "Most of the day they were just running errands, and everything seemed to be fine. Right before you called me, though, he took her into one of these abandoned warehouses, and she looked reluctant to go inside. That's why I was about to call you."

"Which building are they in?"

He steps around the side of the building and points. "Two buildings down."

The sun has completely set now, but the heat from the day is still out in full force. The alcove we've been standing in feels more like a steam room than a hideout.

"My dad said to wait out here," Jordan says as I start walking toward the warehouse. "They're on their way."

"And *you* should absolutely do that." I stop, placing my hands on his chest as I push him gently back toward the alcove. "But I can't leave Mama in there with him for one more minute."

I don't miss the fact that I haven't thought about Daddy or used his name since I read Mr. Masters's letter. I can't face that now, not until I know Mama is safe.

"I won't let you go in there alone, Riley." Jordan's words are hard as steel and I know he doesn't want to give me a chance to argue.

I do anyway. "He won't hurt me, Jordan."

"You can't know that," Jordan pleads.

"I *do* know that. Trust me." I kiss him softly on the lips before turning and sprinting toward the warehouse. Only when I silently pull open a broken door on the opposite end of the building do I realize Jordan is barely a step behind me.

When I frown up at him, he looks at me with grim determination. "I trust you completely, Riley, but there's no way in hell I'm going to trust *him* not to hurt you."

37

WE MAKE OUR WAY AS QUIETLY as possible through the dark warehouse. If the alcove outside was a steam room, this place is an oven. I hear scurrying around us that makes my skin crawl. Waiting for our eyes to adjust, I hear the first sign that we aren't the only people in this decrepit building.

A sob followed by a long moan makes my heart pound in my ears. I glance at Jordan, and he squeezes my hand before we both move in the direction of the sound. It seems like it came from the opposite end of the warehouse—and maybe above us. I point up and raise my eyebrows. Jordan nods and points to an only partially rusted set of stairs to our right.

Just as we reach the top half of the steps, I see a shadow that can only be Daddy's move to block the top of the stairs. A low growl escapes him and I see him crouch a bit like he's preparing to pounce. My body freezes.

I whisper the only word that can stop him cold. "Daddy?"

"Riley?" Daddy jerks upright, sounding startled, and then he seems to make out Jordan standing behind me. In two movements, he's in front of us, has grabbed both of our arms and is dragging us up the stairs behind him. Instead of heading to the left where I thought I heard the moan come from, he takes us to the right before letting us go.

One filthy window lets in the light from a nearby streetlamp and I can see sheer panic in my father's eyes. "Wh—why are you here, honey? Why did you bring *him*?"

I try to slow down and think, knowing it probably won't work to pretend we don't know why he's here, but I need to buy time. The silence from the other side of the stairs is chilling. What if she's hurt? I have to help her. As long as we can stay calm until Chief Vega gets here, as long as I can get Daddy to let me see her, we may be okay.

"Where's Mama?" I ask, fighting to mask the terror I'm feeling and keeping my voice steady. He can't hear the adrenaline in my veins or the pace of my heart.

The tiniest flash of irritation passes through Daddy's expression before his face is suddenly serene. "Why would your mama be here?"

It shocks me how much better he is at the game I'm striving to play.

Good lawyers are one part actor, one part confidant, and one part shark.

Daddy's old saying floats up in my mind, and I swallow back the nausea that comes with it. He definitely has two-thirds of the combination down, I have to give him that.

"Because of the note she left this morning. It said she was coming with you today." I tentatively step toward him. "Is she here, Daddy?"

He takes an abrupt step back and his eyes shift from side to side. He looks out of his depth. The light from the streetlamp outside suddenly shines on his face and I see deep red scratches down one cheek. His other eye is almost swollen shut.

I gasp. "What happened?" The words come out on instinct, even though it's immediately clear what happened to Daddy's face. Mama happened.

Daddy's hand goes up to the scratches and he winces before his face turns hard. Sudden and ice-cold hatred flows through his eyes. "What always happens: your mother knows just how to ruin everything."

Without giving him a chance to say another word, I bolt for the room on the opposite side and duck under the hand Daddy shoots out to stop me. The room over here is actually better lit than the first. I see Mama immediately. Her body is crumpled into a ball in the middle of the floor.

"Mama!" I stop running and skid across on my knees as I land beside her. She's breathing still, but she can't seem to focus on me. She's barely conscious. One of her arms is bent at an awkward angle, and she has bruises all over her legs. My knees feel wet and I realize I'm kneeling in a small puddle of her blood. Her injuries look like those that were on his victims' bodies. My throat feels like it's closing off. He's trying to do the same thing to Mama.

I hear grunts and crashes from Jordan and Daddy, who are fighting by the stairs. I search around frantically for something to stop my father. I see a bloody knife sitting a few feet away on the ground. Grabbing it, I run to the doorway and stick the shaking hand with the knife out toward Daddy. He has Jordan in a choke-hold.

"Let him go!" I scream as I watch a drop of blood roll down the side of Jordan's cheek from a nasty cut near his eye.

They both freeze and Daddy looks straight at me before laughing softly. "You don't want to hurt me, Riley."

"No," I say, trying to get a better grip on my knife as tears run down my face. "But y-you have to stop this."

Daddy's eyes fill with genuine remorse as he meets my gaze. "Things are going to be better, Riley, I promise, but there are some things I have to clean up first." And then with one immense shove, he pushes Jordan at just the right angle. Jordan's panicked eyes meet mine for half a heartbeat . . . and then he disappears, tumbling with horrific thuds and crunches back down the rusty metal stairs.

And then all I hear is silence.

"No!" The knife drops from my hands and I run for Jordan without another thought. Daddy catches me around the waist, easily lifts me, and brings me back into the room with Mama. He ties my hands to a pipe in the corner, kicks my knife out of the way, and moves back toward Mama.

"If you're going to kill all of us, why not start with me?" My voice comes out hoarse and low. My heart still thuds hard in my chest, but I don't know how. It feels like it's been decimated by seeing Mama like this and watching Jordan's expression as he fell.

Please, God, let them be okay.

Daddy looks shocked. "I'm not going to hurt you. I could never do that, sweetie."

Daddy kicks Mama's thigh hard with the toe of his boot and another rush of panic fills me at the idea of sitting here, watching him beat Mama to death. I let all the emotion out, hoping that somehow his love for me will stop this insanity. Tears roll down my face and I clasp my tied hands in front of me, sobbing and pleading. "Please, Daddy. Please don't hurt her anymore."

He stops and turns back to face me with a shake of his head. He looks at me like I'm some sort of poor lost lamb. "I need you to listen. You don't understand."

"Okay, I'm l-listening," I stutter, striving to keep him busy and not hitting or kicking anyone.

"I have to leave this hellhole of a state, and I want you to come with me." As he speaks, he moves over to a bag that sits open nearby. Anything to keep him away from Mama and Jordan for a few more minutes sounds good to me. Then he pulls something out of the bag and runs it through his fingers. I realize with a jolt that it's a long navy length of rope. Images of the bruises on the East End Killer's—on *Daddy's* victims' necks from the crime scene photos flood my mind, and my stomach clenches against nauseating waves of fear. I can barely find words to respond.

"If I go with you now, will you please not hurt them anymore?" I speak slowly, trying to come up with a plan that doesn't end with all of us dead. Why isn't Chief Vega here yet?

"Oh no." He shakes his head with a laugh. Daddy looks at me like I'm that six-year-old girl from the courtroom all over again. "They're dying either way, honey."

A tiny whimper escapes me before I can stop it, but I find strength to keep my voice steady as I ask, "Why?"

Daddy tilts his head in the direction of the stairs he'd pushed Jordan down and gives a half shrug. "Him, because I had to watch him touch my daughter—and because I know it will kill Vega to lose him."

Then without any prodding, he turns toward Mama, and his face fills with the most intense mixture of hate and rage that I've ever seen. "Her, because I've been waiting to do this for an incredibly long time."

When he turns back to face me, I notice Mama's eyes fluttering as she tries hard to open them.

Seeing her fighting so hard despite everything he's done to her gives me strength. I will *not* let him hurt her again. "Why do you want to hurt her at all? She's your wife. She loves you."

He looks at me like I've just said something ludicrous. "She hates me." He shakes his head and laughs. "She killed my son and ripped my daughter away from me. You call that love?"

I glance back at Mama. Her eyes are open now. They're wide and terrified. Still, in the midst of all this, she looks at me and her mouth seems to be forming one word over and over again. I have a sudden flashback to the last word Mr. Masters said to me in the grove.

Run.

But even if I weren't currently tied to a pipe, I would still be done running.

If I'm the only one Daddy doesn't want to hurt, then I have to find a way to use that to my advantage.

Besides, I'll be damned if I have to sit here and watch whatever he's planning to do to my mother with that rope.

"How?" I shout out in desperation as he approaches Mama again and her eyes slide closed.

"What?" He glances back at me in annoyance, like I just interrupted his preparation for an important case rather than another murder.

"How did Mama rip me away from you?"

He blows out a puff of air and the hair on his forehead ruffles. Then he steps over to me and touches the side of my face gently. I force myself not to jerk away. "She could've lied about being my alibi and kept me from ever going to prison. I might have forgiven her for killing your brother if she'd done that. But she didn't. She said she didn't want to lie, but she was just being selfish. She knew she would get you all to herself if I was locked away. But you didn't forget about me, sweetheart. You just kept coming. Even when your mother stopped, you kept coming."

Then he looks straight at me with so much love in his eyes that I truly feel pity and sorrow for whatever has gone so desperately wrong in my father's mind. "You're the only one I really need, Riley. No one else, just you."

"Me?" I cry softly to myself, for my fear about Jordan, for the horrible pain I see on Mama's face—and for the loss of the father that I loved so much. He's undoubtedly sick and incredibly dangerous, but somewhere inside this monstrous person, the man I love still exists.

But no matter what else happens today, I will never be able to see that man again.

"My love for you, Riley. That's the only reason your mother wasn't my first victim." He turns his gaze on Mama again and the rage and hatred return. "She was the key to your life, to raising you right. Without her, our lives wouldn't have looked the way I wanted. What you show the world is what they believe you to be. Nothing else matters. Image matters."

I stop trying to understand him. Reason and logic don't apply here.

"But Daddy, I love them. Why would I go with you willingly if you kill Mama and Jordan?" I lean forward, trying to find some way to convince him to back down.

"Well, you don't have to." He's calm and thoughtful, like we're debating a chess move instead of him murdering everyone I care about. "It just depends on how much pain you want them to go through before they die. For example . . ." He picks up the small but deadly sharp knife I had earlier, steps next to Mama, and I scream as he plunges the blade halfway into the right side of her stomach.

"Stop! Please stop!" I yell out. Mama closes her eyes and all fluttering stops. The knife simply hangs there, half in and half out. Blood spills across the clean side of her shirt and down the front.

"That blade isn't hitting any crucial organs right now, but an inch to the left or right and it will be." Daddy looks at me the same way he used to when he taught me a particularly fascinating chess move.

I watch Mama and can't seem to catch my breath. I'm panting and I just want it all to stop. Daddy notices my distress and pulls out the blade with a sigh, turning to set the knife back on the table. I see the tiniest movement on the stairs and realize Chief Vega is here. He crouches on the top step with his gun raised, but at his current angle, Daddy is too far to the right for the chief to even see my father, let alone get a good shot.

"I know it's hard at first, but you'll get used to it." Daddy waves his hand at me like I'm upset that he had to prune my favorite rosebush or something. "Stacia was scared at first, too, but she changed her mind. It's all about pressure points—you find the right ones and people will do anything you want."

Daddy turns back to face me, and I put my eyes on him and only him. I know what I need to do. I need to lure my father closer to me so that Chief Vega can shoot him while Mama still has a chance to survive.

But he's my father . . .

"I'm nothing like Stacia. Daddy, *please* don't do that again," I whisper so softly that Daddy steps toward me, his eyes filling with confusion and regret.

"I'm sorry, Riley," he states simply as he moves a little closer.

"I know you are." I look up into his eyes and sob freely as I say one final thing. It's the thing I most need him to hear as I see Chief Vega line up his gun for a shot.

"I love you, Daddy."

I hear two loud blasts and Daddy crashes down next to me. The shots are through his chest, and he doesn't try to move. His eyes land on me as he takes his last breath, then he says the one thing I want to remember him saying for the rest of my life.

"I'm sorry, sweetie."

Then he is still as he stares at me with open, lifeless eyes, and I can't seem to look away. Vega scrambles back to the stairs, calling out orders. I hear many sets of pounding footsteps coming up. Vega checks Mama's pulse and yells for paramedics in a tone that tells me nothing about how she is. He moves over to me and cuts the ropes that bind me to the pipe. The paramedics rush up and go to Mama first.

"Are they going to be okay?" I whisper so softly that Chief Vega doesn't hear me, my eyes still on Daddy. Then I tear them away and look up at the chief.

"Chief Vega, are Jordan and my mom going to be okay?" I try to grab his arm but I can't get a grip. I'm shaking all over.

"Jordan is going to be fine." We both watch the paramedics lift Mama on a stretcher and carry her out of sight. "I don't know about your mom, but you gave her the best chance you could."

I feel the slightest bit of relief at hearing that Jordan will be okay, but I don't trust myself to really feel it until I see him for myself. Once I start talking, it's difficult to stop. "I'm so sorry he got hurt. I understand if you don't want me to ever see him again, as long as I know he's all right. Maybe we'll even move away if—*when* Mama is better. They just both *have* to be okay."

Vega looks from Daddy's lifeless form and back to me, then gently takes my arm and places it around his shoulders. He helps me to my feet and a small smile plays at his mouth as he links my arm through his and steadies me on my way to the stairs. "Did you know that Jordan was trying to crawl back up the stairs when I got here? He only made it about six steps up because he was trying to move silently with what looked to be a broken foot."

I see the gentleness in his eyes that I always find in Jordan's.

"You've been really good for him. He had shut down after his mom passed—he didn't want to be a part of anything anymore. You changed that." Chief Vega's eyes are damp. "My boy sure does care about you. If we get down these stairs and he finds out I've encouraged the idea of you moving to another state, I will never hear the end of it."

He waits until I glance up at him again. "And what you did up there for your father . . . was one of the bravest and kindest things I've ever seen, Riley."

"Thank you." As I murmur the words, the tiniest bit of warmth flows from my hand on his arm and up to my heart.

"I knew anyone who could make Jordan smile again like you have these last few weeks had to be impressive." He helps me slowly and shakily to the bottom of the stairs and leads me off to one side. "Now I'm certain that even *that* was an underestimation of you."

I am not sure how to respond to the things he is saying. This is the monster from all my nightmares. Only now I've finally discovered who the true monster was.

"You are so much like Jordan. So if I may, I'd like to give you a bit of the fatherly advice I think your father would've given you if he hadn't been sick . . ." He waits until I nod before continuing. "You need to stop taking the world on by yourself. No one has shoulders that wide."

My whole body shudders at the thought of what I lost today. That was absolutely something that the Daddy I loved so much would've said. I can actually picture him saying something similar over the table at Polunsky. I lean against Chief Vega as my legs start to wobble.

He helps keep me upright as he continues. "You saved Jordan, hopefully your mother, and yourself today. Try carrying *that* truth around for a little while. Lean on the weight of what that says about you. Hopefully then the rest will settle into place."

I don't dare speak. All I can do is hope that he's right.

"Oh, and Riley?" he asks as he pivots me gently toward Jordan's stretcher. "Please, call me Nick."

The aching all over my body dulls slightly and I think of the conversation I had with Mr. Masters so long ago. I smile to myself at the memory. I turn back to face Jordan's father. "How about Mr. Vega?"

He gives me a curious look and then shrugs. "Whichever you prefer."

I find my strength once I meet Jordan's eyes. He sits as far forward as he can on a nearby stretcher and I notice a paramedic trying to make him lie down. I run to his side and try to wrap my arms around him, but he winces while stopping me short, putting both hands on my shoulders as his eyes scan over me. "Are you really okay?"

"No, but I think I will be." I stare down at the bandages around his foot as well as the bumps and cuts all over him. A huge bandage covers his head and I see some blood has seeped through onto the thick white gauze. Before I can examine him any further, he pulls me in tight against his chest. "I was so worried about you. I didn't want my dad to wait for the other officer to take me outside before he went upstairs. I needed him to hurry to get to you—to your mom."

"Why didn't you go to the hospital?" I reach my fingers up to touch the corner of his swollen bottom lip where a deeper cut extends down nearly to his chin.

"I couldn't go without you." His skin pales, and he leans back against the stretcher again. He gently prods his forehead and winces. "They just took your mom on the other one. Will you ride over with me?"

"Yes, please." My desperation to make sure Mama is okay overrides my fear of finding out she might not be. The paramedics lift Jordan's stretcher into the ambulance.

I get myself in and seated, and my whole body trembles as I try to tell myself that Mama will be fine. As the paramedic is about to hop in and close the door, Jordan's dad runs up and grabs the handle.

"I'll lead the way," he says with a glance at Jordan before looking over at me. "We'll get you back to your mother as fast as we can."

Jordan frowns like he thinks he heard him wrong. "Wait, you—you're coming?"

Mr. Vega nods, his voice gruff with emotion. "I want to be there . . . with you. I asked Detective Jackson to take over processing the scene."

Jordan still looks startled, but he finds the words he needs to say. "I—thank you, Dad."

"I love you, Jordan—always," he says quietly, before shutting the door and jogging over to his car.

38

I STAND BESIDE BRAYS BAYOU in Mason Park and let the warm breeze ruffle my hair. Jordan stands on my left, his hand curled around mine. Four days later, some of the swelling on Jordan's face has started to go down. He wears a boot on his foot and will probably have a scar forever from the stitches up the right side of his forehead. When I look at him he smiles wide, and it feels like everything may honestly, truly be okay.

Today would've been Daddy's last day if he'd stayed in prison. Tonight, just after midnight, would've been the time of Daddy's execution. Instead, he's already gone, and I stand here mourning everyone that I've lost.

Reaching in my pocket, I pull out the bag containing my paper chess set and clench it tight in my hand. My fingers tremble as I reach in and draw out a few pieces.

I stare out across the water and scatter white paper pawns into the air as I whisper the names: "To Maren Jameson, Sarah Casey, Hillary Vanderstaff, Valynne Kemp. We'll never forget what you lost."

Reaching back into the bag, I pull out the white king. I kiss it before releasing it. "And to Benjamin Masters. Thank you for sacrificing everything to keep us safe."

The white king catches an updraft and disappears against the sky. I stop watching, happy with the idea that it may never land. Jordan squeezes my hand and finishes, "Rest in peace."

I glance back at the car and see Mama watching us closely from the front passenger seat. She was released from the hospital less than an hour ago. The surgeon stopped her internal bleeding, and she's improving daily, but nothing but time will heal the multiple broken bones, cuts, and bruises everywhere. Until then, she's on strict orders to stay off her feet for the next several weeks.

Still, when I told her I wanted to come say goodbye, she asked me to do it on our way home from the hospital so she could be with me. Even after I told her she'd have to stay in the car and rest, she said she didn't care. She just didn't want me to be alone.

I'd almost lost her. I'd almost been without her forever. Today, when I'm so grateful that I'm *not* alone, it's impossible to say no to a request like that.

She gives me a small wave and a weak smile, but her skin is still so pale it scares me.

Jordan gives me a tight hug and then moves back toward the car. "I'll go make sure your mom is comfortable."

I hesitate, knowing that I'm not done here. "I'll be right behind you. Just give me one more minute."

When Jordan stops and his eyes linger on mine, he seems to understand. Once he gets to the car and opens the door, I hear him say something to Mama so low I can't hear him. She laughs in response, and I smile to myself.

Reaching again into my plastic chess bag, I carefully remove the black king from the paper chess set and hold it tight in my hand.

I think for a minute before saying the only thing that can possibly match all of my confusing emotions. "To you, Daddy. I'll always love and remember the part of you that never forgot to write me letters, didn't let me win at chess, and will always love me forever. I hope you find the peace you're looking for, too."

Then I lift my palm to the sky, opening my fingers. The tiny piece flutters on the wind and eventually lands on the water. It floats lazily across the bayou until it slips beneath the lapping ripples and sinks out of sight. As I turn back toward the car, Daddy's voice echoes through my head one final time.

Checkmate.

ACKNOWLEDGMENTS

THIS BOOK WOULDN'T EXIST without a specific TV show. I got the idea while watching *Last Week Tonight with John Oliver*. The program did a segment on the percentage of the U.S. population that is in prison (1 percent of all adult males), and I started thinking about how underrepresented the children of those prisoners are in fiction. So John Oliver started all of this, and I thank him for that.

Thank you to my mom and my sister, Krista, for always supporting me and reading *all the books*. I love you. Thanks to Bill, Eric, Amanda, and Matt for all of your love and excitement. Thanks to my husband, Ande, and our boys, Cameron and Parker. You make me happy each and every day. My heart is yours.

To my Forever Agent Mafioso, Kathleen Rushall—you are the reason any of these ideas hit the shelves. Thank you for always buying into my shenanigans.

To my fantastic editor, Angie Chen, thank you for truly understanding me and my stories and sharing my love for fluffy feline creatures. You made this story something I'm proud of. Thank you to Janine O'Malley for seeing the shine in the story and helping it land in a great place. Thanks to Simon Boughton and Joy Peskin for making me feel like I belong. Andrew Arnold, you are a visionary genius and I feel so lucky to have you putting a face on my stories. Thanks to Nicole Banholzer for fielding weird publicist questions and always being willing to help. Thanks to Katie Fee and Caitlin Sweeny for helping people hear about my stories. And massive thanks to the rest of the team at FSG: I wish I could send you cookies every day so you would understand how much I appreciate every little thing you do.

My dearest friends in the world are writers. They are the reason I am (mostly) still sane. All my love to my girls: Renee Collins, Bree Despain, Natalie Whipple, Sara Raasch, Kasie West, and Candice Kennington. I'll never stop being grateful to all of you for being in my life. And for the other kindred authors nearby and around the globe who make this community the best—Nichole Giles, L. T. Elliot, Jennifer Bosworth, Jessica Brody, Marie Lu, Brodi Ashton, Morgan Matson, Jessica Khoury, Emmy Laybourne, J. Scott Savage, Leigh Bardugo, Gretchen McNeil, Tera Lynn Childs, Anna Carey, and so many others. I feel so lucky to call you all my friends.

Amazing author groups abound, and I'm grateful for my fellow Lucky 13s, the Friday the Thirteeners, the Binders Full of YA Writers, and the YA Scream Queens. Thank you for walking this path beside me.

Thanks to my weekly critique group, the Seizure Ninjas, for helping me whip all these words into shape. Janci Patterson, James Goldberg, Heather Clark, Michelle Argyle, Heidi Summers, Christopher Husberg, Cavan Helps, Leeann Setzer, and Megan Grey—I'm so happy I found you!

I've saved the best for last: thank you to my wonderfully amazing readers. Each email, tweet, and piece of fan art makes me excited to keep writing more stories. You're the best. Thank you for taking time out of your busy lives for my books.